Dark Days
for
White Knights

by
Dick Jackson

Dedication

For my family, in honor of those who have served and continue to serve, with special thanks to my wife, Julie, for her love, courage and perseverance.

ISBN 978-0615811987

DARK DAYS FOR WHITE KNIGHTS

Prelude

More Vietnam veterans have committed suicide than died in combat. Veterans in general make up a disproportionate share of the homeless, imprisoned and indigent population of America...why?

Boys growing up in post World War Two America gleefully plucked down their quarters on a Saturday afternoon to cheer on their big screen heroes as they rid the world of myriad ruthless, bi-speckled Nips and goose-stepping Krauts. Most dreamed of someday becoming heroes themselves—modern day white knights—whisking away damsels in distress and saving the world from tyranny.

With reports of Americans dying in Vietnam, many rushed off to join the service, afraid the war might end too soon for them to prove themselves. They arrived in Vietnam wide-eyed and as cocky as first round draft choices, certain of their manifest right to be there and a quick victory over the surly communist infiltrators. The day to day reality of war eroded that certainty and slowly transformed some into the villains of their childhood dreams.

In time, many would drag screaming villagers from their homes, destroy their meager belongings and set torch to their abodes. Torture and death awaited those who resisted. It wasn't, as the government later insisted, that they had become drug-crazed murderers and out-of-control marauders, like barbarians plundering Rome. They were simply implementing a policy handed down from the highest chains of command. "Pacification", "Search and

Destroy" and "Free Kill Zones" were some of the elements of a policy that was a sure formula for atrocity. For many serving in combat zones, atrocity became a daily fact of life...as routine as burning off leeches. Those who survived physically were often deeply wounded emotionally and spiritually. They knew they weren't the heroes of their youth... but they had followed orders and survived. Now it was time to go home.

Unfortunately, this is not unique to Vietnam veterans. Combat veterans of every war and from every nation have been scarred by the atrocities of war. However, because of the rotation system implemented by the pentagon during the Vietnam War, the veterans of Vietnam straggled home, one by one, to be scattered across an increasingly hostile America. The country was torn by racial violence and antiwar demonstrations. Women were burning their bras, Black Panthers were burning the cities and SDS antiwar radicals were blowing up college campus buildings. To returning veterans, America seemed as foreign as Vietnam had once been, but these were no longer the boys who had dreamed of serving America. The dreams of many had died in the soul-sucking mud of fetid rice paddies.

Survivors hoped to put Vietnam behind them, but the experience clung like the stench of death. An impenetrable darkness engulfed many returning veterans, creating loneliness so pervasive it could cause physical pain. Alcohol, drugs, violence and ostracism added force to a downward spiral into inconsolable hopelessness. Some believed it was a justifiable punishment for their failures...a kind of self-imposed sentence to an eternity of solitary confinement in a hell of their own making. For many, suicide was the only escape. For those who chose life, healing was an arduous journey down a lonely, dark corridor.

Dark Days for White Knights is the story of one Veteran's loss of innocence and his sojourn down the lonely corridor...a chronicle of his quest to recover something of what he lost in Vietnam. It occurs over a six week period as he hitchhikes across Texas. There are encounters with drug couriers, sharks, Mexican whores and a bar room mystic, plus bouts of delirium and a few epiphanies. It is written in a personal narrative style. The author spent time as a Marine rifleman in Vietnam. The story draws from his experience in Vietnam plus many years of healing...all synthesized into six weeks on the road in Texas in 1969. Hold on...there are a few bumps that might rattle your perceptions along the way.

There are a lot of novels about Vietnam, most highlighting heroic actions in combat. Heroes are a part of all wars and their stories are exciting and important. Vietnam was no exception. The devotion the warriors shared for one another spawned many heroic actions, but perhaps the important lessons from Vietnam were about personal responsibility, misplaced trust, and the ultimate cost of survival. In that light, *Dark Days for White Knights* is a unique perspective on a still controversial time in American history.

Chapter One
A Fall from Grace

"Now that I'm here, we should have this mess cleaned up in the next six months."
Z to Jack upon his arrival in Vietnam, December 1967

They haunt me still... the glistening wild-eyed stares of dirty-faced children and the withered, stoic faces of the old ones as they disappear into the bunker. The "sing-song" gibberish of a language I loathed, extinguished by the murky dankness of the earthen confinement.

"Take care of them," was all Sergeant James had said, but his intent was clear.

Barnes, with a wry grin and grenade in hand, stands ready on one side of the entrance and I on the other. We nod at one another as we press our backs against the red clay wall, then I yell, "Fire in the hole!"

We fling our grenades hard against the back firewall of the L-shaped tunnel entrance to insure the explosion will plug off the deadly entrapment. The "whomp - whomp" of muffled blasts preludes an eerie silence. I crouch by the door to listen, as detached as the gray smoke that drifts up from the musty tomb. When I'm sure, I nod at Barnes, and walk away from the last remnant of my shattered humanity.

How had things gone so wrong, so quickly? I did not go to Vietnam to become a remorseless killer. I joined the Marines with lofty aspirations. I believed there was no higher purpose than to serve, and, if need be, to die for your country. I hoped, as I believed my father, uncle and grandfather before me had done, that I would be able to protect those who could not protect themselves. I was fully trained and jerking at the tether, literally praying for my chance to fight to save the world from the spread of communism. I was sure, to the very core of my being, that what I believed was right.

My Uncle Bob died fighting the Japanese on Peleliu Island, in the South Pacific, during WW II. He was shot while rescuing a wounded friend from the battlefield. As he tried to pull the man to cover, a sniper shot him in the back, puncturing his lung. He suffered a horrible death, struggling to breathe until he eventually suffocated. He drowned in his own blood, while hospital transports floundered amidst the wreckage and human carnage in the shallow, blood-red waves a couple of hundred yards from shore.

His picture hung like a shrine above my grandmother's mantel, a Purple Heart and a Bronze Star pinned on either side of a chubby-cheeked young man in the dress blue uniform of the United States Marine Corps. He was our family hero. I shared his middle name, and I wanted to someday wear that uniform and have my decorated picture on someone's mantel.

When I was fourteen, my grandmother gave me Bobby's tattered Marine Corps manual. His scribbled notes along the margins of the frayed pages reached out from the past to pull me ever closer to my own future. Many nights, after the house had gone quiet, I would stick a towel under my door to conceal the light and reverently study the manual. For me, it was like reading an ancient, sacred manuscript. It became my Bible. I practiced marching in my socks and performed the manual of arms with a broomstick in the secrecy of my room.

My favorite haunts were surplus stores. To me, it was like history magically springing to life. I would wander the aisles smelling and touching...my imagination conjuring up momentous battles and the men who fought them. I saved my allowance and worked extra on weekends to buy banged up old helmets and worn web gear. I started a Marine Club. Being the oldest and strongest boy on the block, I quickly persuaded all the neighborhood boys to become members. We dug a maze of foxholes and cardboard covered trenches in a vacant lot at the edge of town, fighting off hoards of Krauts, Nips and Yankees. I scoured the library for books about war, especially Marines at war, in exotic far-flung places like Tripoli, Belleau Woods, Iwo Jima, and the frozen Chosin. I eagerly plopped down my quarters to watch my heroes on the big screen: Van Johnson, John Wayne, Robert Mitchum...they were all so gallant and brave...and always on the right side.

Life was simple. The "good guys" always won, and there was never any doubt about who wore the white hats, never a question as to motives, or methods of operation. America represented all that was right with the world. We supplied the heroes, and someday, I knew, I would be one of those heroes.

Most children outgrow their childhood dreams; mine grew ever stronger. When the Marines went ashore at Da Nang in 1965, I was a sophomore in high school. I prayed that the war would last long enough for me to see action. Afraid my prayers might not be answered, I managed to get thrown out of high school two months before my 17th birthday. I became a general pain in the ass for the next two months. By the time my birthday rolled around, my mother was convinced by circumstances to sign an age waiver. A month later, I was on my way to MCRD in San Diego.

Boot camp was enlightening. I soon discovered the manual I had been studying was indeed a relic.

"LET'S SEE THAT ABOUT FACE AGAIN, YOU FUCKIN' MAGGOT!"

I performed the maneuver to perfection, just as I had practiced it for years.

"Where the fuck did you learn that, Private?"

"Sir! From the Marine Corps Manual, Sir."

"Whose Marine Corps Manual?" My DI yelled, his face an inch from mine, his spittle splattering my face.

"My Uncle Bob's manual, sir!"

"You think you're a fuckin' Marine, do you, Private?" He yelled with a practiced staccato rhythm, "You're nothing but a fuckin' maggot!" He finished, and turned away in pretend disgust. "Get down and give me fifty you dumb son of a bitch, and don't," he paused and stuck his nose back into my face, "Don't you ever again presume to quote the Marine Corps' manual to me."

"Yes sir!" I yelled, as I hit the deck and began to pump out pushups.

I felt lucky to escape with my life, and I knew my manual, my Bible, was defunct.

The war waited, as I lingered in California. I was assigned to Force Recon, the Marines Corps' most elite. The unit was deployed to Vietnam a month after my arrival, but I was one of the few left behind to form a replacement unit. My disappointment was epic, and my waning performance reflected my deprived attitude.

One weekend, while on duty as the company driver, two of the newer Recon Marines dropped by to get acquainted. One of them had a fifth of Jack. The only regular duty of the company driver was to rescue Sgt. Carter from the NCO club. He had an early night, so we broke out the Jack. One toast led to another, and before the fun had really started, we were out of whiskey. We weighed the risk against the rewards for a few minutes before deciding to take the PC (3/4 ton personnel carrier) to Oceanside to "procure additional liquid refreshments".

We couldn't leave the base without a trip ticket, so I forged Colonel Bass' name to the ticket (a trick I had picked up from Corporal Williams a week earlier, when we had taken the Colonel's staff car to Tijuana).

Walter, my new best friend, and I misappropriated the PC, and I drove to Oceanside. First, we stopped for cheeseburgers. I parked off the main drag and we slipped into a booth in one of the popular burger joints. Dressed in our utilities, which were not permitted off base, we drew a bit of unwanted attention; and it wasn't long before I was flinging catsup coated fries at our detractors. A call to the police sent us fleeing towards the liquor mart. For some inexplicable reason, the owner of the liquor mart agreed to sell us...two drunk, 17 year old Marines, dressed in utilities with a PC parked in front...several bottles of cheap wine, which was all we could afford on our $92 per month pay. Having succeeded in our quest, we uncapped a bottle each upon reaching the PC, and toasted our bravado.

"Let's coast the beach and check out the girls before we head back," suggested Walter.

"Yes sir," I replied, with a snappy salute to seal his new status as Commander-in-Chief.

About a mile south of the lighted pier area, along a seedier part of the beach drive, we came to a red light.

There, leaning against a power pole smoking cigarettes, were two drunken Marines. From their haircuts and general demeanor we quickly surmised, they had just finished boot camp. Walter tapped my leg and smiled before rolling down the window.

"Hey you maggots, put out those cigarettes and get your asses squared away," he ordered.

"Who says so?" One of the insubordinate boots slurred back in reply.

"Lieutenant Walters, that's who says so!" Walter replied with stern implications.

"Fuck you!" the two reprobates answered in unison.

I stepped out of the PC and walked towards the pole. "You sons-a-bitches better shape up and do what the Lieutenant says."

The more vocal of the two, who I would soon learn was actually a pissed off Lance Corporal named Rhoads, flipped me the bird and shot back, "fuck you, too!"

The suddenness of my attack surprised both men, and they took flight. The fleeter of the two made it up a small rise, but I caught Rhoads. I roughed him up a bit and made him apologize to, and salute Walter. I strutted back to the PC laughing and took a pull off my jug.

We left Rhoads cowering in shame, at his power pole. He wrote down the PC number and ran to the nearest MP station to file a report.

An hour later, when the wine and fun had both run out, I pulled up to the gate at Camp Delmar.

"Please pull to the side," the guard directed with a friendly wave.

I pulled over, still full of myself. A civilian, dressed in a suit coat and tie, crossed the street, heading for my PC.

"Who the hell is that?" Walter wondered aloud.

My mind spun, trying to remember if we had somehow pissed off a civilian.

"I'll handle it," I assured Walter.

The civilian stopped a few feet from the window. "Would you please step out of the vehicle," he demanded.

I didn't like being ordered about by a civilian, so I stepped out, ready for action.

"Jim Robbins, CID," he announced, stepping closer.

"Dennis Jackson, USMC," I answered, rocking back to add power to my right cross.

He quickly produced a pistol from beneath his jacket, and that ended the night.

I didn't know my CIDs (civilian intelligence division) from my ABCs until he had me cuffed and behind bars. But...I would learn a lot of legalese in the next couple of months.

I was charged with drinking under age, drinking on duty, being absent from my post, assault, misappropriation of a military vehicle, and impersonating an officer. I was scheduled for a Special Court Martial. My appointed council was a Second Lieutenant, just out of law school. We were both being initiated into the bizarre world of the military justice system. The entire proceedings were prepared before we stepped into court. I was presented with a copy of the proceedings with my replies underlined in red pencil. I was to follow along... my council handed me a file card so I wouldn't lose my place...until we reached the red high-lighted parts, then read verbatim from the proceedings. My defense was that I was 17, homesick, and wanted nothing more in life than to be a Marine. Nothing was said that wasn't written, and as it was written,

I was busted, lost all pay for six months, and was sentenced to four months in the Camp Pendleton brig.

Chesty Puller, the Marine Corps' most distinguished and most beloved Commandant, is quoted as having said that any Marine worth his salt had served some brig time. I was on my way to becoming a very salty Marine.

Marine Corp brig time is hard time. It's a jigger of boot camp, a dollop of prison and a dash of pure hell. We were sorely treated by our tormentors, the brig guards, some of which had only recently finished boot camp, and were still a little pissed off themselves. The only requirement to become a brig guard, or so it appeared, was to have a tendency towards cruelty.

We had one payback. The prisoners pulled mess duty, and one prisoner was assigned a clicker to count off the men as they entered the mess hall. He would whisper, "Piss in the Jell-O," or "Boogers in the salad," as the prisoners passed. Prisoners would take the offending item, but only the unaware guards would eat it.

After two months in the brig, including a two-week stint of solitary confinement in a four-by-six foot cement cage, I was called before the officer of the day.

"Sir! Prisoner #510, Jackson, D.J. reporting as ordered, sir!" I said, standing at rigid attention before his desk. My mind was buzzing, wondering what rule had I broken this time.

"At ease prisoner," he said, as he tossed two manila envelopes on the desk between us.

"We've received two sets of orders for you, Jackson. You have a decision to make. One set is for a rifle company in Vietnam, the other for the Naval Prison at Portsmouth."

I was elated. I had been trying to get to Vietnam since my first day of boot camp. It took a year and a half, and a trip to the brig, but my time had finally come.

"I'll be going to Vietnam sir," I answered with a smile.

I had one last train wreck that almost derailed my departure for Vietnam. One week before I was scheduled to ship out, I bought a half pint of Jack Daniels, slipped it into my jacket pocket, and went to the theater in Oceanside to see the movie *Bonnie and Clyde*. I had the misfortune to sit behind a big-mouthed sergeant who also happened to be a brig guard. He didn't recognize me, but I remembered him. He was acting the big shot...bragging to his companion about his treatment of prisoners.

The story of Bonnie and Clyde was presented in a way that romanticized their life of crime. By the end of the movie, most viewers were emotional, and firmly anti-authoritarian. My emotion was anger. I was angry, drunk, and I had an authority figure within easy reach.

I attacked the sergeant as soon as he stepped outside the movie theater. He bolted, and I chased him around the block. I was pummeling him in front of Taco Bell when the MPs arrived. I had dealt with the MPs on a previous occasion. That time, I had made the mistake of being verbally abusive while still handcuffed. Landing face first on the cement floor of a holding cell is a good lesson in holding your tongue. This time, I was very cooperative until they removed the cuffs. As soon as they removed the cuffs, I jumped onto the desk of the sergeant of the guard, and it took all three MPs to get me into the cell. By the time the cell door was locked, they were bleeding at least as profusely as I was.

Monday morning, I was standing at attention in front of my commanding officer, eyes swollen and head hung low. He read through the charges: "Drunk! Disorderly! Assault!" He shook his head slowly, and then looked me in the eyes. "You're a slow learner aren't you? I guess we're going to have to Court Martial you again!" he concluded.

My heart fell into my stomach. I couldn't take another day of brig time. I raised my hands, interlocked my fingers in the classic begging posture, and whimpered like a child, "Please sir, let me have one more chance...I'll never drink again. I promise."

"You're God-damned right you won't, son! You'll be in here swabbing decks 'til midnight, every fucking night after training until we ship out! Now get out of my office and get back to your unit!" he yelled, as he slapped my personnel file folder shut.

One month later, the Continental stewardess was instructing me to buckle my seat belt as we circled to land at Da Nang Air Base. My first impression of Vietnam was green. Growing up in the Texas panhandle, sagebrush and rows of cotton were my green. This was an overpowering green that pushed itself to the edges of every road and building...enveloping everything in its path.

Chapter Two
A Recipe for Racism

"You never know, sonny, some nigger might have had that quarter in his pocket!"

A Grandmother's warning to a young child about putting money in his mouth.

I arrived in Vietnam in October of 1967. Back in the world, the anti-war movement was just hitting its stride and irate women were burning their bras. Throngs of angry blacks were marching across the south and burning cities in the north. I thought maybe that would all be behind me, but the simmering racial crisis in America was coming to a boil under the torrid tropical sun of Vietnam.

My mother was raised in the Oklahoma panhandle during the dust bowl days of the depression. It was there that she developed a mortal fear of blowing sand. West Texas was no place for a person with a fear of blowing sand. Sand and wind in west Texas are like salt water and breaking waves on a stormy sea, they are ubiquitous. When my mother would see the vast clouds of churning red sand on the horizon, she would gather us all under the dining room table, like a mother hen with her brood of chicks. She would sob softly and quake with fear as the howling wind covered our four step high back porch with sand. After the storm had passed, I would climb out a window and shovel the sand away from the doors, so we could escape our refuge. And so it was on a Saturday, the summer of my tenth year, we were building a sand barrier for my mother.

We had hired a black man named Willy Rose to help us build a five-foot high wooden fence around our backyard sand lot. When we stopped for lunch, my father, younger brother and I stepped into the kitchen. My mother placed Willy's lunch on the back porch, under the blazing west Texas sun. She was very polite. She gave him a big quart pickle jar of ice water to go with his baloney sandwich, but he was outside with a baloney sandwich, and we were eating fried chicken, mashed potatoes with gravy and corn on the cob in the comfort of our water vapor cooled home.

"Why can't Willy eat in here with us, mom?" I interceded on his behalf, having formed a working man's bond with the friendly black man.

"Oh, son, they like eating outside," she assured me.

Through the ensuing years, I was also assured that "they" liked living in tarpaper shacks; that "they" preferred not to shop in our stores, attend our schools, or drink from our fountains. My preacher said "they" had perverse sexual appetites and were a danger to our women, and that their color was a sure indication they were not loved by God. My coach told me the smell of a nigger would peel paint off the outhouse walls. My grandmother warned me not to put money in my mouth because, "You never know, sonny, some nigger might have had that quarter in his pocket."

How could every person I loved or respected be wrong? Living in a segregated state, my only knowledge of black people and their lives was limited to what I had been told by my elders, who had also grown up in a segregated America. We were ignorance incarnate.

When I was 13, Willy took a job at our Mobil filling station. He worked in the back bay, changing oil and washing cars. He was not allowed to serve customers, or even to come into the front office.

I worked with Willy most days, at least until we had washed and detailed all the cars. Willy was the only black person I knew. He was a handsome man with thick, curly hair graying around the temples. He had broad shoulders and huge hands, and probably would have been one hell of an athlete had he been allowed to attend school. He was always clean-shaven, and came to work in clean clothes, smelling slightly of lye soap. He was a jovial man who loved music...we always turned up the radios on the cars as we detailed the interiors. At 6'2" and over two hundred pounds, he appeared to me to be a gentle giant. He reminded me of Hoss Cartwright from the televised western, "Bonanza".

Like most black men in west Texas, Willy seemingly accepted the status quo. He lived in a dilapidated two-room shack with his wife and two young daughters. There was no electricity or running water, and burlap sacks covered the broken out windows. My stepfather treated Willy like a half-witted child, and paid him twenty-five cents for each car he serviced and washed, but I never heard Willy complain about anything.

Willy didn't have a car of his own, so sometimes I drove him home after work in my old model-A Ford, even though I was forbidden by my stepfather from going to "nigger town" alone. I never had any fear of being there. I was treated with respect, or at least ignored, by everyone I passed, but it was obvious to me that they didn't, and in fact could not have liked living in the kind of poverty I saw there. Some of the children went barefoot through the winter. Most of the tarpaper shacks used old rugs or gunnysacks to cover broken doors and windows. They were denied basic education and medical services that even the poorest of their white neighbors received. The caliche roads were unpaved and became quagmires in the infrequent summer downpours. It was the mud that ended my detours through Willy's side of town.

I was pulling back onto the highway after dropping off Willy, when I saw my stepfather's red El Camino pull up behind me. He waved me to the side of the road and strode to my open window.

"Where you been knucklehead?" he asked angrily.

I could smell the Vaseline tonic in his hair and the whiskey on his breath. "I was just heading back to the station," I replied. I wasn't a very proficient liar.

"You're headed in the wrong direction then, fuck head," he said, as he reached into my wheel well and extracted some caked caliche.

He smeared the caliche on my face, then stepped back to get a better view of his target. He drew back his meaty fist and flung it through the open window. It ricocheted off my shoulder on the way to my jaw.

"You lying sack of shit. Get your ass back to work!" he yelled as he stomped back to his pickup. It would be the last time he hit me. I ran away from home two weeks later.

I never saw Willy again. I met a black recruit in Oklahoma City named Jimmy Bell. We spent a couple of days getting acquainted on our way to boot camp, and I met a few other black Marines there, but color no longer mattered. We were all equal, all fuckin' maggots according to our drill instructors.

Before I had been assigned to my unit, I knew things were different with the blacks in Vietnam. At the processing center, black Marines on their way home from their tours in-country, stood off together in one corner, speaking a language of their own making. Many sported "fros" with hair pics jutting out at rakish angles. There was a boom box at their feet blaring out the latest Motown hits. Their anger was palpable. Everything about them was non-regulation; their uniforms, their hair, their profanity, their very demeanor was anti -Marine. They were heavily armed "ditty boppers" and it seemed, there was no one willing to take them to task.

I stayed away from the group, far enough that I could hear the corporal making assignments above the pounding music. I got my orders, and piled into the back of a six by six with eight other "newbies". We were lurching down a deeply rutted country road when I recognized a familiar face. Washington had been in my platoon in boot camp. He was an 18-year-old black Marine from Lubbock, Texas. We weren't tight by any means, but we had spent some time talking about home while in boot camp. I stepped across the truck, taking a seat next to Washington.

"Hey Washington, what's up?"

He looked at me puzzled for a second before recognition spread across his face. "Jack!" He yelped with surprise, "God damned, it's good to see a familiar face!"

We caught up a little, before I asked, "What's up with those black guys?"

"Hell if I know," he began, "I went through AIT with one of those dudes, but when I tried to talk to him, he told me to back the fuck off and called me an Oreo," he paused, shaking his head. "There must be some sort of weird shit going on over here," he surmised.

We bounced over a pass, and wound down a red dirt road into a shining tin-roofed city built on a muddy hillside overlooking a patchwork of intertwining rice paddies. We debarked from the truck and went our separate ways. Washington was assigned to 2nd platoon of Fox Company. I was assigned to 3rd platoon in Echo.

Our living quarters were a line of 60' by 20' plywood hooches with screened in sides and overhanging corrugated metal roofs. The black Marines had segregated themselves. All but a brave few were living in two hooches at the end of the row, their screens covered by camouflaged netting. Whenever two of the segregated black Marines would pass one another, they would go through a hand slapping ritual of mutual recognition. Many, if not most, were heavy into drugs. They called themselves the "Splib" brothers.

With the popularity of the war falling, the Marines were no longer able to meet their quota of volunteers, so a traditional all volunteer force was being diminished by the draft. Most of the discontented blacks were drafted. An inordinate number of those drafted were inner-city blacks. Many were bitter because of the racial problems back in Chicago, Philly, or Detroit. They also believed that a disproportionate number of blacks were being drafted as compared to "Whitey". The Splib brothers made life hell for those traditional black Marines who had volunteered to serve in the corps, and still espoused the values of duty and honor. They were Oreos, black on the outside, white in the middle. I was not sympathetic to the Splib's complaints. This was Vietnam...fuck what might be happening stateside. Our lives were on the line.

I hadn't been in-country very long when I got a pass to spend the day on Freedom Hill. Freedom Hill was a paradise just outside the perimeter of the Da Nang Air Base. The area was replete with an air-conditioned movie theater, a shopping mall size PX, a Red Cross headquarters serviced by several round eyed doughnut dollies, and most importantly, an outside beer garden.

I did it all...I sat at a round table with half a dozen other fucked up Marines and two doughnut dollies, trying my best to craft the story that would earn their affection. Alas, they had heard it all. I slept through 'The Green Berets', angry at John Wayne for deserting the Corps, but at least the theater was cool. I walked starry eyed through the PX, amazed at the variety of American goods here in this most impoverished country. They had washers and dryers, I was dumbfounded. I finished at the beer garden.

The beer ration in Vietnam was two beers per day per man. It cost a dime a beer, and beers were always served two at a time. Since most Marines were in the field or otherwise unable to drink their ration, Marines with free time had to work extra hard to ensure the daily ration was consumed. I got my two beers and sat at a table with three guys from my unit who had also traveled to Freedom Hill for the day. I drank several rations of beer before I noticed that the Splib brothers had taken control of the jukebox. They would kick the jukebox, causing it to skip over any song that was not performed by a black artist. I pointed out my revelation to my friends. They told me to be cool, the music was good and the beer was cold, but it didn't jibe with my soddened sensibilities. There was one tall, white Marine, with an alcohol-charged, Texas drawl, that seemed to agree with me. He was pushing his way through the Splib brothers to get to the jukebox. While he had them distracted, I stepped over and made a selection...Jim Reeves singing "Distant Drums".

I had spent my last night in Oklahoma with a high school friend, on his way to the army. We partied in the living room of a divorced woman's trailer, hoping at least one of us might get lucky. We drank into the early hours of the morning, listening to 'Distant Drums' while we told our hostess sob stories in hopes of winning her short-term affection. Larry was apparently a better story teller. I slept on the couch, but it was still a fond memory of my last night at home. I'd be damned if I wouldn't hear Jim Reeves sing. I sat close by the jukebox until Jim started to croon, then stood up and announced, "You boys don't wanna fuck with that song."

The fight was instantaneous, the drunk Texan and myself grappling with five Splib brothers. I was rolling on the red clay road that ran past the beer garden with one of the brothers, when my right hand found a fist-sized rock. I came up on top, astride the brother, but just as I was about to strike, another Splib brother jumped on my back. I grabbed a fist full of his hair with my left hand, and with the jagged rock in my right, I began to alternate between bashing the skull of the man on my back and the man between my knees. The other three brothers were busy, working over the Texan.

Gunshots rang out and we all scattered in the general direction of the back wall of the PX, where we had deposited our weapons. The MPs who fired the shots quickly cordoned off the area, closed down the beer garden, and regulated the dispersal of weapons to insure a hasty but orderly shutdown of Freedom Hill. I caught a 6 by 6 heading back to camp.

The story of the fight spread quickly through the company, and by the end of the week, a group of the Splib brothers had threatened that I wouldn't return from our next operation. The blacks were angry and heavily armed, however, in the Marines, they were still a small minority. I went to their hovel with a contingent of my own heavily armed men. We made a counter offer...if anything happened to me, they were all dead men.

"What if the NVA waste you?" They seemed suddenly concerned for my welfare.

"Same fuckin' result, you're all dead men!" we warned.

When Sergeant James, my platoon sergeant from Tennessee, heard about my negotiating skills with the Splib brothers, he made me a team leader. He placed the three most worthless black Marines in our platoon under my leadership.

Tarver came to the Marines via the draft from Phoenix, Arizona, where both of his parents were college professors at the university. He was 21, and he had a college degree of his own. He was an Oreo, detested and constantly berated by the radical blacks. He did not use drugs or drink. He was a wonderful young man who was completely overwhelmed by his fear. Every time a firefight would break out, he would roll up into a ball and start crying. Tarver was not a coward. I watched him wade into a mob of Splib brothers with a metal lunch tray. He was the loneliest man in the company; too intelligent for most of the white Marines and hated by most of the blacks.

In our first contact with me serving as his team leader, we were using team rushes to try and dislodge a platoon of

NVA from a tree line. In team rushes, two rifle teams lay down a covering fire while the other team rushes forward, then, ideally, you alternate rushing and firing until you have overrun your objective. My team rushed forward, exposing ourselves to the marksmanship of a platoon of regular NVA. It felt damn good to be safely back on my belly, ready to lay down fire for the next team. Then, I hear the booming voice of Sergeant James.

"Jack, get your man forward."

I looked back to our previous position. Tarver lay there curled up in the fetal position. I ran back screaming, "Tarver, get your fuckin' ass up here."

He laid there motionless, I was hoping maybe he was dead, but no...he's crying too loud to be dead. I threw myself to the ground beside him and screamed in his ear, "Get your ass forward now!"

"I can't do it Jack," he sobbed, but I wasn't sympathetic.

I jerked him to his feet, dragged him forward, and pushed him back to the ground. Not a pretty sight, but we both survived. That evening was the first of many that I asked Sergeant James to transfer Tarver to the rear.

"He's a good guy, Sarge, but he can't control his fear. He's gonna get himself or someone else killed. Let him work in an office at headquarters or be a cook or something, anything but this."

"Shit, Jack, there are a lot of guys that'd like to get out of here, and most deserve it more than him. He'll either get used to it, or we'll haul his ass out in a body bag."

Harris was a malingerer from Cincinnati. He was lazy...he was a liar...he was a stoner, and he was a coward. Harris was a Splib brother not because of some deeply held belief, but because there was security in numbers. On more than one occasion, when we were taking incoming mortar fire, he sliced himself up with his P-38 (can opener) and started yelling for the Corpsman. He got a purple heart the first time, but he got stoned and bragged to the wrong person. After that, the Corpsman would bandage him up, and warn him to quit cutting himself.

Green was the worst, a true hard case. He was drafted out of Detroit, where he had been through the riots. He said his fight was with whitey, and he refused to fight the NVA, whom he considered an ally. He vowed that he would only kill the NVA to save his own life. On an operation outside Chi Lai, a group of six Marines from another company were blown to hell when they stopped to warm themselves by a campfire our company had left burning. Two grenades had been discarded in the fire. As team leaders, we were each saddled with the responsibility of inventorying our men's equipment to try and determine the source of the grenades. Green was absent his frag grenades. He said he had buried them, because they were heavy, and he never intended to use them anyway. Nothing could be proven, but we all knew Green had killed several of his fellow Marines. Green was a menace and I could have, and probably should have, killed him.

In a fire fight, my fire team consisted of one Marine rolled up in a ball sobbing, one slashing himself with a P-38, and the other refusing to shoot at his comrades. When it was my team's turn to take the point, I was the only one I could trust. Through the long darkness of night, who could I trust to stand watch? The ignorance of my youth was quickly being replaced with a deep hatred, but not for the reasons I had been taught. It wasn't sexual perversion, or laziness, or the smell...God we all stank! My life was in constant peril because of black men who were refusing to fulfill their obligation as Marines. For the most part, they were using race as a reason, and I was quickly becoming a vocally belligerent racist.

Chapter Three
To Protect the Innocent

"It's their people, it's their war."

Sgt. James excusing the atrocities perpetuated by the South Vietnamese Army against the people of South Vietnam.

I spent most of my first two months in Vietnam standing perimeter watch in a thirty-foot tall sandbagged tower. Days were spent stringing concertina wire, filling sand bags and building or strengthening defensive positions. We were rocketed a couple of times a month, but the rockets were mostly aimed toward the middle of the base, so the perimeter was the safest place to be. Rats and boredom became my biggest enemies. One I could kill, the other was killing me. I started volunteering for night patrols. We would patrol the darkened streets along the outskirts of Da Nang, or along the edges of smaller villages, looking for any VC activity. It was eerie, but mostly uneventful, until I encountered the girl.

When I arrived in-country, I thought the Vietnamese women were absolutely disgusting. Most dressed in filthy looking black pajamas and chewed betel nut, which produced a nasty dribble of red juice down their chins. They squatted to pee when and wherever the urge arose. They would squat in a circle, babbling and picking lice out of one another's hair. It was all too much for an old Texas hand. I vowed to go without for the duration of my tour.

We were patrolling the outskirts of Da Nang. It was late, and very quiet on the deserted street. I was crouched in the middle of the street, waiting for orders. A small figure emerged from one of the darkened doorways. In dainty steps, she flittered to my ear. Her aroma was alluring. My belly ached with desire. "Come inside," she invited. I couldn't remember ever wanting anything so badly.

"Saddle up!" Smitty ordered, and we moved out.

No one else saw the girl, maybe she was an apparition. Whatever she was, it marked the end to my abstinence. We would bring prostitutes to the bunkers at night, and use a radio code to make all the perimeter guards aware of their offerings. It cost two dollars for ten minutes of bliss, and as often as not, three days of agony. We were warned about black syphilis and razor blades implanted in the walls of women's vaginas, but we were young men in our sexual prime, 10,000 miles away from round-eyed women. Thirteen months of Playboy magazines and doughnut dolly dreams seemed unbearable.

The first time I caught the clap, I felt dirty to the very core of my being, and the pain was excruciating. It took two weeks after treatment before my desire for the girls overrode the memory of the pain.

It was during this time that I had my first contact with the enemy. They were VC, an old man and what we guessed was probably his grandson, a boy about 14 or 15 years old. The NVA had given them a relic bolt-action rifle and a few precious rounds of ammo, with instructions to kill Americans. They were holed-up in an abandoned well when we entered their village. We set up a command post near the well. We left the first sergeant and his radioman there while the rest of the company began a search of the village.

The two VC crawled out of their hole, killed the radioman and shot the first sergeant in the back. We quickly drove them back into the well under a hail of gunfire. We threw seven fragmentation grenades down the hole, then spent the next hour digging them out...to rectify our body count.

The bodies were pasty, and riddled with divots...as if someone had thrown a handful of gravel into wet cement. The boy's left arm was gone. The left side of his chest was churned to a pulpy jelly. The grandfather's right leg was mangled and twisted...held together by a few frayed tendons. His body was face up, but his right foot was turned completely around and extended at least two feet past his left foot. As we dragged the old man from the well, his brain slid from its broken skull, gurgling into the red dirt. Ski began to stir the grey matter with a stick. "Wonder what the old son of a bitch is thinking about now?" he joked.

It was the first human brain I had ever seen, the first time I had witnessed the results of our firepower; dead humans I had helped to kill. It flipped a circuit in my brain. I was suddenly filled with the certainty that I could die in Vietnam.

We were ordered to hang the bodies in the village temple as a warning to others. When we tried to hoist the old man into the rafters, his head came off. Undaunted, we hung him by his good leg. I didn't sleep well that night.

My first Christmas in-country, I was alone in the watch tower looking out across an empty rice paddy. A lot of the guys had gotten passes to attend the Bob Hope Christmas Show in Da Nang. I was offered a pass, but had volunteered to stay behind...too many months left in Nam to be enticed by half naked starlets.

Two children walked out into the paddy from the village in the tree line at the far edge of the muddy quagmire. I watched them through binoculars as they approached the wire. The older of the two, a thin boy in black shorts and a tattered t-shirt, was leading a menacing looking water buffalo by a ring through its nose. A diminutive girl followed behind, flicking the ass of the beast with a leafy branch. They made a beeline straight to the concertina wire in front of my bunker. The girl shouted across the wire.

"Marine, you gib us food please, Mai Ling berri hungry!"

She may have been small, but her voice was not pleading, it was more like she was placing her order for lunch. It being almost Christmas, I was in a generous mood. I grabbed a few cans of sea rations, climbed down the ladder and waved them closer. The boy, I would later know as Hang, appeared frightened and lowered his head. They were holding hands, and when Mai Ling started forward, Hang tried to pull her back. She turned to Hang, saying something rash in Vietnamese, then shook off his grasp. She came to the wire armed with a devastating smile.

Mai Ling was also dressed in tattered hand-me-downs and barefoot. Thick, black, blood-bloated leeches covered her feet and had climbed half way to her knees, but she seemed oblivious to the menace. Her coal black hair was pulled back, but her shaggy bangs hung crookedly over sparkling dollops of chocolate colored eyes. Her skin seemed aglow, the color of autumn straw, smeared of course with the requisite patches of paddy mud. She was, after all, only seven years old.

I stood mesmerized by this child of poverty and war. I, on my side of the wire, a citizen of the world's most wealthy nation...our base had more food stores and medical facilities than most large Vietnamese cities. On the other side of the wire stood this child of one of the world's most wretched nations...torn by war, poverty, hunger, and rampant with exotic diseases. Why was she emanating such joy?

"You OK, Marine?"

She roused me from my reverie. "You throw food Mai Ling now. We berri hungry, you Numba 1 Marine, gib us food, OK?"

I tossed over the cans I had brought down and asked them to wait. I went back up in the tower and filled a sand bag with several more green cans. I threw the bag across the wire and wished them a Merry Christmas.

"Vietnam no hab Christmas," Mai Ling informed me, "We hab big time New Year."

"Well, then Happy New Year," I said.

"New Year no come now, big party come soon, you likey berri much Marine, OK?"

"Sure...I likey much."

"We come again tomorrow, you numba 1 Marine bring more food, OK?"

"Sure, I'll bring more food."

"What name you hab, Marine?"

"My name is Jack," I answered, and I was hooked.

She rejoined Hang. He forced the head of the buffalo down by exerting pressure on the nose ring, and the children stepped onto his horns. As the animal raised its head, they slid nimbly onto his back. Mai Ling smiled at me, slapped the butt of the buffalo with her switch, and they ambled back towards the village.

I began to appropriate a case of sea rations every evening on my way to the tower. The number of children increased. The ragtag group would congregate at the small gate near our tower, anxiously awaiting my arrival. Mai Ling was the mouthpiece for the gang. She was small, even for a seven year old, perpetually barefoot, with those lively brown eyes always partially hidden behind her shaggy bangs. Mai Ling was one of the youngest of the children, but clearly the brightest. She had decided the Americans represented her best chance for survival, so she taught herself to speak English.

At first, I would open a case of sea rations, and let the kids dig in, but the bigger boys like Hang would always grab the lion's share and run back towards the village. I started shooing away the older boys and giving all of the rations to Mai Ling. I let her divvy them out, knowing she would be fair with the younger children. She always set back meals for the older boys I had shooed away. When the children were finished eating, I would wrestle in the sand with the younger boys, just as I had with my nephews back in the states. Mai Ling would laugh and throw sand in my hair, yelling, "You crazy numba 1 Marine, Jack!"

Even though it was against regulations, I often let Mai Ling come inside the wire. I showed her how to target and fire our 81 mortar, and took her up into the tower to let her look through the binoculars. She loved to watch the people in her village. She would tell me who they were, and what they were like.

Mai Ling was an orphan. Her parents had been killed by the local VC before she was old enough to remember what they looked like. Mai Ling was afraid of the VC. She said, "VC berri bad, they numba 10...come kill many people in Miloc...you be berri careful Jack...before VC come kill you."

Mai Ling was being raised by the village, but even at her tender age she was expected to provide for her own sustenance. She had matured far beyond her years, yet she retained an innocence and zest for life that won my heart. I knew that in a scant few years she would be sold into prostitution by her elders. I could not bear the thought of her becoming a boom-boom girl. Although I knew it would be virtually impossible for a single enlisted man to adopt a Vietnamese child, I had fallen in love with Mai Ling, and decided to try. My only option, it turned out, was for one of my married family members back in the states to adopt Mai Ling. When I talked to Mai Ling about becoming part of my family, she laughed, "People in America not like Mai Ling."

"They'll love you," I protested.

"No, they no like Mai Ling, Mai Ling not same people in America," she said, with a wisdom that belied her age.

She was right. When I approached my family about trying to get Mai Ling moved stateside, they said they weren't ready to have a little slant-eyed kid running around the house.

Mai Ling became my reason for being in Vietnam. Back in the states, people were burning American flags and spitting on guys coming home from Nam. The communist threat didn't seem that eminent. The Marine Corps was being destroyed by dissension from within, but maybe I could protect this one small Vietnamese child.

Tet 1968 started with fireworks and random gunfire, all part of the Lunar New Year celebration Mai Ling had promised, or so we thought; then we saw the rockets hit Da Nang, and my world changed. We became prisoners in our own compound. NVA flags fluttered in the wind above the children's village, partially hidden by the tree line just three hundred yards outside our gate. American jets were dropping 500 pound bombs and canisters of napalm on the village. We were suppressing fire from the village with mortars and machine guns. I was distraught. Days turned into weeks before we were able to drive the VC and NVA back into their jungle fortress.

The children did not return. We found them in a mass grave near the center of their bombed out village. I held my breath long enough to peek into the ditch. Mai Ling's contorted, naked body lay near the top of the pile of children, her rotting flesh pulled taut across her cheeks, her lively eyes pecked out by crows, her once silky black hair matted with dried blood. The stench was unbearable. I ran to the edge of the village, retching in anguish. The remaining villagers told us the NVA had bound their hands with wire, bashed in their skulls with a ball peen hammer, then tossed their twitching bodies into the shallow mass grave as a warning to others not to befriend Americans. I couldn't understand how anyone could be so cruel. It was the first time I actually hated the NVA.

We scattered lime over the corpses and called in a dozer to cover the grave, then bulldozed the entire village. The village, several hundred years old according to some of its inhabitants, was destroyed to deny cover or comfort to the enemy. Every structure and all the graceful old palms were knocked down and covered with sand. The dazed villagers, with chickens tucked under their arms and the few possessions they could carry stowed in baskets balanced on their heads, were loaded into amtracks and moved to a resettlement camp on the outskirts of Da Nang. Within a week, there was nothing but sterile white sand and the stones of an ancient cemetery visible from the tower where Mai Ling and I had so often watched the life of her village unfold. A big piece of my heart lay buried with that village.

It was the beginning of a new policy in Vietnam. Before Tet, we had been trying to win the hearts and minds of the Vietnamese people. We had units in the villages dispersing health care, digging new wells and building new schools. After Tet, all of Vietnam except for a few coastal cities became a free fire zone. Our job was to clear the countryside of all Vietnamese and destroy anything that might give comfort or aid to the NVA and VC forces. This included the destruction of entire villages, destroying all crops and food stores and the killing of all livestock. We were told that the people were warned to move to safe havens and anybody left was fair game. It came down from the top, "If it moves, it's VC."

A few weeks later, we passed through a village along the edge of the mountains on a search and destroy mission. The village was in a free fire zone, but still populated. While Sergeant James was interrogating one of the village elders, I found a cool refuge in the shade of an arbor near one of the thatched huts that composed the village. I had no sooner sat down than a young girl emerged from the hut and offered me a bowl of rice. It smelled ok, none of the manioc fish sauce that the Vietnamese preferred, so I took the rice. She sat next to me as I ate, chirping away like a mother bird protecting her nest. I didn't understand a word she was saying, but I smiled and nodded a lot, which seemed to please her immensely. I figured she was between 12 to 14 years old, about the age of my sister.

Sergeant James finished his questioning and we were ordered to saddle up. I handed back the bowl, said thank you, and roughed her hair as I turned to leave. She smiled, then whirled around and ran giggling back to her hut. It was one of those moments of connection, like two halves of a broken stone bumping together in their journey down river, suddenly remembering their oneness, then being tossed again into the raging torrent. I looked back as we left the village. She was standing in the doorway smiling. I waved and returned the smile, knowing it was unlikely our paths would cross again.

I was wrong. After a day of patrolling the pine covered foothills near the village, we returned there to set up our CP for the night. Z and I set up our shared poncho shelter at the edge of the CP, near the girl's hut. We were lying with our backs against our packs, sharing a moment over a can of peaches, when we heard a scream. We burst through the thicket separating our encampment from the girl's hut. In the clearing, behind the hut, two South Vietnamese soldiers were holding the girls arms while a third beat her across the back with a bamboo cane.

I yelled for them to stop. They looked at me with disdain, and continued to beat the girl. I chambered a round and stuck my M-16 into the face of the man with the cane.

"Dee Dee Mau motherfucker," I screamed, leaving no doubt I would kill them all if they didn't leave immediately. They were screwed...their own weapons were stacked against a nearby tree. They pushed the girl to the ground and fumed away. She lay on the ground sobbing, her white blouse torn and bloody, her face discolored and swollen. I helped her to her feet and let her use me for support as she staggered back toward her porch. Her wide-eyed parents met me half way, pulling their child from my grasp and chasing me away with angry prattle.

"Hell, you'd think I was the one beating her!" I complained to Z, as we returned to our shelter.

"We'll be leaving soon, they'll still be here," Z replied.

"What do you mean?" I asked, defensively, knowing exactly what he meant.

"All I'm saying is you can't keep doing this shit. I know...I've seen it!"

We were out on ambush that night, when the South Vietnamese soldiers returned. They tortured and raped the girl and her mother, before cutting their throats. The father was forced to watch, then mercifully, he was shot in the back of the head. It happened right under the noses of our officers manning the CP.

When I returned from ambush, I saw the bodies laid out in a row in the clearing behind the hut. I turned to head to the South Vietnamese camp, but Sergeant James stepped into my path.

"You can't go there!" he warned.

"Those mother fuckers can't get away with this shit," I protested.

"You might as well have killed those folks yourself as to have made those assholes lose face," he said in his slow Tennessee drawl. "It's their people, it's their war."

"But why should we allow them to rape, pillage and murder the people we're here to protect?"

"It's not our business to wonder why...just to do or die," he concluded in his sergeanty way.

"Well they better sure as fuck not count them as dead combatants," I yelled, loud enough to be heard at the Command Post.

"You know they will," James said quietly, then turned to walk away and repeated, "You know they will."

I knew James was right. If I had not interfered, the bastards would have raped the girl, robbed the parents and gone on their merry way. That was their *modus operandi*.

The Vietnamese were part of a ten-man detachment assigned to our company as a liaison between us and the civilian population. Instead, they treated us like their hired thugs. We would secure a ville...they would come in behind us and rape the women, steal anything of value, and murder anyone who questioned their authority. Of course, anyone they killed was VC, and thereby eligible for our body count. I swore a private oath to kill them when the opportunity arose.

That day marked the end of my compassion for the suffering of the Vietnamese people. I decided that being raped, murdered, or blown to bits in your sleep was just the price you paid for being born in Vietnam. Their own army, our policies and our air power were as much to blame for their suffering as the VC or NVA. There was just nothing I could do...nobody I could save! My fantasy of being a white knight vaporized into the steamy jungle, like Lieutenant Sumpter when he stepped on the booby trapped 500 pound bomb. This was not the war of our fathers or the John Wayne movies. There was no clear distinction in my mind between the good guys and the bad guys. The only winners were the survivors.

One day folded into another, broken by a few hours of sleep rolled up in our ponchos. Sometimes we were cold, sometimes the heat was so intense men passed out from dehydration. We were soaked through when it rained and soaked in sweat when it didn't. We lugged 70 to 80 pounds of gear, sloshing through paddies and rivers, cutting our way through jungles and working our way up into the mountains, always searching for the elusive NVA. It was mostly long days of boredom punctuated by moments of intense adrenalin surges during firefights or mortar and rocket attacks. The NVA were always watching, setting mines and ambushes...waiting for us to make the big mistake.

Our operations took us through many small villages. Sometimes we just passed through peacefully. Sometimes we stopped to ransack and burn the village, destroying all the food stores and killing the chickens, pigs and water buffalo. One time we passed through a village on the way out to an operation, then stopped on the road overlooking the village on the way back, and lit it up. It seemed random to me, like maybe it depended on whether or not some General back in Da Nang got laid that night.

"To deny food and comfort to the enemy," we were told, if we bothered to ask. After a while, you just quit asking.

We didn't seek out innocents to kill, but we were operating in free kill zones, where everyone was considered a target of opportunity. We operated under standing orders: "If they run, they're VC."

Our air power was much less selective and struck with less warning. You could hear a company of Marines coming from a half mile away. A jet could swoop from the sky in an instant, and incinerate an entire village and its occupants.

The undercurrent of racial tension was churning into a tidal wave of antagonism that often exploded into violence. It was often between two or more of the Splib brothers, usually, because one of the brothers wasn't being black enough. As much as we all may have desired to be green, the violence back in the states was infusing an increasingly radical point of view into our midst. The brothers seemed more attuned to the fallacies of our policies, and in general, had more empathy with the Vietnamese people, but after Sgt. James' experiment of using me as the team leader for the malingering blacks, I had lost all tolerance for things not white.

I began to mark off the days on a calendar I kept stuffed in my helmet liner. Scientists tell us that the human body completely replaces itself, cell by cell, every seven years. My metamorphosis had been much quicker. I hadn't spent even a full cycling of the season in Vietnam, but the young man with the high ideas was no more. I no longer loved God or country, nor did I retain my passion to save the world from evil. An overpowering darkness had replaced the light, and I was filled with hatred. I hated God. I despised the leaders, if you could call them that, of my own country, the South Vietnamese, the NVA, our policies, blacks, and hippies. I could see that we were not trying to win the war, or the hearts and minds of the people. I couldn't tell what we were trying to accomplish, but the "whys" and "what fors" didn't make a diddley shit any more. I had become entirely desensitized to the pain of anyone except my band of brothers.

My world consisted of a company of Marines. We all had one set of utilities, a WW II era soft pack, a helmet, a poncho, a web belt with as many canteens as you could physically tolerate, one pair of jungle boots, an M-16, and as much ammo and ordinance as we could carry. We were rationed two meals a day, and resupplied every third day. We seldom had an occasion to bathe, and we all smelled like shit. We had to drink water where we found it, so everyone had some degree of dysentery. Toilet tissue was a tradable commodity, and trench foot was epidemic.

I was sure the NVA were watching, just waiting for me to take off my boots. It felt like every time I did, a firefight would erupt. There was no way I would take my boots off at night. Dry socks were rarer than a rice paddy without leeches, so our feet were constantly wet. My feet turned green on the bottoms, and large chunks of rotted flesh routinely fell into my rancid socks.

Not only did we share the same hopes, fears and discomforts, we spent all of our time together, 24/7. We ate together, slept together, and showered together when the opportunity arose. Our lives were inexorably intertwined. The failure of one could mean the death of us all. We became brothers. We would do whatever we deemed necessary to ensure the survival of any member of our brotherhood, and for some, nothing outside that brotherhood mattered. It was a powerful sense of belonging; but even that comfort was being whittled away.

Sergeant Billings and I trained together before shipping out to Nam. A week after our arrival, he lost his face when he rolled a dead VC off a live grenade. Marshal and Rico were cut down by machine gun fire when they rushed an NVA bunker. Jake, Cotton Top and Travis we lost to booby traps. Jake was gone before we got him to the chopper. Bruce killed his own best friend, Brown, when Brown came in from a busted ambush in poor visibility. Bruce was hauled from the field in shackles a month later, after he wrapped a pound of C-4 around a mortar round and set it on fire outside the CO's tent. He was cognizant enough to know the C-4 wouldn't explode without a blasting cap. It was his way of cutting his ties with the people he thought he had failed.

McCall, Snider, and Pierce were relatively lucky. McCall and Snider caught malaria, and Pierce came down with Elephantiasis. They all left on their backs, but in one piece.

Most we lost to rotation. I didn't know who had decided we would fight harder if we had a limited term of service, a tour of duty; but he was sorely mistaken. It was severely detrimental to unit cohesion.

For Marines, the tour was thirteen months. New guys were assigned where the need was greatest, which didn't always match their MOS (military occupational specialty). A rifleman might be assigned as an A-gunner to mortars, rockets or machine guns just to heft around the heavy ammo. If he had any inkling of how a Pric 25 radio worked, he might be assigned to communications. The casualty rate for radio operators was so high, no one else wanted the job.

New guys were a pox. No one wanted a newby assigned to their squad or team. They were an unknown quantity, a dangerous liability. They were prone to make stupid mistakes...like trying to recover an SKS from beneath the body of a dead VC, or standing an LP with the pin pulled on their grenade...mistakes that could, and sometimes did, kill others. Depending on the man and the level of activity, it could take two weeks to a couple of months before they became a trusted member of the unit. Until then, they were an outsider...an awful, lonely thing to be 10,000 miles away from home.

Short timers were another kind of problem. When a man was down to a month left in country, he would begin work on his short timer's stick. He would begin with a five or six foot hiking cane and carve on it daily. His goal was to carve a tooth pick to clean the olive pits out of his teeth, left from the martinis he would drink on his flight home. Once a man started on his stick, he was generally consumed by dread, anxiety, and sometimes a foreboding that he might not finish the stick. Maybe he had used up all his luck. We would all try to lighten the mood, sometimes with short timer jokes – you're so short you have to stand on your tiptoes to piss in a foxhole! But we all knew that being too cautious could be just as dangerous as being a newby. We would all do whatever we could to keep a short timer out of bad situations and get him home. Those who made it home were often racked by guilt because of the friends they left behind. Many ended up volunteering to return.

With an ever-shifting landscape of new faces replacing our losses, and the most experienced men rotating, it was near impossible to maintain the unit cohesion and *espirit de corps* needed to succeed. For most it became a perverse exercise in survival; 13 months and a wake up, then back to the world.

Between the stories we heard from those who went stateside and returned, and what we were hearing from the newbies, some of us decided going home wasn't for us. In

September, I discarded my calendar, and Jake, Z and I made a pact to stay in Nam until the war was over. We all went to the CO and signed a six months extension.

Z's loss was the toughest for me. He got his while eating a can of ham and motherfuckers. We were sitting back against a tree, talking about our mother's best home cooked meals, when I heard a shot and a loud "ding." I looked around the tree and saw Z slumped over with a wisp of grey smoke coming from a hole in the side of his helmet. He wasn't dead... unconscious and probably brain dead...but his heart was still beating.

I remembered early in our tours, when we were all talking about being wounded, and we all shared what amount of maiming was acceptable for us to still want to return home. Z had said," If there's nothing left but my head and my jaws still flapping...throw it on a poncho and get me the fuck out of here."

A resupply chopper was on the ground, so we loaded Z onto a poncho and rushed to get him there before it took off. As we were running toward the chopper, I looked down to check Z's status. Little bits of gray matter were leaking from his wound into the folds of the poncho. I remembered the old man, his brain sloshing from its skull, and was reminded that war has no favorite sons. It reduces us all to the base elements of shit, sweat, piss, blood and tears.

It was the same old story...a brother loaded on a chopper, disappears into the sky, and he's gone forever. We never heard if Z lived or died; he was just gone, and I would miss him.

A week after Z got hit, Sgt. James stopped me as I was walking past him on a jungle trail.

"I was looking over your records and saw you haven't taken your extension R and R yet," he said.

"I don't need R and R! Shit! Some of these new guys don't know which way to point a claymore!" I protested.

"They'll be fine. Everyone needs to get out of this shit hole for a while."

"Sarge, I really don't think this is the best time."

"Bull shit! You're leaving on the resupply chopper tonight. You're going to Okinawa. You're gonna get drunk, you're gonna get laid, and you're gonna fuckin' like it, and that's an order Jack! You get your gear together and find me as soon as we set in...understood?"

My bird came in at dusk. I sat in the door of the chopper as we lifted off, looking down through the jungle at my platoon digging in for the night. A feeling of peace flowed through my body as I realized I would not be going out on ambush tonight. There would be no listening post or standing watch of any kind for the next week.

Chapter Four
Rest and Recreation

"Do you think she really loves me, or is she just doing it for the money?"
Question from a lonely, and very drunk Marine, Okinawa, November 1968.

Okinawa was every bit as green as Vietnam, but no one was shooting at me. Bars, brothels and bath houses lined the streets of Kosa. I checked into my hotel room, and spent the first hour in a steamy tub, trying to wash away the stench of war. I found the brown paper bag wrapped bottle of Jack Daniels in the bottom of my ditty bag, uncorked it and took a long pull from the bottle, then opened the curtains to look out on the street below.

Mind numbing neon signs competed for the attention of a throng of young, drunken Americans. A few were in uniform, but most wore civvies, anxious to put the military behind them if only for a few hours. I nursed the warm whiskey as I dressed in a pair of khaki slacks and an outlandish, bleeding madras shirt I had picked up at the R and R welcome center. I staggered down the stairs and into the street, ducking into the first club. I stood in the darkened doorway until my eyes adjusted, then spied an empty bar stool at the end of the bar. A harlot, well past her prime, pushed her way between the stools and slid up beside me.

"You buy me drink, GI?" she cooed thickly.

Bleary-eyed and wearing a stained and rumpled, red silk kimono, she smelled absolutely flammable. A lethal mixture of slow gin, passionate perspiration and two dollar a gallon perfume, I surmised.

"Not tonight honey," I deferred, as I turned to order a drink.

I felt her hand brush my pocket as she staggered off toward another mark. I didn't need to check my pocket...my money was tucked safely inside my sock.

I sat at the bar drinking Jack and coke, assessing the possibilities. There were a few couples slow dancing in the back of the club near a seldom used stairway. The stairway led to a row of thinly partitioned boom-boom rooms. Most of the action was along the front wall. Drunken soldiers sprawled in pink naugahyde booths, paying two dollars a pop for watered down "champagne", to keep scantily clad Okinawan women at their tables. The women, many themselves just teenagers, would sit on their laps and let the boys feel them up enough to hold their attention. When the money was gone, so were the girls. Periodically, one of the boys would wise up to the game, realizing he was too low on cash to keep the girl interested, and start to complain. The offender was quietly escorted from the club. If he refused to leave, the Military Police were quick to respond; a sudden and unhappy end to a man's R and R. I had no intention of leaving Okinawa broke and horny.

I stepped back into the street, walked past the neon signs and turned down an alley. There, painted women dawdled in front of cramped stalls. These were business women, no watered down drinks or slow dances.

I picked a girl in a clinging, yellow print dress. Her aroma was that of floral soap and scented face powder. She had pretty dark eyes and silky black hair pulled back into a bun, but I was especially drawn by the lively bounce of her ample, pear shaped breasts.

"You look lonely," she said in almost perfect English, as she brushed her fingers across my temple. Like a bow drawn across the strings of a violin, her touch sent a melodious vibration through my body.

"Come in and I'll help you forget your troubles," she promised.

She kept her promise. She gave me a sponge bath in warm, soapy water, and for the next couple of hours we talked, laughed and screwed. I was just a young man sharing time and affection with a young woman. Vietnam was light years away, in another dimension. It was the best ten dollar investment I had ever made.

Satisfied that my night had been well spent, I started back to the hotel. As I walked past the club, I decided to slip in for a night cap. I sat at the bar next to three uniformed army privates. They were heading for Nam.

The nearest man leaned over and yelled in my ear, "You fuckin' Army, man?"

"Marine," I responded, looking straight ahead.

"We got a fuckin' Marine here," he reported to his friends.

"Fuckin' jar head huh," the middle man said, craning his neck around his friend to get a closer look.

He was the biggest of the three...handsome, with piercing blue eyes and slightly chubby cheeks. He looked too young to be shaving...way too young to be drunk in a brothel on his way to war.

"You jarheads got yourselves into some deep shit up in Kahn Sahn didn't cha? Don't worry, the cavalry is on its way. We're gonna save your sorry asses," the big boy taunted.

"We'll be OK," I answered, already sorry I had responded.

"Move over jarheads! 1st Cav is coming to the rescue!" He yelled to no one in particular.

I faced the trio and fired back a salvo, "You guys must already be fuckin' heroes or generals."

"Whatcha fuckin' mean jarhead?" the nearest man answered defensively.

"All those pretty ribbons, and that fuckin' braid, what the hell does it all mean? You look like a bunch of fuckin' pussy ass drum majors," I was getting wound up. "Now you're going to join the cav and wear that silly-ass patch with the horse you never rode, the line you never crossed, and that yellow there," I tapped the yellow part of his 1st Cavalry shoulder patch for emphasis, "That's the fuckin' reason why."

The big boy slammed down his beer mug, shattering it on the bar. "You jarhead sons-a-bitch, I'll kick your ass!" he threatened, swinging his legs away from the bar.

Alerted to the trouble by the breaking glass, Mamma Sahn came running down the bar screaming, "No have fight in here! MPs come, take you all brig!"

"Let's take it outside," I said, dismounting my bar stool and quickly walking toward the door.

The three very drunk army privates stumbled behind in single file. I walked out into the street and quickly turned to surprise who ever came through the door first. It was the big boy. I caught him with a quick jab to the jaw, which startled him just enough for me to move in close. I grabbed his shirt, spun him out into the street and up against the outside wall. The impact with the wall knocked the wind from his lungs. I stepped behind him, threw my arm around his throat, and dragged him to the ground in a choke hold. With my back to the wall and big boy's large, nearly unconscious frame between me and his friends, I was spared any interference. I turned his head toward mine and bit a large chuck out of his chubby cheek, then stuck my thumb into the corner of his right eye and popped his electric blue eye onto his bloody cheek.

The struggle of his friends to wrestle him free snapped me back to a puke-tainted side street in Okinawa.

"Stop it! Don't hurt him anymore!" they pleaded.

I looked up. A crowd had gathered, most aghast by what I had done. I pushed the limp body aside, and stood to walk away. A black Marine wearing a khaki summer dress uniform sporting the ribbons of a Nam vet, including the Purple Heart, blocked my path.

"What the fuck did you do man?"

I looked down at the mess at my feet...the one-eyed big boy, his friends now at his side trying to haul him to his feet.

"I probably saved his life. That sorry-assed mother fucker won't be going to Nam anytime soon," I answered, then I sidestepped the Marine and pushed my way through the crowd.

I felt sick to my stomach. I was as stunned by my actions as the crowd of onlookers. What had I done and why? I went back to my room and stuffed my whiskey and clean underwear back into my ditty bag. I walked to a corner and hailed a mini cab.

"Get me the fuck out of here!" I said, my voice laced with desperation.

"Where you want go?"

"Some place quiet...and far away."

"I take you Henoko," he promised, as we pulled away from the curb.

I rolled down the window to inhale the heavy moisture laden air as the bright lights of Kosa dimmed in the rear view mirror. We slid quickly into peaceful rolling hills, with sheltered inner valley rice paddies. There, nestled in the trees, quiet, candle-lit homes and the melodious croaking of frogs replaced the blinking neon and the incessantly honking horns of the city. A trailing sliver of moon-lit ocean glimmered between sinuous, boulder jetties, lulling me into a peaceful contentment, and for a moment there was nothing...no past, no future, nothing but a peace filled now.

I'm lying on the carpeted floor of my grandmother's living room in Oklahoma. The room is filled with my aunts and uncles, cousins, my grandparents, my mother, and my brothers and sister. I'm filled with excitement; it must be Thanksgiving, our annual reunion. But my grandmother and mother are huddled together on the couch crying, my grandfather is leaning across the arm of the couch trying to comfort them. I move closer to see why they are crying.

"He was always such a pretty boy," my grandmother sobs, "Why did he have to lose his pretty blue eyes?"

"I should have never signed the papers," my mother cries out in remorse.

My grandfather grabs my mother's hand and softly intones, "You could never have stopped him, that's what he wanted, just like Bobby."

"I'm right here, mom!" I try to intervene, but no one can hear or see me. "I'm OK mom!" I yell, but am I? Am I OK?

"Are you OK? Are You OK?" The cab driver yells, shaking me awake.

Startled, I grab the driver's shirt, but he quickly pulls away.

"We here Henoko now, you pay now and go please."

I paid the driver and started down the empty street toward a collection of cement buildings, Henoko I presumed. I found a scattering of bars and restaurants, but none of the noise or neon of Kosa. I walked past a couple of crowded bars to a side street, where I found a gaudy, green door open to an almost empty bar. All I wanted was a quiet drink, no more excitement for me.

Mama Sahn smiled from behind the bar as I walked in. Two older harlots sat near the end of the bar, making swans out of folded napkins. I sat on a stool at the other end. Mama Sahn was sugar sweet, anxious to please her one and only customer. I ordered, and she mixed me a Jack and Coke, then said, "You come sit with Tommyco, she very sad and need friend."

I resisted, thinking she was talking about one of the older women at the bar, but she pulled me away from the bar toward a table half hidden in a darkened corner of the room. There at the table sat a beautiful young girl, her silken black hair drawn back in a ponytail framing her high cheek bones and almond-shaped, chocolate eyes. She was dressed in a new gather-top, green blouse, and brown pleated skirt that reached to the middle of her thighs. Her legs were pressed tightly together, and she continually tugged at the end of her skirt, struggling to cover as much of her thighs as possible. Her head was slightly bowed, her eyes glued to the table.

"You buy Tommyco a Coke, she no drinky champagne," Mama Sahn explained, as she walked away. I stood for a moment transfixed by the innocence and beauty of this young Okinawan girl.

"May I sit down?" I asked, afraid she might actually say no.

She nodded nervously and glanced at the chair next to her. I sat down and imbibed her entrancing fragrance. Love at first sight may have been too strong a sentiment, but she was the only true thing I had experienced since my arrival in Okinawa. She was like a light, illuminating the darkness that had become my soul.

As we began to talk, I learned that Tommyco was seventeen, and this was her first night in a bar. Her parents had taken a loan from Mama Sahn and Tommyco would work off the loan, business as usual in Okinawa. A week ago, Tommyco slept peacefully in one of the quiet homes nestled in the trees that I had passed on the way to Henoko. Now she was Mama Sahn's hope and salvation, a young, pretty country girl to fill up her dying bar. For now, Tommyco would draw them in and the old harlots at the bar would handle the action.

As Mama Sahn later explained, "You no want to wear her out too fast." Because I had come in sober and alone, I would be her one last fling with innocence, and her induction into a life of prostitution.

We spent a couple of hours getting acquainted, then took a long walk, holding hands, along the deserted, moon-lit beach. She was delightful; easy to laugh, easy to cry, openly afraid of her new life and as much in need of a friend as me. She brought out the best in me. The past was a fog, the future not worth dwelling on. We were lost in each other, living for each moment.

We snuck into her room after midnight. Mama Sahn wouldn't want her to give it away and Tommyco didn't want to be a whore. Her quarters were in a cement block building divided into six 8' square rooms. The rooms were connected by a dark, narrow hallway. The room at the end of the hall was used as a toilet. It was empty, with a one foot circle cut through the floor. All the other rooms had a door, a tiny window and an electrical outlet. Tommyco's walls were covered with colorful posters of Japanese bands and comic book characters. She had a bed, a night table, a small lamp with a frazzled pink shade, a pile of comic books, a small record player and a half dozen records. This would be her world for at least ten years.

We spent the next several days snuggling in her room as much as possible. She would sneak me food. We would listen to her records and make love. She would go to work in the afternoon and I would thumb through her comics or walk along the beach. When she got off work, we would go the beach and make love in the moon light, or stay in the room and make love 'til dawn. We both knew our time together was measured in hours, not years, that she was destined to become a prostitute and I would soon return to Nam. We talked about running away, but we both had commitments. She had to honor her parents. I was a Marine...I had my own commitments to honor.

It was overcast and drizzly on the day I had to catch a flight back to Nam. The weather outside was a perfect match for how I felt inside.

"You stay here in Henoko with Tommyco," she begged, knowing I couldn't. I didn't promise to come back for her; knowing I wouldn't. We held each other knowing that when we let go, both our lives would disintegrate into the madness of war; her to begin a life servicing men on their way to and from Nam, and me...back to the killing fields.

"I have something to keep you safe," she said, pulling a silver crucifix from her pocket. I put the crucifix around my neck.

"I will never take this off," I promised. "And I will never forget you Tommyco," I said, kissing her on the forehead.

"I never forget you too, Jack!" she called out, as I turned toward the door. I didn't look back...it would have broken my heart.

As my cab pulled away from Henoko, I was saddened by the realization that Tommyco was just one more innocent person whose life was being destroyed by the war...one more person I could not save.

Chapter Five
A Very Long Day

"We're all gonna fuckin' die!"
Jack, explaining the squad's rescue plan to Tarver, November 1968.

The flight back to Vietnam was eerily quiet. On the flight to Okinawa, we had all been drinking and filled with excitement about our coming adventure, now each man was lost in his own thoughts. As the plane circled through the gray stratus clouds above the Da Nang airport, my stomach tightened. I was torn by the mixed emotions of excitement about rejoining my friends, and a deep foreboding. I touched the crucifix, thinking of Tommyco. Could reconnecting with my humanity cause me to make a fatal mistake in Nam?

I thought about the guys back at the company. Were they all right, had we lost anyone? I thought of Z. Who was there in his place? Each operation brought new casualties and bright shiny faces to fill the ranks. Some were gone before we knew their names. One in particular held the record as having served the shortest tour with the company. He joined the company while we were on an operation in Arizona territory, a wild, dark place along the Ho Chi Minh Trail, where death lurked behind every tree line.

I saw him step from the supply chopper, its lights blinking against a dying sun. He was assigned to first platoon as the sun set, and sent out on a listening post. He blew himself up before midnight...alone, afraid and with his own grenade. I wondered what his parents must have thought. Before they were notified of his arrival in-country, their boy was on his way back home in a box. Would he be considered the family hero? Would his picture be displayed on the mantel alongside his purple heart? How much more could he have given? On the positive side, if you were going to die in Vietnam, the first day would be the best day...at least your beliefs and soul would still be intact.

The newbies told us about football games played on chilly fall nights, and cuddling with their pretty round eyed girlfriends. They were innocent young men who reminded me of myself eleven months earlier. They still carried the pictures of their girlfriends and received their perfumed envelopes in the mail. If they lasted long enough, the letters would come less frequently, until that one arrived without the perfume. We tried to tell them, "That pretty young thing will wither away in a year without some loving."

They would get angry, and defend the honor of their girl with phrases so similar you would think they came from a training manual: "My girl's not that way. We're in love. We're going to get married as soon as I get home!"

The stronger their belief, the harder they fell, but it was all part of the hardening process. After the letter, they usually made better Marines. They were ready to be taken under wing. We taught them to burn villages without remorse, to mutilate bodies of the dead enemy, to ignore the plight of civilians caught in the crossfire. It was simple; get callus or die, and we were teaching the art of survival.

Death pervaded our lives. We killed the enemy, and at times, we had to watch our friends die. We sometimes came across decomposing, bloated bodies, often writhing with maggots. We collected souvenirs from the bodies, including gold filled teeth and skulls. We took safari pictures of ourselves standing over piles of mutilated bodies, or of one of us sharing a moment with a headless corpse or a bodiless head. Death was like the smog of a smoky bar room. It was all around us, it permeated our very being. It was the subject of our conversations...the death we had witnessed or the death we feared. It was our very reason for being... to kill the enemy, or as Sgt. James had said, "To do or to die."

On occasion, we became ghouls, digging up fresh graves to make sure the NVA hadn't used the grave as a cover for a weapons cache. The smell of death would saturate our clothing, making it impossible to eat. Some of the food was Korean War surplus, and the smell of death on your hands as you brought a greasy, twenty year old meat patty to your mouth would send convulsions through your body. I became a fatalist. First thing each morning I would step off into a rice paddy, go ahead and get wet, and let the leeches have their breakfast. It was my way of saying, "Go ahead and fuck me Vietnam, I don't give a shit anymore!"

We displayed the visible signs of our callused souls like campaign ribbons. I had a woman's scalp tied to my pack and wore the bloodied rain hat of a dead NVA. Lieutenant Howard had a film canister filled with gold teeth on a chain around his neck, teeth he had personally extracted from dead NVA. Doc Murry carried a skull tied to his pack. It became our official platoon mascot. We named it Charlie, of course.

Now I was back...ever deeper into the shit. I rejoined the company one day before the beginning of Operation Meade River. We would be making a helicopter assault into Dodge City territory. The Viet Minh had held the region when the French were fighting in Vietnam, and the NVA had been entrenched there since the French left. We had lost eight men there in August. It was the most spooked I had ever seen the company, the old hands especially so. Men flocked to see the Padre and Preachers the morning of the assault, November 20, 1968.

We came in low, skimming just above the tree line, and jumped from the rear cargo doors of the Chinooks. We ran for cover, hearts pounding, not sure if the LZ was hot. The noise from the choppers and outgoing fire from the door gunners made it hard to determine if we had incoming fire. We wouldn't be sure until AK rounds began piercing the thin skin of the chopper, or someone slumped over dead onto the floor.

When the choppers withdrew, it fell silent. There was no return fire. Marines in other sectors were not so lucky. One chopper was brought down by ground fire with 13 Marines killed and a truck was blown up by a booby trap with seven Marines lost.

We moved into the tree line, finding cover behind fallen trees along the southern bank of a tributary of the Ky Lam River. Golf Company crossed the river and immediately drew heavy fire from an entrenched NVA position. I watched the action with my fire team from a protected position behind the thick trunk of a downed tree. We were the blocking force, deployed to kill any NVA that tried to retreat back to our side of the river. The NVA were ready and well dug in. They quickly repulsed the attack. Golf company retreated back across the river, leaving six of their dead behind.

In history books, battles seem impersonal, as if the same thing happened to all the combatants at the same time. I once read in a story about Napoleon that "On June 18th, 1815, Napoleon's army of 70,000 men attacked Wellington's allied force of 65,000 men at Waterloo, near Brussels in Belgium. By the end of the day, 45,000 men lay dead in the field, including 26,000 of Napoleon's troops." As if battles are won and lost by some war board technician swiping cardboard soldiers off the map. Whoever has the most pieces remaining, wins.

In reality, nothing is more personal, or more position perceptional than combat. One man can be drinking a cup of coffee, while 50 yards away another is in hand-to-hand combat, rolling in the mud with a bayonet at his throat. And so it was for us on day one of the operation. Bullets were tearing through the trees around us...we could see the explosions and hear the screams of dying men, but we never fired a shot. We sat tucked safely behind the trees eating lunch, watching the action unfold and waiting for our turn.

When our guys had made it back to our side of the river, we called in Marine, Phantom jets from Da Nang. The jets dropped napalm and HE rounds on the NVA positions. As evening fell, the NVA were still repulsing all attempts to cross the river, and six Marine bodies remained in enemy hands. We pulled back to a packed dirt road near the LZ, and set in for the night. The ground was too hard to dig in. It was already dark...too late to set out listening posts or ambushes. We set up our perimeter in the ditches along either side of the road, using our packs and helmets for cover. We were severely exposed and expected an attack, but none came.

On day two, we skirted around the edge of a long bend in the river to get north of the NVA stronghold. We sloshed through knee-deep mud all day to get in position for a day three assault on what was now being called the horseshoe. We set in for the night along the bank of the river. It was third platoon's day to take the point, so we would be leading the assault. The mood in camp was very subdued. We knew the NVA were surrounded and determined to hold their ground. We were in their back yard. Intel was sketchy but we knew there were over a thousand NVA. Many were concealed in cement hardened bunkers, with heavy weapons that included RPG's, 12.7 MM heavy machine guns, and 82 MM mortars. The bunkers were connected to miles and miles of tunnels that probably went right under, around and behind us. Echo Company numbered slightly over a hundred men with probably four M-60 machine guns, two 60MM mortars, one 3.5 bazooka, a half dozen bloopers (M79 Grenade Launchers) and a couple of hundred LAWs. Hell, maybe we were the ones that were surrounded.

The night was quiet...scary quiet. We were within a few hundred yards of our objective. We expected sniper fire, maybe a probe, possibly an all out attack, but there was nothing. The gurgle of the river was occasionally interrupted by an artillery round fired from the Marine base on Hill 55...sometimes followed by the eerie whine of burning parachute flares as they floated down above the river. We could have slept through the night.

We were up at dawn. Some sat on their haunches over burning chunks of C-4, heating up their morning coffee.

Others were cleaning their rifles, or loading extra clips of ammo. I was ready...leaning back against my pack thinking of Tommyco, wishing I would have stolen her from Mamma Sahn and run away into the hills. It was hard to believe, it was just four days ago.

We were all roused from our individual activities by the sound of heavy machine gun fire and the whoosh-bang of incoming RPGs. The radio crackled, "This is Charlie 1, we've been hit! We've been hit, the Captain's down! We need"... then nothing. We were all ears, leaning toward the Pric 25 radio, anxious for more information from Adams, the CO's radio operator.

Sgt. James's newbie radioman, Johnson, tried frantically to raise Adams, but there was no reply.

Blood, sticky, thick and warm pooling in his lap, Adams lies propped against a downed tree, a front row seat to the battle unfolding before him. The camouflaged NVA to his right are firing heavy machine guns, RPGs, and tossing grenades at his friends to the left, who are falling back in disarray, still dumbfounded at the surprise and heavy volume of fire. Most are desperately trying to drag their wounded comrades out of the kill zone, back to the relative safety of the river; but he sees the Captain in full retreat, loping toward the river with his hands over his ears. At first, Dawson and his A-gunner, Robinson, provide cover for the retreating men with a barrage of 3.5 rockets into the bunkers, but they are soon silenced by snipers, concealed high in the trees overlooking the ambush kill zone.

The sounds of explosions and screaming men fills the air. The crackle of the Pric 25 strapped to his back has been silenced by the 12.7 mm machine gun round that punched through his abdomen, smashing the radio. The steaming pile of intestines slips through his fingers when he tries to force them back into the ruptured cavity. "How did all this stuff ever fit in there?" he wonders.

He tries to scream for help but only coughs up blood. The metallic taste of the blood mixed with the smell of urine and partially digested beef patties, spilling from his torn intestines, causes him to vomit. The cleansing gives him back his voice.

"Momma, Momma," he moans softly, the words a balm to his tortured body, invoking the memory of his mother's soothing touch. Louder now he cries out, "MOMMA! MOMMA!"

He sees the jungle boots and follows them up. Padilla, his face smudged with powder and smeared with blood, kneels at his side. A jagged hunk of bloodied meat and the stub of a shattered bone jut from the shoulder hole on the left side of his flak jacket. He holds his 45 in his right hand.

Adams and Padilla, good friends and teammates in first platoon, are too far forward to have any hope of rescue, any chance for survival. Adams feels the cold metal barrel of the 45 against his forehead.

Thank you Padilla," he whispers.

"Saddle up! We have to move out now," Sgt. James screamed, jerking men to their feet and pushing them towards the sound of battle. Many left their coffee cooking and a couple of the newer guys were carrying their boots.

We followed Sgt. James double time along the bank of the river. As we moved, Johnson hailed second platoon and got the XO, Lt. Howard, on the hook. We paused and knelt down for a few minutes to let Sgt. James apprise the LT of our movement. It wouldn't be good to rush into our own guys and risk a friendly fire incident.

Lt. Howard said the CO had walked up on a couple of NVA scouts. The NVA had dee-dee'd across the paddy, making for the trees. The CO had followed with 1st platoon and weapons platoon in hot pursuit. The fleeing NVA led the men into an open paddy fringed by a tree line where several hundred of their fellow NVA waited, concealed in cement hardened bunkers. It was a classic NVA ruse. We had started the morning with just over a hundred men, thirty were hit in the initial burst...eight of those were known dead, including both of the COs radiomen. Several were unaccounted for...still pinned down or dead in the kill zone. The CO had made it back across and caught a chopper out. His ear had been shot off, according to the XO's report.

Lt. Howard was a mustang officer, having worked his way up from private with a battlefield commission earned during the Korean War. It was now his company to lead. He had set up second platoon along the river to provide cover fire for the retreating remnants of first and weapons platoons. He said there was a ville between us and second platoon. The NVA were very adept at setting secondary ambushes to maul units rushing to aid those caught in the primary ambush.

"The ville is the perfect spot. I'd bet it's full of NVA. If they take you out, we'll be surrounded," Howard warned.

"Maybe we should call in arty or a gunship and force their hand," Sgt. James suggested.

"No time, and we're all too close anyway," the mike went silent for a second, then sputtered back to life. "You're going to have to clear the ville and set up a defensive perimeter behind it in case the NVA try to hit us from the rear. Go in hot and watch your ass!"

"Roger that," James confirmed, and handed the mike back to Johnson.

Sgt. James relayed the orders to the squad leaders and we moved out as quietly as 30 men carrying 70 pounds of gear apiece can move. The continuous clatter of heavy machine guns, RPGs, and small arms fire from across the river was a constant reminder of the peril we faced.

We reached the edge of a small oxbow lake that guarded the northern approach to the village. Sgt. James motioned for everyone to get down, and sent word back down the line for me to come forward. I found Sgt. James lying on a muddy bank, concealed behind a tall stand of horsetail reeds. We were close enough to the ambush site that stray bullets were ripping bark off the trees around us while others were skimming across the water.

I crawled in alongside James. He parted the reeds and looked out across the shallow lake through his binoculars. "Howard's right, this is a fine damn site for an ambush!' he affirmed, handing me the binoculars.

I could see a few thatched huts and a lot of sandbagged bunkers through the trees on the far side of the lake. There was no movement in the ville, but the stray bullets skipping across the lake gave me pause.

"We have to secure that village and we're gonna have to cross this lake to get there." He turned on his side to face me.

"OK," I paused, unsure of his intentions.

"I want you to cross the lake and recon the other side. Make sure the way is clear."

"Sarge! There's..." I tried to point out some of the potential problems with his plan, and perhaps propose one of my own, but he cut me off abruptly.

"Now! Goddamn it! Move out!" he ordered.

Sgt. James was my hero and mentor. Even though I was only a PFC, thanks to my brig time, he made me a team leader over Corporals and Lance Corporals. He continually tried to get me promoted against the wishes of the CO, whose retort was "I'll just have to bust him first time he gets liberty." While the rest of us would be trying to make love to the ground during a fire fight, Sgt. James would be up walking around, calmly directing fire. He was a poster Marine and a great leader. I would follow him to hell, but I wasn't that interested in leading him there.

I rose and stepped into the water. I began to run hunched over, zig-zagging towards the far shore. It was maybe 75 yards, but it felt like running through honey. As the water deepened, my zig-zags slowed. Near shore, it was chest high. I could barely push forward through the thick waterborne vegetation. I was a sitting duck, but as a seasoned point man, I figured, the NVA would most likely wait until I motioned the platoon into the lake to spring the ambush.

I pulled myself onto the bank, rolled into the brush, and took my first real breath in the past three minutes. I peered through the tree line into the bunkers looking for signs of an ambush. Finding nothing in the trees along the edge of the lake, I checked the village. It appeared to be deserted. I rushed back to the edge of the lake and signaled James. He sent men across in three and four man fire teams to establish a perimeter on my side of the lake, before proceeding with the main body of the platoon. When we were all across, we moved into the village, treating it as if it were an ambush site. We peppered the huts with M-60 machine gun fire and tossed grenades into every bunker. James found a protected clearing behind the village. We cut away brush to establish an LZ, so we could begin to haul out the wounded. My squad set up behind a paddy dike along the outer edge of the LZ to provide security.

"Here they come!" Thompson, our squad's black blooper-man was the first to see a group of gooks coming through the trees, headed towards the ville.

We waited until they were in the open, 100 yards out, caught between our concealed position and the tree line. They were hunkered down, zig-zagging through a thick stand of elephant grass. I made sure my selector switch was on single fire, and took aim. We waited for the M-60 to open up, then hit them full in the face with everything, including a 60 mortar. The group was knocked flat by the volley. I figured I had hit at least two myself. It felt good...the sons of bitches were butchering us on the other side of the river, now we had some pay back.

The radio crackled. Johnson, set up behind a bunker near the middle of the village, relayed the message. The group we ambushed was our own Vietnamese army detachment. They were badly mauled, several were dead, the rest wounded. They wanted permission to come inside our perimeter.

"Fuck 'em." There was venom in James' retort. "Who fuckin' knows if they're friendlies...it could be the NVA with a stolen radio! Tell 'em to pull back or we'll finish 'em off."

We all cheered as they retreated, dragging their wounded back into the tree line. That was the last we saw of our South Vietnamese detachment.

My squad was sent to the edge of the river to begin hauling the wounded back to the LZ. We passed several walking wounded stumbling through a cane field along the edge of the river. They were lost, but moving in a general direction away from the kill zone. We stationed a couple of men to direct the walkers back to the LZ. The rest of us continued to the river. We were drawn to the triage area by the screams and moaning of the wounded. Doc Pile had set up triage behind a berm at the edge of the river. He was doing what he could with morphine and band aids to stabilize and calm a growing number of bloodied men. Men were lying on ponchos in the wet sand, filling the ponchos with their blood. Some were screaming for their mothers...some were moaning and reaching out for help. Sgt. Ski was leaning against a tree, quietly smoking a Lucky Strike. His right leg was severed below the knee, and a bullet had passed through his abdomen. Doc Pile had bandaged the wounds and given Ski some morphine. Smitty told us to let him be. Ski had requested he not be evacuated. He had no desire to live the rest of his life in a wheelchair.

Doc Pile had the demeanor of a ship's captain in a gale. He was calm, purposeful, and in control. He pointed out the men we would take out first, those with the worst wounds, but still a good chance for survival. We each grabbed the corner of a poncho, four men to a litter, and headed back towards the LZ. We would drop off a wounded man and race back toward the river. I left my rifle at the LZ after the first trip. It was just in the way. I could be more effective at moving the wounded with both hands free. If I needed a rifle, there would be one lying nearby.

Many of the men would scream and kick all the way back through the cane, pulling the blood slickened poncho from our grips, sending the wounded man crashing to the earth. We would roll them back onto the poncho and onward to the LZ. By our third trip back to the river, Ski had died. I hoped that if I was badly wounded, I would die with the quiet dignity that he had exhibited.

I spent the morning and into the afternoon hauling men to the LZ, and loading dead and wounded into the rear cargo bays of Chinooks. We stacked the dead toward the front of the chopper...two men to a body... tossed like bags of rice, to get them out of the way. By the second trip, the flight crews had put wooden pallets on the decks of the choppers to keep us from slipping and sliding on the blood and spilled body fluids. The heat in the chopper fuselage was stifling, the smell horrendous. Some men cleared their bowels and pissed their pants when faced with their own eminent mortality. The flies were feasting on gelatin-like masses of congealing blood and feces, and still, I wanted to climb in and lay there among the dead, to escape the death that lurked outside.

By mid-afternoon, the last few survivors were dribbling back across the river. Seven remained unaccounted for, still down in the ambush kill zone. As each of the wounded returned, we questioned them to determine the status of the men left behind. Four were dead, two or three maybe still alive, one of those, almost surely still living. A couple of men had rushed out on their own to try and recover their friends. They were both now among the badly wounded. There was a reason they called it a kill zone.

I went back to the river one last time. Doc Pile had taken a round through the chest while helping a wounded man across the river. He was confused about how to treat himself. The man who had calmly triaged 40 or more men was suddenly totally baffled about how to treat a chest wound. His lung was collapsing. He was going into shock. We cut some cellophane off the cigarette package still lying in Ski's lap and covered the entry and exit wounds. By then, Doc Murry had made it down from the LZ to take care of his last remaining fellow Corpsman. We rushed him to the LZ, but he died of shock before we could get him to a chopper.

Newsome and I took the last of the walking wounded between us and started back to the LZ. He was a newbie I didn't recognize. He had been shot once through the thigh, nothing fatal, but he was scared and in a lot of pain. He was alternating between screaming, "It hurts! It hurts!" and babbling incoherently.

The NVA had run out of targets, but they kept up a constant fusillade of small arms fire. Bullets were snapping through the cane and peeling bark off the trees. We were moving along a paddy dike, just below a large berm where Sgt. James and Lt. Howard had established the CP. Johnson was lying between them, relaying coordinates over his Pric 25 and directing artillery fire into the NVA bunkers across the river.

Suddenly, a stray round slashed through the wounded man's throat. He shook himself loose from our grip. With both hands grasped around his throat to try and stop the surging blood, he ran splashing through the paddy. When he had run out of wind, he threw himself to the ground at the base of the berm. He thrashed about like a headless chicken, fighting hopelessly for one last breath of air. Five of us watched...frozen in our tracks...paralyzed by our inability to stop his suffering. It was the worst death I had witnessed in Vietnam.

When he stopped kicking, I returned to the LZ to help load the last of our wounded. Smitty, my squad leader, found me resting there. He passes the word that Sgt. James had ordered my fire team back to the village to stand watch over the villagers. I thought the village was empty, the inhabitants either dead or having run away. But we found them under guard near the center of the ville. They were all either too old or too young to be of service. Everyone of fighting age was across the river with the NVA. They stared blankly ahead, avoiding eye contact...their faces filled with malice. I knew they had counted our dead and wounded, knew our strengths and weaknesses. They were gathering information for their brethren across the river. I was disgusted by the way the old ones squatted on their withered haunches, picking nits from one another's hair, then squashing the filthy lice between their betel nut stained teeth. I hated those people... they were my enemy, a threat to my survival.

After an hour guarding the villagers, James sent word for my squad to assemble in the river bed below the CP. We were relieved of guard duty, and started for the river. Phantoms were swooping low over the ambush site, dropping bombs and napalm. The long white cylinders hit the ground and tumbled forward, spreading a wall of fire in their wake. After the jets had dropped their loads, and while they were back loading more ordinance, Huey and

Cobra gunships peppered the area with rockets and bursts from their mini-guns. All outgoing gunfire from the area was suppressed, but we knew the NVA were underground, waiting for our air support to leave the field.

We found Sgt. James sitting on a bleached and twisted trunk of driftwood, smoking a Camel. As we slid down the six foot embankment to join James on the spit of sand that had entrapped the driftwood, he field-stripped the cigarette, rolled up the paper and flicked it into the river. I giggled, thinking this guy is a Marine tried and true. Here we are in the middle of nowhere, fighting for our lives, and he's still field-stripping his smokes.

"Take a knee men...no use in giving them sons-o'-bitches a target," Sgt. James warned.

I glanced toward the unfriendly side of the river. I could see the trees, so any sniper in the trees could see me. I quickly knelt and the trees disappeared from view.

Sgt. James looked into the eyes of the ten men kneeling before him. "You men are the only full strength squad left in the company," he paused and ran his fingers through his hair. "We have seven unaccounted for. Most of them have been confirmed as KIA, but McKinney and Dawson were reported to still be alive when the last of wounded made it back across." He paused long enough for us to contemplate the fate of the stranded men.

McKinney had been with the company just over a month. He was Newsome's best friend. They had gone to high school together, joined the Marines on the buddy plan, and come to Echo Company together. McKinney had been assigned to first platoon. Newsome was kneeling beside me...we were teammates in third platoon.

Dawson was "the rocket man." He carried and was proficient with a 3.5 bazooka, an antitank weapon from WW II that had proven itself to be an excellent bunker buster in Vietnam. Eleven months with the company, two purple hearts, and courage enough for three men had insured his place as one of the most popular men in the company.

"The fuckin' colonel hoverin' around up there from the safety of his chopper," Sgt. James pointed to the sky, "has ordered us to pull back and leave our dead behind." He leaned forward, making sure we were all with him. "We're Marines...we don't leave our dead to the enemy."

"That's right," Smitty confirmed, looking back to see us all shaking our heads in agreement.

Sgt. James continued, "We're not gonna get any help. The fly boys are going home, and arty's got another mission. It's up to you men. Talk it over and come up with a plan." He finished and climbed up the bank, back toward the CP.

The silence was deafening. I thought of my Uncle Bob. Was this how he "volunteered" to go save his buddy?

Smitty broke the silence, "Give me some ideas guys, how we going to do this thing?"

We developed a plan. One man with a rope would go forward while the rest of us laid down cover fire. The rope man would tie a knot around the leg of a dead Marine, and the rest of us would pull the body back to the river, then throw the rope back to our hero, but...who would be the hero?

Smitty, who was now sitting on the driftwood log, looked out over his squad, "Any volunteers?" he asked.

The silence was monumentally deafening. We were all checking out our boots; but how many times can you count your own two feet?

Finally, Smitty broke the silence, "We'll draw straws, that's the only fair way," he decided. He pulled some straw from the bank of the river, broke it into ten pieces and declared, "Short straw goes."

Each of us in turn smiled and sighed relief as we pulled a long straw, until Thompson pulled the short straw. He was resolved to go, but how could we, in good faith, send him? It was suicide. The NVA would be back in their bunkers overlooking the ambush kill zone, and that's where Thompson would have to go to recover the bodies. Thompson was good. He might get one...maybe two, but eventually the NVA would get Thompson. Then, who would go get Thompson? At the end of the day, we would all probably be dead...bad plan!

"Let's all go." I don't know who said it, but I don't think it was me.

The new plan...we would split up, two men to a body. The entire company would open up for two minutes. James would fire a red flare as a signal to stop shooting, and we would all run to our designated body and drag it back to the river.

We met with James and Howard at the CP to gather Intel as to the location of each body and to split up into our two man teams. I would be with Newsome. Smitty and Barnes were teamed up, but they would cross with us. Dawson and Robinson were last seen lying next to each other at our destination.

As I was leaving the CP, Tarver, the intellectual, black Marine from Phoenix, pulled me aside. I wasn't his team leader any longer, but, for whatever reason, he thought I might be sympathetic.

"What's going to happen to us, Jack?" he asked, with tears welling in his eyes.

I had my own mortality to worry about. "We're all gonna fuckin' die," I answered, pushing him aside to start for the river.

We slithered up through the mud on the far bank of the river. We kept our heads down, concealing ourselves behind the berm, waiting for everyone to get into position. I switched my weapon to full auto. It wasn't about hitting a target...just a volume of directed fire. We waited for the mortar barrage to begin, then sprayed everything we had toward the bunker complex. When the red flare appeared over the field, I threw down my M-16 and ran zig-zagging through the kill zone. There, lying dead behind a dike, were two Marines...Dawson and Robinson. Dawson was a big man, 6'2" and well over two hundred pounds. It would all be dead weight. Newsome was by my side. We quickly surmised we could not recover both bodies. I grabbed one of Dawson's legs, Newsome grabbed the other, and we hauled ass back towards the river. The NVA were wise to our ploy by now and they were back in business. Machine gun rounds tore at the earth at our ankles as we ran for our lives. When Dawson's body had cleared the berm, we both released our hold and dove into the river. By the time we had crawled back to our weapons we were fully engaged in a fire fight. Newsome looked back and watched as another team dragged his best friend, McKinney, up the far bank. There were no survivors, but now only three bodies remained to be recovered.

Barnes peered back over his shoulder and yelled, "You guys go get that other body...we'll cover you!"

"Fuck you! We got our body, that one's yours!" I answered angrily.

"I outrank you...I'm ordering you to go!" Barnes spat back.

I had never liked Barnes. He was all talk in the rear but green around the gills in the field. I didn't mind talk, and I understood fear, but both coming from the same individual sickened me. Smitty and Barnes were friends. Smitty made excuses for Barnes, but they didn't fly with me.

"You can kiss my mother fuckin' ass Barnes, I'll cut your God Damned ..."

"I'll go," Newsome volunteered.

The guy had just seen his best friend dragged across the river, and he was volunteering to go back a second time. Newsome was our hero.

"Let's go, Newsome," Smitty jumped in, and the pair rose and sprinted toward the second body.

We fired towards the bunkers until they returned with the body in tow. We tossed Dawson and Robinson into the river, floated them across and dragged them up behind the berm on the other side. Tarver and Harris had been hit by mortar fragments (I'm thinking p-38) while recovering their body. Other than that, we were all safely back across the river.

The bodies were lined up on ponchos awaiting transport back to the LZ...five of our friends in various states of disassembly. Some with broken limbs, skewed at unnatural angles, one with his skull split open, seeping gray matter. Dawson had a single bullet wound in his upper right arm. He must have bled to death waiting for his rescue. Except for the bandage on his arm and the mud caking his face, he looked like he could just sit up and tell us about his latest adventure. The company would miss Dawson's commanding presence. I looked down at his perfectly waxed, handle-bar moustache and vowed to never shave my upper lip again. It was the least I could do.

Most of the wounds were bandaged. Hinds, First Platoon's Corpsman, had done his job well, exposing himself to withering fire several times before he was killed. Two men, Adams and Padilla, were still missing. They were too far forward to recover, and had already been confirmed KIA, they would have to wait another day. We hoped the NVA wouldn't mutilate the bodies.

We were all sitting or kneeling around our five fallen comrades with our heads hung. It was quiet...almost peaceful, for the first time that day. Mortar rounds began to rain down 25 yards upriver, breaking our trance. The NVA would adjust their fire and have us in the next barrage.

"Move out! Get these men to the LZ!" James yelled, as he began to herd us away from the river.

We were all exhausted...mentally, physically and emotionally. The NVA weren't inclined to give us a minutes rest. We begrudgingly trudged those final mud sucking steps to the LZ and loaded our dead onto the last incoming Chinook of the day.

The sun was sinking behind the trees when James called me to his side, "Jack, you and Barnes need to go back and take care of those villagers."

We finished the villagers with no more emotion than putting the cat out for the night. We set up for the night in an ancient graveyard. There were no stones...just a field of eight foot high earthen mounds separated by a maze of two foot wide passageways. The mounds were covered with foot high vegetation.

From more than a hundred men in the morning, less than 40 remained. James and Howard divided us into two-man teams, with several unmanned mounds between each team. Our positions defined a wide circle around a centrally located CP. We lay prone on our ponchos using the tall vegetation for cover...facing away from the CP. The NVA could come from any or all directions.

I was teamed with Newsome. Between us, all we had remaining were 5 clips of ammo, seven grenades, and two claymore mines. We placed our mines on either side of the mound directly to our front... pointing the business end into the pathway to protect the approach. The remaining ammo, our grenades and entrenching tools were laid out between us to share as needed. James came up just as darkness approached.

"Jack, did you take care of the un-friendlies?"

"It's done."

"Good, we don't need any extra bullshit tonight. This could get hairy boys. We need to maintain strict fire discipline."

"We know. If we're shooting, the shit's done hit the fan," I answered.

"Good, we have coordinates called in, and arty's on call. Just stay alert."

"Sure thing Sarge," we replied in unison.

He turned to walk away, then turned back. "By the way, Howard wants to write third squad up for some sort of medal for today."

Newsome and I looked at one another. I spoke for us both, "Everyone?"

"Yeah, it's an all or nothing sort of thing," James answered, with a tinge of anger creeping into his voice.

"Well, I can't speak for everyone, but if Barnes gets written up, I don't want the fuckin' medal."

"Same for me," injected Newsome.

We both knew our medal would end up buried in a drawer. Barnes would organize a parade for himself.

"You fuckin' guys!" James shook his head and disappeared down the pathway toward the next outpost.

We lay quietly for a few minutes. I contemplated our predicament. Forty desperate men out of food, low on ammo, no M-60s left in operation. The M-60s had drawn such intense fire that the gunners were all wounded or dead and the machine guns themselves were destroyed. We had one remaining Corpsman and two working radios. We were spread way too thin and the fucking pathways between the mounds provided protected inroads right up to our positions. As far as I could figure, there was no reason for the NVA not to try and finish the job they had started that morning.

"You know the worst thing about McKinney?" Newsome broke the silence.

"I'm sorry buddy. That's some bad shit. Who ever thought of that buddy plan thing should have his ass kicked."

"Naw, it was great. We did everything together. We lived right across the street from each other back in Orem, and that's the problem. Our mothers talk every day."

"We've been writing...telling them what a beautiful country it is...all the pretty girls, you know, that kind of bullshit, so they wouldn't worry. Now my mother will know we're in the shit and she'll worry all the time."

"Your mother was already worried."

"Yeah, I know, but not like this. They will probably get together for Thanksgiving, and that's about when the news will arrive."

"There will be a lot of families having a shitty Thanksgiving this year," I surmised.

"Yeah, and the day ain't over yet," Newsome finished.

As the light faded, the incoming began. Green tracers screamed overhead, seemingly originating from every point of the compass. It was untargeted harassment fire meant to prod us into returning fire, thus giving away our positions. It would very likely be a fatal mistake. We traded two hour watches. I trusted Newsome with my life. While he was on watch, I slept like a baby.

Chapter Six
MOMMA

"Why the hell do they scream for their momma? She sure as hell can't help 'em."
Z's comment on the last words of dying men, September 1968.

The night passed with only one new casualty. A sergeant in the CP, sleeping between two other men, took a stray round through the jaw. He lay bleeding into his poncho until dawn, our first opportunity to bring in a chopper. I carried his gear to the chopper. I stopped in the rice paddy to wash the stinking, congealed blood out of his poncho. I was sick and tired of blood.

Choppers came in early, delivering C-rations and ammo, and hauling off the few walking wounded from the previous day who had stayed the night to help shore up our defenses. The last chopper deposited six newbies in shiny black boots and bright green stateside utilities. They were as out of place as a piñata at a funeral. It was a bad time to have to babysit, and I prayed none would be assigned to me.

Gunships and jets had been working over the bunker complex since first light. There had been no return fire. It was now time for us to move back across the river and take the complex. My team was on point. We scouted out a shallow crossing north of the bunkers. I waded across first and slithered into the woods. I crawled on my elbows and belly into a thicket, and lay there silently watching and listening for any signs of the NVA. Newsome moved in behind me, then crawled forward, facing in the opposite direction. We reconnoitered in silence for several minutes before signaling the remaining two members of our team across. We fanned out, forming a protective perimeter, and James moved the rest of third platoon into position. We continued to leapfrog forward until the platoon was dug in along a line at the edge of the trees on the northern fringe of the bunker complex.

I could see several concrete reinforced bunkers with narrow firing slits open towards the rice paddy where first platoon had been ambushed. There were a lot of downed trees, dozens of bomb and rocket craters and huge patches of burned over vegetation from our two days of bombardment, but the bunkers looked to be mostly intact.

"Give 'em hell boys!" Sergeant James yelled, and we all began firing at the bunkers. Hundreds of rounds kicked up puffs of dust and law antitank rockets knocked chunks of cement off the edges of the bunkers, but our onslaught failed to elicit a response

After two minutes of fury, James yelled, "Cease fire!" and all was quiet.

"Jack, take your team and check it out...on the double," he ordered.

I assigned a bunker to each of my three team members. We all ran to our designated bunker, and tossed a grenade through the firing slit. The complex was deserted...the NVA had pulled out overnight.

We spent the rest of the morning searching the complex for Adams and Padilla, weapons caches and signs of dead NVA. We found nothing of the NVA, no blood trails, no dead and no weapons. What we did find were the ruins of previous bunkers. On the side of one was a message left by one of our own: "In memory of six brothers from Delta 1/7 who died taking this bunker on June 6, 1966." It was signed by Myron Adkins of Attica, New York, with the subscript Oct 65 to ?? . I wondered if Myron had finished his tour.

"Jesus fuckin' Christ!" Smitty commented upon reading the inscription, then added, "What a fuckin' waste!"

Newsome and I started back towards Sgt. James' position, working our way through a thickly wooded depression just forward of one of the NVA bunkers. That's where we found them. Adams slumped against a tree...his hands buried in a maggot-seething pile of intestines, the top of his head from above the eyes blown completely away. Padilla lay at his feet. The right side of his skull was crushed by the impact of the heavy 45 caliber slug. The pistol was still clutched in his cold, dead hand.

Both men were covered by swarms of black flies, digesting and laying the eggs of their offspring in the rotting flesh. The shock and smell caused us to back away. We were so revolted by our discovery that we conspired to leave them there with their secret. We agreed not to report our find to Sgt. James, unaware of what our failure might mean to their grieving families.

We knew within a few days they would melt into the jungle floor like ice cream dropped on a hot Texas sidewalk. I imagined that their bodies would nurture the soil; that someday, if the war ever ended, a farmer might take notice of the richer soil and decide to plant a garden there. He might dig up a decaying piece of broken bone and possibly find Adam's dog tags, or maybe the journal he kept wrapped in plastic to keep out the mildew. If the farmer can read English, he would learn something of Adam's dreams and fears. Or maybe he would find Padilla's likewise wrapped wallet, and see the fading pictures of his wife and baby daughter. If the farmer is a sensitive man, he would be saddened by his discoveries. He would wonder what happened to these men. Maybe he would collect the things he finds and take them back to his home, build a small shrine, and pray for their souls.

I wondered how many millions of men, women and children have thus nurtured the soil in the forest of Belleau Woods, and the fields of Flanders and Appomattox, in the bombed over cities of Hiroshima and Manila...the list seemingly endless and ever growing. What is it that we, as a race of civilized men, have learned from this violence? We measure the progress of our civilization by the improvements in our weapons systems: from stone tipped arrows to automatic rifles that can kill at over a thousand yards; from crude catapults that could lob a stone a few hundred yards to modern missiles that can deliver a payload over 10,000 miles, and kill everyone within a hundred-mile radius. I'm not sure the world started with a big bang, but it doesn't take a propulsion scientist to see that it will likely end with one, and the last sound will probably be some poor private screaming for his mother – "MOMMA!"

We found Sgt. James and Johnson sitting on one of the NVA bunkers. James waved me over. He was on the hook with headquarters giving the General an after action report. As I drew near, I heard him say, "Yes sir, that's right, an estimated 300 enemy dead." He listened to the general a few seconds then answered, "We don't have an exact count yet, sir, but our casualties were moderate."

I fumed as I waited for him to finish his report, then I attacked. "What the fuck are you talking about Sarge? I loaded dead and wounded in choppers all day yesterday, and I haven't seen one fuckin' dead gook!"

"We have to estimate based on the size of the unit our intelligence says was here...and the amount of ordinance we used to displace the unit," he tried to explain.

"Bull fuckin' shit, that's what it is, it's fuckin' bullshit. Maybe if we were honest about what's fuckin' happening over here, the people in America would lend us a little support!" I was boiling hot.

"It don't matter what you think Jack. It's bigger than you and me. Just get your team rounded up. We're moving up to the railroad berm."

The railroad berm had been our first day's objective. We were supposed to be the blocking force...the anvil. We were supposed to walk three clicks to the berm on day one, dig in along the high ground and wait for other units...the hammers... to drive the NVA into our trap. It would be like buffalo hunts in the old west, a bunch of dumb ass NVA just stumbling into our sights. Yet, here it was day four...we had lost two thirds of our men and were still two clicks from the railroad berm.

We spent the afternoon walking, rather carelessly I thought, towards the berm. We strode down a path criss-crossed by heavily trodden trenches. The NVA were on the move. At one point, we came upon a row of NVA ruck-sacks loaded down with ammo and rice. Several of the packs had pith helmets strapped to their sides. Some had pictures of sweethearts or children and letters stuffed inside. It appeared we had startled the men while they were resting... causing them to run off and abandon their gear. We burned everything and moved on.

We arrived at the railroad berm late in the afternoon. The railroad had been deserted since the French were thrown out of Vietnam in 1953. We set up our CP in a graveyard near a dilapidated French plantation house. You could still imagine its former grandeur from the storm shutters and marble balcony balusters that now hung askew from the burned out second story. We moved inside Golf Company's defensive perimeter for the night. It would be a night of rest for Echo.

Smitty, Newsome and I snapped our ponchos together and stretched them between two headstones near the center of the cemetery. We gathered all the peaches and pound cake we could pilfer and moved into our cozy abode. We told stories and laughed late into the night, like three boys on a camping trip. It was a memorable night. Little did I know, it would be my last night in the field.

It happened before nine the next morning. Newbies started arriving at dawn. Smitty was medivacked for foot problems and Sgt. James assigned a survivor from first platoon as our new squad leader. We went out on patrol to search the area around the plantation house, and before I had a chance to ask the new squad leader his name, he set off a mine.

It was a bouncing betty...a deadly contraption made in America to kill communists. It tosses a grenade up to waist level before it explodes, killing without question or remorse. This one worked to perfection...tearing our new squad leader nearly in half.

It was like watching a slow motion movie. I saw the squad leader being ripped into chunks of flesh, bone and innards that came rushing towards me...pelting my chest and face. I was disgusted by the grossness of his macerated torso splattering into my eyes, up my nose and into my open mouth. I reached up to wipe away the carnage and found my own eye dangling from its socket by a strand of tendon. The movie ended, and the reality of pain rolled through me like a tank through a thatched hut.

"You OK, Jack?" I heard Newsome's voice through the ringing.

"Naw, I don't think so. I have my eye in my hand."

I heard screaming until Doc Murray knelt at my side. "Ok Jack, I'm here," he said.

The screaming ended. It had been me screaming for a Corpsman. When Doc started to give me a shot of morphine, I protested, "No! Doc, it's a head wound!"

"Shut up Jack, let me do the doctoring."

As he cut away my boot strings and utilities, I complained, but he continued to cut away my clothing and bandage my wounds. Finally, the morphine kicked in and I relaxed. James began to question me.

"What's your serial number Jack?"

"2256423," I answered.

"What's your rank?"

I looked at him quizzically, "You know my fuckin' rank."

I was getting weak. I wanted very badly to go to sleep. I didn't have the time or energy to answer a bunch of bull shit questions meant only to keep me conscious. I wasn't sure if I was dying, but I had deep feelings of regret for the pain I had caused my mother and grandparents. With that thought, I began to drift away into the darkness.

"Where's your home town?" Sergeant James was still asking questions, but I was finished trying to find the answers.

Finally, he bent over my face and yelled, "Can you hear me, Jack?"

I began to nod my head affirmatively.

He smiled and said, "If you keep shaking your head up and down, your fuckin' brain's gonna slosh out your eyehole!"

I wanted to laugh. Didn't he know he was supposed to keep me calm so I wouldn't go into shock? Of course he did, that's why I loved the guy.

I heard the thudding of a chopper setting down. Johnson, Barnes, Newsome and James each grabbed a corner of my poncho and ran toward the LZ. They tossed me through the door and we thundered skyward. I looked up at the impassive door gunner, and the lights went out.

I awoke a few days later, prostrate on a dolly in a hangar at the Da Nang Airbase. There was a disconcerting absence of light. I could hear the clanging of metal trays. I knew someone was being fed. *Why weren't they feeding me?*

I reached towards my eyes to discover that my head and both hands were heavily bandaged. Slowly, the memory of being wounded crept back into my consciousness. I remembered the doctor at the medevac hospital telling me just before I went to surgery, "Your right eye is badly lacerated. We probably can't save it; but I think your left eye will be OK."

I pushed the bandages up, exposing my left eye. I could see a long row of silver caskets along the wall to my right. To my left and behind me, men in various states of altered consciousness lay silent on wheeled dollies. Since I wasn't being fed, I worried, maybe one of the caskets was for me.

The next morning they loaded us all on a C-130 bound for Japan. I lifted my bandage one last time, as they loaded me on the plane, to get a final glimpse of the place that had robbed me of my humanity.

Vietnam had sucked away my beliefs and perceptions of truth like loose sand in an Oklahoma whirlwind. My perception of God was the first casualty. I believed my faith was strong, but in reality, it was based on a shaky foundation of fear and reward. My religion had been fed to me as the unquestionable truth. I had no spiritual knowledge grounded in experience. I had gained a new perception of God, and I hated him for all I had seen.

My belief in the ultimate rightness of my way of life was the next victim. I saw first-hand the deception and treachery perpetuated by my government in the name of democracy and freedom. Thousands were dying, lives were being destroyed, and the men responsible were being praised and growing wealthy. I hated those men more than I had ever hated the NVA.

My perception of blacks was totally altered. I was taught that blacks were inferior and that whites should not associate with "colored people." But, I had always felt empathy for the black community in Texas. I knew that they were driven by the same hopes and dreams as the white community. Being raised in a segregated state, I was ignorant to most black issues. The violent undercurrent of racial tension in Vietnam had morphed my ignorance into prejudice and a deep hatred for all things black.

Worst of all was the loss of my humanity. I had become a remorseless killer, with no hopes or dreams beyond my own survival. Nothing beyond that mattered.

When I returned to the states, I was greeted by demonstrators. From my hospital window, I could see them picketing outside the front gate. To them, we were all murderers and "baby burners". I knew they were partly right, but their perceptions were limited by their lack of experience.

I could see from the TV coverage that the government was ready to use the veterans as a scapegoat for their failed policies in Vietnam. We were being labeled as out of control, drug addicts, and blamed for the perverse turn the war had taken.

I received a letter from Newsome while I was at the naval hospital in Corpus Christi, Texas. He had taken his R and R in Okinawa. He said he had tried to find Tommyco, but the bar was shut down. Sgt. James, Johnson and Tarver had all been killed in December. According to the letter, Tarver had been posthumously recommended for a medal. He had thrown himself in the line of fire to save Thompson. I didn't answer the letter...I was too depressed to function.

When I finally arrived home, even my own friends and family seemed unsure of how to treat me. Certainly, I was no returning hero, but I didn't want to be treated like a disease. Suddenly, Vietnam didn't seem like such a foreign place. At least there, I knew where I fit in. I was a shell of the young man who had gone off to war. Nothing remained but a dark emptiness, oozing rage.

Chapter Seven
OKLAHOMA 1969

"Marines are dinky dow! You have much food to eat but you complain about food. You have dry place to sleep but you complain about rain. You could learn a lot from us."

Mai Ling's commentary on Marines, December 1967.

A bitter wind howls across the Oklahoma panhandle, bouncing giant tumbleweeds across fields of stubble to be snagged in sagging barbed wire fences. The icy wind had driven me from my job as a laborer on the Optima Dam project to the relative warmth of the Jolly Tavern, a pine log shack at the edge of Guymon.

"Shut the fuckin' door," we all yelled in unison, as the grey metal door on the north side of the bar flung open and a chill cut through the room.

A stranger in his early thirties slipped through the door and pushed it shut behind him. He paused for a moment in the sudden darkness to let his eyes refocus, then he found his way down the bar, to plop on the stool next to me. He was a bulky man with bagging bulldog jowls that knew their way around a cheeseburger. He had stuffed his blubbery frame into an undersized, green plaid business suit, and even with the top button and tie loosened, his neck was squeezed up in rolls above his collar. His ivory white hands and two inches of wrist protruded from the ends of his jacket. The hands looked to be as soft as a new born baby's butt. I figured him as an office "gofer", who had never worked a day in his life. He ordered a beer and began hitting on the bartender, Viola, a fading rose of indeterminate age, bragging about his high paying job with Bridger- Knutson.

"They're the largest contractor in Vietnam, and as their Midwestern buyer, I'm personally responsible for a big part of Vietnam's economic boom," he began. "And I do mean boom!" he added, with emphasis on the boom. "Every time we build something the Goddamned Vietcong blow it up. I love those bastards, they're great for business. We can't keep up," he chuckled, stopping long enough to quaff some beer.

"You've got to love those fuckin' gooks," he continued. "I get a brand new company car every six months and I'm pulling down four figures just in commissions...plus my salary. If this war lasts long enough I'll be a fuckin' millionaire!" he laughed again.

His laugh was irritating me. He raised his beer as if to propose a toast. "This is the greatest little fuckin' war ever."

I was slumped over my beer trying to ignore the asshole, but the beer had a mind of its own. "It's not worth it," I mumbled, without looking up.

"Hell boy, it's the American way!" he spoke loud enough for everyone in the bar to hear. "We send over a few boys to keep things stirred up. The American economy booms and everybody comes out a winner."

Tom and Paul, two of my old school mates, were playing pool behind us. Both shook their heads in disbelief, knowing what was about to unfold.

"Not the Vietnamese people or the men being sacrificed," I muttered, as I raised my head to look him in the eye.

He had a lingering smirk, sure he could outwit me. "Some win and some lose," he flashed a big grin, "It's the American way."

I lunged forward and had both hands around his throat before he knew he was in a fight. I squeezed until my fingers were digging through the fat into his windpipe. He grabbed my wrist and tried to pull away, but I tightened my grip until he stopped struggling. I watched his eyes go glassy, then put my nose against his cold, fat cheek and whispered in his ear, "How does it feel to die for what you believe, motherfucker?"

"Come on Dennis, let him go...It ain't worth it!" the bartender intervened, standing over me with a sawed off pool cue.

Paul dropped his cue and grabbed me by the shoulders, while Tom worked to pry my hands loose and pull the choking man away. I stared into his glassy eyes until he was free. He stumbled back to catch his breath. "Ya...you...your fuckin' crazy man! I'll have your ass arrested!" he coughed out in spasms, charging toward the door.

"Good idea man! Then I'll have your name and address... I'll know where to come to finish the job!" I warned, as the grey metal door slammed shut behind him.

Viola slipped the sawed off cue beneath the bar. "Jesus, Dennis, sometimes I think you've lost your mind!"

"You know you love me Viola," I answered in defense.

She picked up a bottle of deviled eggs and took a swipe at the dusty bar. "I hope you'll remember that if I ever have to crack your skull," she said.

I knew Viola was right, I had changed, and I was more than just a little crazy. Before I went to Vietnam, I fought on adrenaline. I could feel the rush as it surged through my body. It might take the rest of the night for the rush to subside. Now I fought with a cold detachment... and always went for the quick kill.

I slid the half-emptied beer of the fleeing businessman next to mine and said to no one in particular, "I don't reckon he'll be needin' this."

I was chugging down the bonus beer when Max ambled through the door, his boyish face aglow with mirth.

"What's up with the fat cat?" he laughed, and continued, " He was moving so fast he tripped and fell on his ass, rolled onto his belly, then split his pants trying to get back to his feet. He was still on his knees trying to open his car door when I came in. He seems to be in a pretty big hurry to leave."

"I think he had a near death experience," I explained.

Max sat on the stool the businessman had abandoned. "I've got your check," he said, handing me an envelope.

Max turned to watch the pool match while I cashed my check. "Who's winning?" he asked.

I glanced back at Paul and Tom. "Hell, I don't know, there're both fuckin' losers as far as I'm concerned. Let's get the fuck out of here."

Max ordered a case of Coors, cashing his payroll check to pay the tab, and agreed, "Have beer will travel."

When I left for Nam, Coors was the drug of choice in the Oklahoma panhandle. When I returned, most guys had longer hair than the ladies, the ladies had burned their bras, country music was for old folks, and marijuana had replaced Coors as the pause that refreshes.

I had seen a lot of grass in Nam but had never smoked it. I had an agreement with the guys in my team...they could smoke back at base camp, but smoking in the field was an automatic death sentence. It was just a matter of the executioner...me or the NVA. I associated pot with draft card burning hippies and ditty-bopping niggers. I hated them, so I hated pot.

Max started smoking pot in Nam. He returned to Guymon a month before me, and we found work together building forms for the spillway on the Optima Dam project. I hated his Jimmi Hendrix tapes and his pot smoking, but he had saved his pay in Nam and bought a 1969 Chevy Super Sport with a 396 engine. I loved his car.

We loaded our beer in the backseat of the Chevy and headed out of town to the lopes, an interlinking complex of dirt roads that crisscrossed the Beaver River. I drove while Max rolled up his joints.

"Why do you smoke that shit?" I asked.

"It alters my perception," he answered without looking up from his work.

"Alters your what?"

"The way I see things," he said, sliding his tongue along the edge of the zigzag.

"What about all the draft dodging hippies and niggers that smoke that shit?" I challenged.

"What about it?"

"They're fuckin' up the country, out blowing up buildings and burning down cities," I said, taking a chug from a beer and sliding it back between my legs.

"Shit, Jack! They ain't fuckin' up nothin'. They're burning down the cities 'cause this country's already fucked up!"

"That's your altered perception talking, because of that shit you smoke," I said, as I pulled off the narrow dirt road onto a bluff overlooking the river.

I turned off the key and was enveloped in the silence. A sliver of silver water reflected under a pale moon wafted me back to simpler times...walking hand in hand with Alisia...bare foot in the wet sand on a warm summer's night...camping, fishing and hunting trips with high school buddies, with nothing more pressing on our minds than a Friday night football game. It must have been a thousand years ago...nothing of that life remained.

I turned to face Max. "If you're right, then what the hell were we doing in Vietnam?" I challenged.

"Shit, Jack, I was drafted, I don't know what the fuck you was thinkin'," he said, snickering through his teeth.

"I believed in America, I believed we went there to protect the people from communism," I answered, with a complete absence of pride.

"And how did that work out for you?"

"Not so good."

"Not so good in-fuckin'-deed!" Max taunted, "We didn't have such high ideas. We took what we wanted. The pot helped me to see it for what it was," he said.

"Then what the hell was it?"

"NDSOBS," he answered, "New day, same old bull shit. It was just bull shit Jack, let it go, it don't mean nothin'."

I didn't like to hear Max put down our involvement in Vietnam, to me it demeaned the memory of our friends that had or would die there. But I knew he was right, and by his service and his own loss, he had earned the right to speak his piece.

"Max...it pisses me off when you say that shit...," I started, but he interrupted.

"Everything pisses you off. You say you hate blacks, you hate hippies, you hate the NVA, you hate the war, but you're trying to get back there. Jack, you're the one who's all fucked up!" He finished his statement laughing.

"Well, at least, I'm not smokin' that shit."

"You should give it a try. It just might change your attitude."

I looked out at the shimmer of water snaking its way through the leafless cottonwoods and opened another beer. "It just doesn't matter anymore anyway," I answered.

Max reached across the car and switched on the key, The Stones' "Satisfaction" reverberated through the car. He rolled another joint and suggested, "Let's head in to BJ's bar and hustle some pool."

"Sounds good to me," I answered, "I think Judy's working tonight. She can pocket my balls anytime."

I took a left at the cross road, mashed the pedal to the floor and power slid onto highway 3. Nine miles north of Guymon the Stones were still wailing about not being able to get no satisfaction as I blasted across the eight mile bridge towards town. Max, his head bobbing in rhythm to the music, was facing the passenger window.

"Shit Jack! How fast are we goin'? That bridge looked like a fuckin' picket fence!"

I glanced down at the speedometer. "We're at 110 but I bet I can get her up to 130 before we hit the three mile bridge."

"Chill out, Jack, and try some of this pot," he said, waving the smoldering joint beneath my nose. "You're way too fuckin' serious."

I was tired of saying no. "Hand me the motherfucker!" I said, snatching the joint from his hand. I took a deep pull. Not being a smoker, the effects on my lungs were immediate. The harsh smoke burned at my lungs and I coughed deeper and deeper, until I almost went into convulsions. I took another hit and passed the joint back to Max. I began to slow down as we passed the three mile bridge, and took one last hit as we passed the Jolly on the outskirts of town.

"How do you feel?" Max asked as I passed him the reefer.

"Just fuckin' grand," I answered, but I had an impulse to say more...a lot more.

A green mustang pulled up behind us and laid on the horn. He swerved out around us on the driver's side, and shot us the finger as he squealed past.

"What the fuck is his problem?" I wondered aloud.

"How fast are you going now?" Max asked, and began his snicker.

I looked at the speedometer. "Twelve miles per hour, but I think I can get her down to five," I answered, as an uncontrollable grin began to spread across my face.

I pulled up to the red light at the intersection of Highways 3 and 54, the busiest intersection in the Oklahoma panhandle, and lost my mind. I left my body...not for long...a few seconds at most, but long enough to look back on myself. Sitting behind the wheel of that SS 396 Coupe was the most serious 20 year old in the world. He looked so pathetic...sitting there simmering in his self pity and broiling in his anger. I couldn't help but to laugh. The laugh was infectious. As I laughed, the serious kid behind the wheel began to laugh. We laughed ourselves into a tremor.

"What's the matter with you, Jack?" Max glared at me in a panic.

The light had turned green, cars were honking and pulling around, but I had cracked up. I was shaking too hard with laughter to function behind the wheel.

"Let me drive!" Max yelled, as he reached across me, opened the door, and shoved me into the street. I fell into the street laughing, but quickly recovered enough to fling the driver's seat forward and dive into the back seat. Max clamored across the console and sped towards the country. Marijuana had saved my life. I had learned to laugh at myself again.

Sweat pours into my eyes, blurring my vision. From out of the misty darkness, apparitions seemingly float towards my position. I search up and down the line for help, but everyone else is dead, their stiffening limbs casting twisted shadows in the wavering light of extinguishing flares. I fire frantic 18 round bursts into the night. Bodies flail and pile up in front of me, but more materialize from out of the steamy haze, coming ever closer. One of the apparitions suddenly breaks free of the mist. I see a face...a young girl with a halo of streaming black hair framing her glistening doe eyes. Tears are rolling down her red clay, smudged cheeks. I pull the trigger...she jerks to a stop, stumbles backwards and falls onto the growing pile of corpses.

I awoke in a cold sweat, with a cool breeze sweeping white lace curtains gently across my face. I knew immediately this was not Vietnam. That was not always the case. I often heard the sounds of gunfire at night when I knew no one was shooting, and I often awoke not knowing whether or not I was still in Nam...but the air in Nam was never this crisp. I knew that I was in the back bedroom of my grandmother's house... my room before I went to Nam, but I had no notion of how I had gotten there.

I rolled towards the window. Ooze from under my glass eye had stuck what was left of my eyelashes together. My mouth felt like it was full of cotton. I pried open my eye, wiped the ooze on my pillow case, then took a swig of a lukewarm, half-empty bottle of Coors perched on the night stand.

I thought of Max's acronym "NDSOBS", and suddenly remembered this day was full of possibilities. This was the day I would leave the frozen Oklahoma panhandle for my VA appointment in San Antonio, Texas. My $34 dollar a month disability retirement from the Marines had been a pleasant surprise. I figured if you lost a body part in the Marines, your reward was a purple heart and a pat on the back. The VA had written saying they would probably pay more, and I might qualify for their rehabilitation program. I didn't know how much more, or what they meant by rehabilitation, so I had been putting the trip off for several months. Just show up for your evaluation and we can get the process started, they had promised, and the chance to leave the "not so chosen frozen" for a few days was too good of a deal to pass up. Hell, I thought, there may be some cash waiting for me in San Antonio.

I dressed in the dark, packing my extra pair of jeans, two denim shirts, a pair of clean underwear and socks, and my weathered Marine utility cap into my surplus Alice pack. From the still darkened kitchen, I collect bologna, bread, and cheese, stuffing them into the quick access pockets with the underwear and socks. After brushing my teeth, I shoved my toothbrush into the pack, and quietly slipped out of the house.

A pink frosting coated the eastern horizon. My frayed jean jacket offered little protection from the chill of morning. I buttoned it up to the collar, stuffed my hands in my pockets and started towards Max's apartment. I found Max there, sitting at a wobbly-legged Formica table, sipping peach brandy from a freshly uncapped pint.

"Have a shot," he offered, pushing the bottle across the table.

I took a hard pull, whipped my mouth on my sleeve and screwed the lid back on the bottle. "Let's hit the road," I said, as I slipped the bottle into my jacket pocket, and headed towards the door.

Max rolled his toothbrush into a clean pair of skivvies and grabbed a half gallon of wine from the now empty fridge. "Let's do it," he replied.

The 396 roared to life. I stuck "Sgt. Peppers" into the eight-track, and Max burned rubber for a block before taking a sharp right towards Highway 54. Turning onto the highway, we soon passed the intersection where my transformation had begun. The intersection incident brought a smile to my face. "That was some trip last night," I said, "I can't remember a thing after the red light."

"You were pretty fucked up, Jack. You laughed for most of the night and kept repeating 'experience is to a man like water to a geranium.'"

"What the hell does that mean?" I wondered aloud.

"I don't have the slightest, but last night you thought it was pretty profound."

"Well, you're right about the marijuana Max...that shit really does change your perception. Hell...I wasn't even in the car after we stopped at the intersection."

"No you weren't, I had to push your ass outta the car."

"No...before that...It was like I was floating outside the car looking back at myself."

"Like I said Jack, you were pretty fucked up."

"I know, but I don't know how anybody could have smoked that shit in Nam, and done the things we had to do."

"I don't know how anybody could have done the things we did without being fucked up," Max said, handing me a joint from his shirt pocket. I lit the joint as we left the Guymon city limits.

Across the high plains of Kansas, Oklahoma and Texas the land is flat and bleak with trees as lonely as a black man at a KKK barbeque. Chalk white grain elevators, the prominent feature of each settlement, jut hundreds of feet into the air, casting stark silhouettes against the expansive azure sky. You can often see the elevator of the town in your future from the city limits of the town you're leaving. Like mile markers along Rome's Appian Via, these giant obelisks track your progress across the high plains. We had a pint of peach brandy, a half a gallon of Chianti wine, and an ounce of Columbian to break the monotony.

South of Dalhart, the distance between towns expands as the land begins to roll towards the Canadian River Breaks. My grandmother often told me stories about crossing the wild Canadian River in the back of a covered wagon, when she was a child heading north to the family's new homestead. Where a mighty river once rolled from bank to bank, nothing remains but scattered rivulets of gleaming water, wandering across a quarter mile of red sand. By the time we crossed the Canadian River Bridge, the half gallon of wine was history. Amarillo came and went, and with it any semblance of scenery. Dry snow swirled across our windshield as we passed Happy, "The home to 672 Smiling Faces" or so the sign promised. But, I couldn't imagine why. The elevators of Panhandle dissolved in our rearview mirror as the last of the peach brandy passed our tongues on the way to burning our bellies. Lubbock would be our last chance to replenish our alcohol supply before setting out across the sand hills of West Texas...a barren plain with no trees, no water, and no legal booze.

The only legal place to buy liquor for a hundred mile radius was a two mile strip of drive-thru liquor stores on the south side of Lubbock. It was lit up like a miniature Las Vegas...its flashing neon attracting Texans like June bugs to a porch light. As we pulled up to the drive thru window, a pretty pink face, framed in golden locks, bobbed out the window. "Whatcha drinkin' boys?" she asked in her soft Texas drawl.

"Whoa wee, you sure are pretty!" Max exclaimed. "Marry me and I'll take you away from all this glitter," he added with a big grin. The pretty face returned the smile. "Gaud damn, you look so good, I'd eat you for breakfast, lunch and supper," he foolishly continued, sticking out his tongue and waggling it, as he gobbled like a turkey.

Now the pretty face twisted with disgust. "You boys best be movin' on before I call the police," she warned, backing away from the window.

"Fuck you if you can't take a joke," Max yelled as he jammed the Super Sport into first and slammed down on the accelerator.

Gravel shot from the spinning rear tires into the windshield of a green Road Runner waiting behind us in line. The lights of the Road Runner blinked on and off and the driver began to pound on the horn as he pulled out in pursuit. Max sped across the highway into an empty lot and slammed on the brakes. The Road Runner swerved to the left, barely clearing our car. It slid to a stop just past Max's door.

I saw a Texas Tech sticker on the rear window and the silhouette of two cowboy hats above the front bucket seats. Max sprung from the car...I reluctantly followed. Two men, wearing tight blue jeans stuffed into glossy cowboy boots, emerged from the Road Runner, each in turn laying his hat onto the seat he had abandoned. They were both tallish and lanky with short chopped hair.

"What the fuck ya think you're doin' asshole? You busted my windshield!" the driver yelled, stepping towards Max.

"Step back...or I'll bust your ass!" I threatened, stepping between Max and the pretend cowboy.

His face reddened, accentuating the white hat ring that encircled his head.

"You and who's ar....." he started, but my fist caught him square on the mouth before he could finish. He staggered back far enough for me to reach down and fill my hand with a fist-sized rock. When he came rushing back, I ducked his awkward windmill right and smacked him right between the eyes with the rock. Blood spurted from his wound, filling his eyes. He stumbled blindly, then fell to his knees.

His buddy charged towards me, screaming, "You son of a bitch!" I side-stepped his onslaught and slammed the rock into the back of his head, just behind his left ear. I heard a crack, and he sprawled face first into the gravel.

"Let's get the fuck out of here!" I yelled, jumping back into the car.

Max reached under the seat and extracted a rusty tire iron.

"Max, let's go now...before the cops show up!" I prodded, not certain of Max's intentions.

Max kicked gravel onto the two down and out cowboys on his way to the Road Runner, and then busted out the windshield, tail lights and headlights of their ride. He kicked more gravel on the boys on his way back to the car, and mumbled something about learning not to fuck with Okies, before crawling back into the driver's seat.

"Why didn't you let me have a crack at 'em?" he complained as we fishtailed out of the empty lot. We slid onto the service road, then headed south on US 62, toward Denver City.

"You know the worst part of it?" Max asked, as we sped down the darkened road.

"No...what?"

"That was our last chance to get beer!" he said, slamming his fist into the dash.

We drove into the night until the lights of Lubbock faded into total darkness, then pulled off under a roadside tree to bed down for the night. I crawled into the back seat and pulled my jean jacket up around my shoulders.

It's that dim time between darkness and light. I'm walking dual point with a man from Fox Company on a red clay road, southwest of Da Nang. We're on opposite sides of the road walking on the slope between the road and the barrow pit to avoid mines we know the NVA has planted in the road. Our companies trail behind, but because of the absence of light, we can only see one another. We are moving very slowly, too slow for Captain Matterson. He sends Lieutenant Sumpter forward to speed us along. Sumpter walks briskly down the middle of the road towards the point, acutely aware of the risk, but anxious to please his superior. An explosion sends a ball of fire into the sky and a concussion rolling through the column of men. As the dust clears, the wailing of the wounded fills the silent void. Bloodied men lie scattered around a 10 foot deep crater in the middle of the road. Cotton Top's leg dangles from the branch of a nearby tree. A light mist falls from the sky. I'm lying on my back, looking up into the filtered light wondering how an explosion can cause rain to fall from a cloudless sky? I look down at my flak jacket...it's covered in blood. I wipe the falling mist from my face, and my fingers are smeared with blood. The mist is Sumpter. I pull a towel from my pack and wipe the blood from my face and hands, but the taste of blood and the stench of death sticks like dug in chiggers.

Captain Matterson runs forward. "Where's Sumpter?" He yells. "Find Lieutenant Sumpter!"

Jake and I move into a tree line pretending to search for Sumpter. Away from the road, we find a tree stump and lean back to share a can of peaches. Mac walks up beside us and smiles, "That was some disappearing act," he jokes.

I add my two cents worth, "It's a little bit "<u>misti</u>fying."
"Maybe he had a "<u>mist</u>tical" experience and left the Nam,"
Jake adds, and we all laugh...but no one thinks what
happened to Sumpter is funny.

With the rising of the sun, the search for Sumpter
intensifies. We look behind the trees, in the trees, in the
barrow pit, even search a nearby village; dragging sleepy
people out of their hutches to look beneath their woven
mats. We expend half the day searching for Sumpter, but
can't find a shred of evidence that he ever existed. Captain
Matterson is not sure whether to report Sumpter as killed
or missing in action. Finally, we put Cotton Top's leg in a
body bag, and label it with Sumpter's name and serial
number. Now his family will have something to revere and
bury.

Chapter Eight
You can never go back home.

"We can't win under these conditions. All I want is to get my ass home in one piece."
Lieutenant Sumpter shortly before operation Starlight, September 1968.

I woke up sick to my stomach...the metallic taste of blood thick in my mouth. Morning brought a new round of dry flurries on the cusp of a frosty north wind. Up front, Max sat with his hands wrapped around the steering wheel, staring through the blowing snow.

"It only snows once a year down here," I offered, stretching to get out the kinks from sleeping curled up under my field jacket in the back seat. "But it blows it around all winter long."

I looked at Max through the rear view mirror. He was working his jaw, his eyes red and puffy. He looked like a coiled viper ready to strike.

"Do you ever sleep?" I asked.

"Not when it's dark, someone has to be on watch!" he answered.

"This is Texas, buddy...we'll be OK."

"Fuckin' A we'll be OK, 'cause I'm on watch."

Mentally, Max was still in Vietnam. The stress of trying to live two realities was tearing at his psyche. He was a hair trigger always ready to go off. A slight man already, he was losing weight and becoming increasingly agitated. He never talked about Vietnam. The only thing he shared with me was the death of his best friend.

Max had shown me a picture of himself and Stu standing in front of an APC at a rubber plantation in Vietnam. Stu was an Alabama redneck, with beaver sized buck teeth, large protruding ears and freckles sprinkled across the bridge of his nose. Even with an M-60 perched across his shoulders, he looked more like a character out of the little rascals than a warrior. Max said they were bunk mates in boot camp, and had gone through infantry training together before being assigned to the same unit in Vietnam. Stu was killed just 37 days short of his rotation date. Max said Stu's manhood had been sheared off by an AK round when the company swept one of Goodyear's rubber plantations near Plu Ku.

"We lost a good man protecting those asshole's fuckin' tires! I held him in my lap while he bled to death," Max had told me, and that was the only time he ever talked about the war.

Max and I had been high school buddies before we went to Nam, so I knew he has always been as wild as a thistle in a corn patch, but now he was surly and unpredictable. If someone crossed him, he'd better be a light sleeper. Shortly after returning from Vietnam, Max bought a pistol that he carried tucked away in his belt. I figured, I might have saved the life of a cowboy or two in that Liquor Mart parking lot.

Max rolled a joint while I slapped together a couple of dry bologna and cheese sandwiches.

"Where's the nearest booze?" he asked, lighting the joint.

He passed me the reefer. I took a deep drag before answering. "My stepfather will have a fridge full of cold beers and a couple quarts of vodka stashed in the barn."

"Yeah, but you don't want to go there after all the shit you've told me about him."

"Fuck him! I need to see my family once in a while. He won't give us any trouble."

Max started the car, and pulled onto the empty four-lane. We sped through Brownfield, turning west on Interstate 83 at Seagraves towards Denver City. I was trying not to remember why I left Texas, as we glided through the shifting sand hills. Miles of oily lease roads dissected the cactus covered dunes. Over the purr of the car's engine, I could hear the forest of clanking pump jacks hungrily humping mother Earth, sucking away her vital body fluids. Below us lay one of the world's largest oil pools. Sulfur gas seeping up through thousands of open wellbores left the whole country smelling of rotten eggs. I hated the god-forsaken desert, the smell of sulfur and the sand, but I especially hated the memories it provoked.

When I started working as an oil field roustabout at the age of 14, my first crew chief said that the oil industry provided the only true American jobs. Stub, a crusty, red headed, ex-driller with two fingers and a thumb missing from his right hand, went on to tell me about a dreamer named Drake who drilled the first oil well in Pennsylvania back in the 1800s.

The discovery of free-flowing oil ignited a cataclysmic shift in the human experience. The towns, the roads, and the people of West Texas all owed their existence to the oil industry. The cars, buses, and trains that scatter families across America and the planes, tanks, and ships that provide the machinery for modern warfare are all by-products of the oil industry.

When I arrived in Vietnam, a college-educated Marine told me the war was being fought over control of oil reserves in the South China Sea. According to him, all of the 20th century wars had been waged to procure oil reserves. Having just arrived in-country, I still believed we were there to stem the tide of communism. I didn't much like college boys anyway...especially an ex-hippy who had been drafted into the Marines. I told him he was full of shit and disregarded the conversation. Later, I heard that Shell Oil made a big discovery off the coast of Vietnam.

The discovery caused me to question, for the first time, my presence in Vietnam. Was I just a pawn in a superpower struggle for control of the world's oil reserves? I began to suspect that my life was being squandered for perverse reasons beyond my control. That, perhaps the government was perpetuating fear and lies to increase the wealth and power of a handful of Americans and their corporations.

We passed through the one stop light of Denver City, turning onto the driveway of a small red farmhouse just west of the city limits. Bob, my younger brother, came rushing out to meet us as we pulled into the drive. His smiling face reminded me of why I made the detour.

At 14, Bob was working hard at becoming a peacemaker, desperately trying to mediate the conflicts that were ripping apart his family. He was short but built like a bull, with broad shoulders and a tapered waist. But, already it was apparent that his shoulders would not be broad enough to bear the responsibilities he bore. He hugged me and pulled me inside where Ann and Justin were playing cards at the kitchen table.

"Dennis is home!" Bob announced, as proudly as if I were his prodigal son.

Ann waved coyly, and looked back down at her cards. Her bout with puberty had left her unsure of how to express her emotions. Mom had warned me that Ann had gone boy crazy. My first thought was, *she's wearing too much makeup*, and I didn't like the way Max eyed her.

Justin, my youngest brother, bounced off his chair to run up and hug me. At 11, he was still living the dream of youth and his eyes were alive with mischief.

"You guys can sleep in my room," he begged, trying to drag me down the hall.

"Mom and dad went to Hobbs, they won't be back 'til late tonight," Bob offered.

It was obvious Ray wasn't home. There was no tension, and I knew Ray wouldn't start back until the bars were closed. It would give me time with the kids. I could be asleep before they got home, and I could sleep in until he went to work the next morning.

I called him Ray now. He had been dad until age 13 when my mother took me aside and explained that I had been living a lie for 12 years, my last name was Jackson, not Fuller. She and Ray had not married until a year after my birth, and he had never bothered with adoption. I lay in bed that night waiting for the man I thought was my father to come home and say something ...anything. He came in late, drunk, porked my mother and went to sleep. He never said anything...not that night, the next day...never! Until that night I had accepted the beatings and emotional abuse -"You'll never amount to shit you sorry-assed Knucklehead!"- as just his way of trying to mold me into a good man. The humiliation of not being enough had always been worse than the physical pain. Now I knew it was something entirely different, and I lost all respect for and fear of my pretend father. He became just an old drunk, and nothing he could say or do would ever hurt me again. I ran away that summer and moved in with my grandparents in Oklahoma.

I pulled up a chair next to Ann, and motioned for Max to sit across the table. We spent the day playing silly games and laughing, trying not to think past the present moment. Ann warmed to me as the day wore on and the boys waited on us like we were visiting royalty. Later, we made popcorn and laid on pillows on the floor watching an old John Wayne western.

When the kids fell asleep in front of the TV, I opened my first beer of the day. I was sitting at the kitchen table downing my second when they pulled up. The car slid to a stop with the motor racing. I heard one door open... then the other...the car was still running.

"Get out of there you slut!" I heard Ray yell.

I looked out the screen door as he pulled Mom from the car by her hair, spinning her to the ground. She landed like a rag doll, dress over her head and her face in the dirt.

"Get up, you filthy slut!" he ordered, as he kicked her in the face.

I raced out the door. "What the fuck do you think you're doing?" I screamed.

Ray turned towards my voice and stumbled back. My sudden appearance had stunned him.

"Hi son," he grinned, looking like the village idiot. "Your mom fell down."

"Yeah, I saw."

I scooped her into my arms...even unconscious she was light as a sunbeam...and carried her towards the house. The kids were all awake, standing inside the door crying.

"Is mom OK?" they asked in unison.

I laid her on the family room couch and checked her pulse and breathing. Her face was a grayish pall, her heartbeat undetectable, she wasn't breathing. I tilted back her head and began to give mouth to mouth resuscitation and chest compressions...glad for the training the Marines had given me.

Ray stumbled into the room. "Get to bed!" he yelled at the kids, shoving Justin to the floor as he passed. "Your mom will be fine, I'll take care of her."

He grabbed me by the shoulder. "I'll take care of her," he repeated, as he tried to pull me aside.

I whirled around, grabbed him by the shirt, and flung him against the wall. "You've done enough...just get the fuck out of my way!" I screamed in his face.

His face was flushed, his fists clenched, but he must have sensed my rage. He slumped against the wall, suddenly acting like a whipped puppy. I was surprised. He was a squat, stout man, with bulging biceps and thick wrists from years of cutting meat. He outweighed me by 40 pounds. Was he too drunk to resist, or just playing his "poor me" game?

I didn't have the time to question his motives. I turned back towards mom and continued the mouth-to-mouth, but Ray wasn't done, he grabbed me from behind again.

"She's my wife, and I'll God-damned sure take care of her!" he yelled.

"You damn well might have!" I answered, slapping his hand away.

I spun around quickly, grabbed him by the throat and shoved him back against the wall. "You're a dead mother fucker!" I spat in his face.

The kids began to scream, "Don't hurt daddy!"

"Listen Ray," I spoke as calmly as possible, with my hands clutched tightly around his throat and my mouth against his ear, "You go out and take care of the car and let me take care of mom." Even though I spoke softly, there was no misunderstanding my murderous intentions. He nodded affirmatively and I loosened my grip. He stormed out of the house. I returned to mom.

After a few tense minutes of mouth-to-mouth and chest compressions, she began to moan and then slowly opened her eyes. On seeing me hovering over her, she smiled and whispered, "I love you son."

"Call the ambulance Ann," I said.

"No, please don't call the ambulance...I'm ok," Mom's plaintive voice, barely audible from the couch, implored. This was not her first rodeo. She would absolutely not let anyone see her in that condition.

I looked into her face...both eyes were swollen almost shut and blood trickled from her lip. Her black evening dress was in tatters, bruises covered her thighs and upper arms.

"Mom...please go to the doctor," I begged. "Let's document this shit and get this guy put away."

She set her jaw. "No son...everything will be fine. Just take care of the kids."

I knew the drill...she was small but persuasively strong willed. The only way she would ever leave the house in this condition would be by way of the morgue.

Ray passed out in the back seat of the car with the passenger side door still flung open and the engine running. I looked in the back window to make sure he was passed out, then quietly closed the door, but left the engine running. Maybe the exhaust would kill him.

With Ray passed out, things quieted down. I put the boys on a pallet on the living room floor, and went back to the family room to check on mom. She was asleep. Max was curled up on a chair in the corner, pretending to be asleep.

I pulled a beer from the fridge and began drinking in earnest. I felt like someone should be on watch, and there was no way I would be able to sleep with Ray in the driveway. I was on my fourth beer when Ann shuffled into the kitchen, her house slippers scuffing against the hardwood floors. She sat down in a chair across the table, pulled her bath robe tight around her shoulders, and began to peel the labels off my empty beer bottles. Her hands were still shaking. I knew she wanted to say something, but she sat in silence, fidgeting with the beer labels.

"What's up, sis?"

She looked up, then quickly returned her attention to a label she had rolled into a funnel.

"Dennis...you drink too much!"

She put down the label and looked up. Her eyes were red and swollen.

"Sometimes you act just like dad when you get drunk. It scares me how much you've changed since you've gotten back from Vietnam."

Her words hurt, but I knew she was right.

"Ann, you don't know me anymore. I'm not the same person who went to Vietnam. That person is dead...killed in action. I've done things that have changed me forever, but I do still love you."

"Why do you keep running away then?" she asked.

"What would I do here? Work at a filling station? There's no future for me here."

"You could work with dad at the packing plant."   .

"Ann...If I stayed, I'd end up killing Ray or he'd kill me. That's not what you want."

"But he seems more settled when you're around." She heaved her shoulders, "Maybe if you worked together it'd be good for you both...like before you went to Vietnam."

"Ann, you're living a fairytale. Things haven't been any good between me and Ray since he started drinking. He used to beat the hell out of me all the time...that's why I left. Don't you remember?"

Ann nodded and went back to her beer labels.

"I'm not a kid anymore Ann. It just won't work."

"But you used to be happy," she said, without looking up.

I opened a beer and sat listening to the night.

"It's worse at night...sometimes I can feel them waiting in the dark." I said.

Ann sat up straight and looked towards the door. "Who's waiting?" she asked.

"I know they're not really there...but I still feel their presence. In Vietnam, the nights belonged to the NVA. We'd be out there...just two men to a listening post, praying for daylight. Every birdcall, every whisper of the wind would send shivers through our bodies. If you stared at something too long...it'd start to move. Pretty soon, you couldn't tell what was real and what was just your imagination.

"I remember one night, when we set in after dark. It was too late to put out listening posts, or ambushes...too dark to set out our claymores, our trip flares, or to dig fighting holes.

"We were spread out along a high ridge, hiding behind rocks and bushes. We didn't know which way to face. They might come from the front, the back... hell, they could have come from underneath us.

"It was a moonless night...so dark you couldn't see the man right next to you. I was afraid maybe everyone had left and I was out there by myself. We were all afraid.

"The NVA knew we weren't ready...they always knew. They watched our every move just waiting for us to screw up. When we did, they'd kick our butts."

I took a swig of beer, remembering the ambush.

"Yeah...they were always there waiting. But it was so dark that night that they weren't really sure where we were, so they drove a herd of pigs through our lines."

"Pigs? Why'd they do that?"

"To find our weaknesses. If we open up, they know where our machine guns are, where our rocket team is set up...they have a better chance of kicking our butt. But that night, not one man fired a shot.

"After the pigs went through, the NVA just melted back into the jungle. I was really proud of our guys. Not one man got spooked."

"You must've gotten pretty close to the guys you were with?"

"We were like brothers...maybe closer. You can't face death with a bunch of guys and not form strong bonds. In fact, I made a pact with two guys to stay in Nam until the war was over...or we were all dead."

"Why? If you really cared about each other, wouldn't you want your friends to make it home?"

"We just didn't want to come home alone... things were too confused."

"Did you really think you might die?"

I laughed. "We pretty much knew we'd either die or get wounded, and one can be about as bad as the other."

"What do you mean?"

"Helicopters could get a man back to the hospital so fast that there might not be much more than a puddle left and the guy would survive. For some that's okay. I remember when Z said, 'If there's nothing left but my head and my jaws still flappin'...throw it on a poncho and send it home'.

"Some of us were more concerned with the quality of life than the quantity. I didn't want to come home missing two of anything. One leg, one arm or one eye was okay...but anymore and Z and Jake promised to keep me off the chopper."

"Keep you off the chopper?"

"Yeah, to do whatever it took to make sure I didn't come home."

"Anything?"

"They promised to put me out of my misery rather than to let me come home and live in misery."

"Did your buddies make it home?"

"Some did, some didn't."

"No, I mean the two guys you made the pact with?"

"No...Z got shot in the head."

"What about Jake?"

"He lost a foot and bled to death waiting for a chopper."

"So you're the only one who made it home?"

"Yeah, I broke our pledge. I'm home, I'm alive and the war's not over."

"But you didn't have any choice."

"It really doesn't matter. I still broke a promise."

Ann pushed away from the table and stood up.

"Well, I'm glad you're home, and you should be too…you know what?"

"What?"

"I bet your two friends would be glad you made it home too." She turned to walk away.

"Thanks for talkin' to me Sis. It really helps."

Looking back, she said, "I want to help, but it's so gory. I'm afraid to hear too much, Dennis."

"I understand Sis."

After Ann left, I pushed a chair up against the door, and fell asleep on the floor next to mom's couch. By the time I woke up, Ray was gone for the day. I was always amazed at his ability to drink a case of beer and a quart of vodka every night, and never miss a day of work.

Chapter Nine
Remember the Alamo

"I didn't sign up for this shit!"
Jake, after the burning of Me Tong Village, May 1968.

We stayed for breakfast. Nobody mentioned the previous night. Mom looked pathetic...her frail frame bound tightly in a nightgown, her face bruised and swollen.

"I must be comin' down with something," she said, hiding the truth from no one but herself.

I finished breakfast, hugged everyone and slipped mom a little money, then gathered my things and headed out to the car.

Bob beat me to the car. I found him there, hunched down in the back seat...a small bag by his side.

"Let me go with you Dennis?" he whispered.

"I can't do that. You know Ray. He'll call the cops and I'll be in jail."

"Don't leave me here! He doesn't have to know I'm with you!"

"He'll know Bob, and besides...who'd take care of mom if you left?"

Just then, mom came running out the door, waving her arms and yelling.

"Is Bobby in there?"

Bob hunkered lower. Mom ran up to the car and peered through the back window. "Bobby Jerrald Fuller, you get out of that car right this minute!" she demanded.

I looked back at Bob. Tears were welling in his eyes.

"I don't know how much longer I can take this," he said.

Justin came out on the porch...crying.

"Is Bobby goin' with Dennis?" he asked in a broken voice.

"No, he's just sayin' good-bye," mom assured him.

"Bob, you know I can't take you, and I can't stay here. Please try to stick it out...for mom's sake," I said.

Tears were rolling down his cheeks, as he reluctantly stepped from the car. Ann came out onto the porch, and they all stood huddled...waving as we pulled away.

I hated to leave my family in the grasp of that lunatic, but the previous night had been no different than a hundred other nights. I knew Ray...he would come home with his head hung, begging to take everyone to supper. He would play on their sympathies until they believed it was their fault he had gotten drunk in the first place. How many times had I tried to talk Mom into leaving? She thought it was more important to keep the family together...or at least, to keep up the appearances of a family.

As the foursome disappeared in the rearview mirror, I knew I would never see them all together again...that I would never go home again.

It was a long, dry run from Denver City to the first wet town on our route. We found a drive-thru liquor store on the south side of Big Springs, where we bought two half gallons of Chianti and a case of Coors, just as insurance.

South of Big Springs, we dropped off the table-flat Cap Rock, down an abrupt escarpment, into the Colorado River drainage, where the road wound lazily through rolling, oak-covered hills. We turned south at Eden, skirting the exposed granite domes of the central mineral region, where the Llano uplift forms the heart of Texas. After crossing the Llano River, we stopped for lunch on the outskirts of Junction City, at the Burger Haven.

"We fought three days to take a rubber plantation north of Da Lat, then gave it back the next day," Max said unexpectedly, after we pulled under the metal awning in front of the drive-up restaurant.

I knew he was soused, and we had smoked a joint between Mernard and Junction, so I wasn't surprised at his disconnected train of thought.

"So?" I said.

"So we had to go back a month later and take it again, and that's when Stu ate it."

"Yeah I know...we kept retaking the same ground over and over too."

"Did the Texans ever recapture the Alamo?" he asked.

"I don't think so."

"You mean all those guys died there and they just let the Mexicans have it."

"I think the war ended right after the battle."

"That's not the point!" Max insisted. "The war ended without the Texans retakin' the Alamo! It's still the property of Mexico!"

"What is your point?" His marijuana logic was beginning to elude me.

"The point is, we have to recapture the Alamo for Texas!"

"We have to what?"

"We have to recapture the Alamo in the name of Texas."

"Who we gonna take it from...a bunch of tourists? The Mexican army is long gone!"

"We'll take it from whoever has it...in the name of Texas," he said, raising his beer in salute.

We ordered cheeseburgers and chocolate milkshakes from the carhop and wolfed them down in silence. We both had a bad case of the munchies, so we ordered hot fudge sundaes for dessert. I couldn't get Max's idea off my mind. I was intrigued by the fantasy of me scaling the walls of the Alamo to recapture it in the name of Texas. It seemed somehow heroic.

We headed south on US 10 with our bellies full of cheeseburgers and our heads filled with a romantic notion. The more we drank and smoked, the more determined we became to recapture the Alamo.

We dropped off the Balconies escarpment onto the mesquite covered questas of the Nueces Plains just as the sun sank into the horizon. The lights of San Antonio beckoned from the plains.

By the time we pulled into a Gulf station on the outskirts of town, its brightly lit orange sign was casting off more light than the disappearing sun. An attendant, dressed in a khaki uniform with the name Bud stitched across the pocket, answered the bell.

"Fill it up?" he asked.

"How do you get to the Alamo?" I asked.

He began to give directions, but neither Max nor I were able to follow them past the first right.

We went as far as we could remember and pulled into another station, where another attendant, dressed in the same khaki uniform, asked the same question.

"Fill it up?"

"How do you get to the Alamo?" I asked.

He leaned into the window and spat out a string of directions that we couldn't follow. We drove to the next station within range of our inebriated understanding. Station after station, for over an hour, took us downtown to East Commerce Street.

Again, a khaki clad attendant asked, "Fill it up?"

"Where the hell is the Alamo?" we asked in unison, and began to laugh.

The attendant pointed across the street and said, "That's the Alamo." And sure enough, it was.

An eight foot rock wall ran the length of the sidewalk, opening onto a plaza in front of the Alamo. The wall framed the plaza, rising in a series of steps to the historic building. We scaled the wall and followed it to the top.

A soft glow emanated from inside the building through the green Plexiglas roof. We searched for a way into the Alamo from the roof; finding none, we climbed down into the Alamo compound to look for an open window or unlocked door. Again we were thwarted.

We started back toward the top of the Alamo. I found a place near the back corner with an abundance of hand and foot holds. As I climbed, I was reminded of the unfortunate soldiers in the Mexican army...forced by a corrupt general to leave their homes and march hundreds of miles to die scaling that very wall. At least the defenders had a choice, and possibly...a cause worth dying for.

Max had taken an easier route. He was looking down at me from the top. When I looked up, he held a finger to his lips, pointing down into the compound. A night watchman stood below...awakened by our invasion. He was searching for intruders. I wasn't sure if he was Mexican, but I snickered at the thought, he was the Alamo's lone defender. I hung on, suppressing a laugh, as he waggled his flashlight from side to side, peering intently into the darkness while I hung a mere 10 feet above his head. When he returned to the building, I climbed within a foot of the roof, then had a sudden vision of myself leaping the last foot, scrambling over the top Mexican style. It was not a well conceived plan.

I lunged upward with both hands as I kicked away from the wall. The minute I let go, I knew I had misjudged my leaping ability and the effects of gravity. I fell...landing in the exact position from which I left the wall. I found my own stupidity irresistibly funny, and began to laugh. Max was shushing me from above, but soon, he was laughing too. After regaining my composure, I used the stepped wall to get back atop the Alamo before the return of the watchman.

We leaned back against the building's facade to catch our breath. In the silence, we could hear the music of a Mexican Mariachi band drifting up from the river walk. Max rolled a joint, and passed it to me.

"Did I ever tell you Stu was gay?" he asked. He had a way of catching me off guard.

"Hell no! This is news to me."

Max looked at me and shook his head.

"It wasn't like that. No one suspected it...not even his own family."

"How did you find out?"

Max took a hit from the joint and began, "We got into some deep shit north of Pleiku. Some sappers got through our lines and started blowin' up APCs. Stu caught a piece of shrapnel in the shoulder. It wasn't bad, but he bled like crazy. Stu thought he was gonna die. He wanted someone to know the truth before he kicked off."

"Lucky you...I'll bet he was embarrassed to live."

Max looked at me and sighed.

"Yeah, he was embarrassed, but relieved. It was a big, dark secret he'd carried around all his life. After he shared it, it didn't seem so bad."

"No one else knew?"

"Nope...he never told another soul."

"Then he never really acted on his impulses?"

"I don't know...certainly not while he was in Nam. He was too ashamed to have anyone know. He joined the Army and volunteered for Nam to show his father he was a real man."

"It's crazy what we'll do to prove ourselves. The men who died here were probably just like Stu...tryin' to prove somethin' to someone," I said.

"Yeah, it's always been the same ole shit. Young men goin' off to war to prove themselves worthy," Max said.

"I spent most of my life tryin' to earn my stepdad's approval," I said. "Even now, I catch myself doin' things to please him and he obviously doesn't give a shit."

"What do you mean...like throwin' him up against the wall?" Max started to giggle.

"So you were awake?"

"Yeah, I was awake."

I shook my head and continued, "No, I mean like gettin' up at six when I'd rather sleep in, because Ray said a man should rise before the sun. Or bustin' my ass to be the best hand on the job, because Ray always measured a man's worth by his work."

"I see what you mean. I do that sometimes," Max agreed.

"I remember one time when I was mowin' the yard...I was a kid...maybe ten or eleven years old. I was doin' the best I could, tryin' to please Ray. He was sittin' on the porch watchin'. Bobby was there with him. Ray was teachin' Bobby how to chew tobacco. Anyway, whenever I'd miss a little strip of grass, Ray would cuss me, then run up, and kick me in the ass with his fuckin', pointy-toed cowboy boots. It hurt all the way up into my stomach. Then he'd give me his old *"If it's worth doin', it's worth doin' right"* speech. But the thing that hurt the most...he'd go back laughin' and tell Bobby how worthless I was. I was so afraid of that man, I'd hide at a neighbor's house when he got home from work."

"Sounds like a real nice fuckin' guy," Max said.

"Yeah, but then one day he came home early and whistled for me to come home. I didn't know what I'd done, but I was sure I was in for an ass kickin'. When I got there, he put his hand on my shoulder and gave me a transistor radio he'd gotten for Christmas. Hell, the thing still worked.

"I was dumbfounded! I guess in his own way, he was tryin' to say he was sorry. He just didn't know how to express himself. You know...I still have that damned old radio stashed away in a box at my grandmother's house."

"Maybe he did love you," Max said.

"I thought so that day, but after that, things just got worse."

"Well, my dad wasn't much better," Max said.

"Really, he always seemed nice to me."

"Seemed is the operative word. He put on a show for everyone else, but when it was just our family, things were different. We'd go to church Sunday mornin', eat out with the neighbors, then, after we got home, he'd get drunk and beat the hell out of the old lady."

"I wonder if everyone's father was like that?" I asked.

"Probably more than we knew," Max replied.

Max thought for a minute, then added, "Why is it that someone would act nice around a stranger...then go home and beat the hell out of the people who love them?"

"I guess some people are just born assholes," I said.

Max scrunched down, pulled his coat up over his ears, and we fell into silent contemplation. From the top of the Alamo, San Antonio was peaceful now, but the humid night air and fragrant aroma of the river took me back to a time I had never known. I wondered what had been going through the minds of those Alamo defenders when they looked out over the prairie 150 years ago to see thousands of campfires flickering in the night...knowing that daylight would bring certain death. I fell asleep propped against the facade.

I'm moving towards the Alamo with a column of men. The drummers beat out the cadence as we march forward, our battle flags snapping in the wind. As the buglers sound the charge, hundreds of muzzles flash from the wall. To my right, a man's head is severed by a bursting canister round. He takes a half step and crumples to the ground. To my left, a man takes a mini-ball in the chest. Crimson bubbles gurgle from his mouth as he falls to his knees. Mini-balls buzz past my ears like hungry horseflies and cannon balls explode in the air. Thick smoke blackens my uniform and burns my lungs, but we close ranks and continue marching forward.

A breach opens in the wall ahead. I see the smoke-smudged faces of the defenders as they fall back, knowing death is imminent. We charge towards the breach, our bayonets gleaming in the sun. A young defender lies wounded against the wall, a pistol cradled in his lap. I rush forward, burying my bayonet into his stomach. He looks up and our eyes lock. I blink...and now I'm the dying defender, looking up at a young Mexican soldier with his bayonet buried in my stomach. I'm the victor and the vanquished...the living and the dying. Then I hear a voice: "It's always been the same ole shit! Young men goin' off to war to prove themselves worthy!"

I jerked awake. Max was silhouetted in the pre-dawn light, peeking down into the Plaza. "What's up Max?"

He jumped, scraping his nose against the wall. "Shit Jack, keep it down!"

"What's the problem?" I asked.

"We have to get off this buildin'...tourists are startin' to show up."

I looked over the facade. A group of people stood reverently admiring the edifice.

"I guess we can go...we've accomplished our mission. The Alamo is now back in the hands of Texas," I said.

We came down from the roof along the rock wall, jumping from the wall onto a flagpole and sliding down into the square. People in the plaza were shocked.

"We took it back from Mexico!" we explained to the wide eyed tourist, as we walked towards the car.

Ravished by our battle at the Alamo, we stopped by Sambo's for pancakes. We then located the VA Regional Center on Houston Street... named after Sam Houston, the Texas patriarch who defeated the Mexican Army at the battle of San Jacinto. We arrived an hour early and spent the time walking through the still deserted streets of downtown San Antonio.

Many of the older buildings were built of native limestone...quarried from the Texas hill country. The cut stones were filled with spiraled ammonites, clams and corals...relics of life from the ancient seas that once covered most of Texas. A plaque on one of the buildings said the rocks were over 100 million years old. They represented life forms that lived in the ocean at the same time dinosaurs ruled the land. The rocks are so old, the plaque said, that the short span of man's existence is like a fleeting second in the passing of a year. Long after man's dominance has ended, these rocks will remain a testament to the earth's ever changing life forms. I wondered, *what kind of message would man leave in the rocks...clues to a tumultuous passing?*

I was standing outside the VA building when the doors opened at eight. A pretty red-headed receptionist directed me to the office of Dr. Walters. I spent the next two hours being probed and tested. It reminded me of my induction into the Marines, except now, instead of standing bent over naked with a hundred other inductees, my cheeks spread while a doctor with a clipboard looked up my ass, I was getting personal attention. Walters, a balding man with glasses perched precariously on the tip of his nose, tested me for latent diseases and thoroughly examined each of my wounds. He used a caliper to measure the length and depth of every scar. Afterwards he sent me down the hall to be photographed. The photographer used creative lighting to cast shadows, showing each wound to its maximum dollar value.

By five o'clock, I had been probed, photographed, and given a battery of intelligence tests. My evaluation was complete. Dan, a darkly tanned VA rep with bushy eyebrows and a handlebar mustache, invited me into his office. I sat down across from his desk. He looked into my eyes with a wry smile on his face.

"Dennis...according to my calculation, you should qualify for $130 per month in VA compensation benefits. That includes $47 per month due to anatomical loss of your eye."

"One hundred and thirty dollars a month! Are you shittin' me...that's almost as much as I made in the Marine Corps."

"You gave a lot...you deserve it."

"Some gave a lot more."

"Of course your VA compensation will be in lieu of your retirement pay. You'll have to give up what you're now receiving from the Marines."

"All thirty dollars?" I joked. "Where do I sign up?"

"I also need to know...what plans have you made for a career?" He asked the question as if he expected me to have an answer.

"My career?" I asked, stalling for time to think of a reply.

"Yes, you know...your future."

No one had asked me that in a long time. The Marines told me when to shave, shower and shit...what to wear, when and what to eat, when to move forward and when to move backwards. Since returning from Vietnam, I was running on auto pilot...doing little, other than working construction and drinking. I owned only blue jeans and denim shirts so I wouldn't have to decide what to wear. I moved back in with my grandparents so I wouldn't have to deal with meals and shelter. Now someone was asking me what I wanted to do with the rest of my life!

"What did the test say?" I asked, hoping it would give me a clue as to how I should spend my future.

"Do you know what a geologist is?" he asked.

"Don't they build bridges?"

"That's an engineer," Dan said. "Geology is a field science...they study the earth. They look at rocks to try and understand how it works."

I had been trying to learn something about the earth from looking at rocks earlier that morning. The coincidence intrigued me.

"That's neat...but what do they do when they find out how it works?" I asked.

"What do you mean?"

"What kind of jobs do they have? Who pays them?"

"Oil and mineral companies hire a lot of geologists and both the state and federal governments use them. Geologists can tell us where to find gold and how to predict earthquakes. They study volcanoes, rivers, and mountains to see how they're formed."

"Sounds like fun...how do I get a job as a geologist?"

"You have to go to college," he said.

"College!" I shook my head. "Hell, I never finished high school! I can't go to college."

Dan pushed my test results in front of me, pointing to a row of numbers with his pencil. "These test scores indicate that you would do very well in college, especially if you pursued courses in the physical or social sciences," he said.

"I can't afford to go to college anyway," I said, pushing the papers back across the table.

Dan smiled, "But you can!" He paused, getting my full attention, "The VA will pay your tuition, buy your books, and pay you $175 a month as a full time student. And, we'll also help you get accepted into the college of your choice."

I was overwhelmed. Not only was I going to get $130 a month VA compensation, the VA was going to pay $175 a month to rehabilitate me.

"Where do you want to go to college?" Dan asked.

My mind whirled.

"Corpus Christi," I suddenly blurted out.

I had spent my last few months as a Marine in the Corpus Christi Naval Hospital. I had been engaged to a girl from there and I loved Padre Island. *What place better for me to pursue my career?* I thought.

"Do they have a college there?" I asked.

Dan pulled a book from the shelf behind his head, and began to thumb through the pages, stopping at a section titled "Texas Colleges and Universities". He ran his finger down the list, then looked up.

"Del Mar College," he said. "It'll be perfect. It's a junior college. You'll have no trouble getting accepted and it'll give you a chance to prove yourself before you transfer to a four year university."

There it was... my future decided in the time it takes to get a burger and fries at McDonalds.

Dan set up an interview for me at Del Mar, and told me my first VA compensation check would arrive within the next six weeks. Then he finished blowing me away.

"Dennis, your first check will be retroactive back to the date of your discharge from the Marines. If my calculations are correct, it should come to about thirteen hundred dollars," he said.

Within the next few weeks I would receive what amounted to more than four month's pay at my construction job back in Oklahoma!

I floated out of his office.

Max was waiting in a darkened bar across the street from the VA building. I found him there hustling beers from an old drunk.

He waved me over to the pool table, and whispered in my ear, "Grab a stick, this place is a gold mine!"

He didn't know the half of it.

"I'm not goin' back to Oklahoma," I said.

Max didn't seem to understand. "What about your job?" he asked.

"I'm gonna to be a geologist."

"What the fuck is a geologist?"

"A geologist studies the earth," I answered.

"Why?"

"To find gold." I smiled.

"Gold is good." He smiled back.

Max decided to start back towards Guymon rather than spend another night in San Antonio. He stopped by a liquor store to pick up some beer for the road. I bought a package of Ritz crackers and some beef jerky for my trip south. I had decided to go to Mexico. It was still several weeks until my check was due. I figured the hundred and twenty bucks in my wallet would last longer in Mexico. Max took the 410 Loop, dropping me off on the south side of San Antonio at the Junction of Highway 281...a direct route to Mexico. Max wanted to join me, but he had a car payment, an apartment, and a job back in Oklahoma. Everything I owned, I carried in my backpack.

"Semper Fi, mother fucker," he said, shaking my hand as he handed me a beer.

I pulled my backpack out of the back seat. "I'll see you, Max."

I would miss Max. He was the only one who understood what I was going through. As he pulled away, I saw a fugitive tear escape from the corner of his eye. He would miss me for the same reason.

It was almost dark...too late to catch a ride. Max had given me the old wool army blanket he kept stashed in the trunk in case he got lucky. I walked several yards into the brush, and rolled up in the blanket. Stars blazed from a moonless sky. I chugged the beer, and fell asleep wondering, *is that real gunfire, or just my imagination?*

I'm in what used to be the front yard of a bombed out French mansion. I can see an abandoned railroad right of way from where I'm squatting, probing around a buried porcelain urn with my bayonet. The urn is filled with pots, pans and colorful china...relics of a lost empire. I stand up, looking towards the berm. Our new squad leader is facing the berm, digging with the toe of his boot in the knee high grass.

"What did you find?" he yells back over his shoulder.

"Nothing but a bunch of pots and pans...ans...ans...ans!"
The word reverberates through my head like a marble

bouncing off the inside of a tin can. The whole world is moving in slow motion.

The squad leader's arms and head begin to quiver then slowly disintegrate into a thousand pieces of tissue and bone. His torso separates at the waist...sailing back towards me in a graceful arch. His legs fold at the knees, and sink into the grass. Bits of his body splatter against me, adhering to the exposed flesh of my face, neck and arms.

I know my eye is gone...that fragments of metal are embedded in my legs, testicles, chest, arms, neck and face, but it doesn't matter. I'm desperately trying to remember what the squad leader's face looked like, before his head exploded.

What will his parents think when they hear that their son died violently on the day before Thanksgiving...in a province they won't be able to pronounce...in a country they probably can't find on a map? Will they ask why?

I woke up shivering. It was light...the air warm and heavy with moisture. At first, I thought I was still in Vietnam.

Had I fallen asleep on a listening post, and been left behind? Fear sent tremors surging through my body, then I remembered the dream, and heard the sounds of passing cars.

Chapter Ten
Senoritas

"No one gives a good goddamned what you think. If the Marine Corps would have wanted you to have an opinion, they would have issued you one."

Capt. Matterson to Jake, following Operation Starlight, October 1968.

It wasn't easy for a shaggy bearded longhair to catch a ride in cowboy country. I walked alongside the road with my thumb in the air for most of the morning, before finally deciding the eye patch might be part of the problem. In town, children sometimes fled at my approach, clinging to their mother's legs as I passed.

"It's a pirate," I would hear them say.

Perhaps, I thought, *even grownups are secretly influenced by the pictures planted in their minds. Hadn't that been part of my problem in Vietnam...believing in things that weren't real?*

I hated to be seen without the patch...the missing eyelid, discolored scar tissue, and glaring glass eye staring off into space...but I didn't want to walk to Mexico. I pulled off the eye patch and pushed it to the bottom of my inside jacket pocket.

Almost immediately, a black Chevy Impala pulled up beside me. Seeing my reflection in the tinted glass, I turned my head to hide the eye. My image disappeared as the smoky glass slid into the door. When I looked into the car, my first thought was *oh shit!*

The driver looked like a professional wrestler, with a thick neck and broad muscular shoulders.

Wrists, the size of my biceps, were connected to huge forearms that rippled as he squeezed the steering wheel. His bulbous head was shaved slick as a watermelon. A black cowboy hat sat on the seat at his side. Remembering all the hippies I had taken to the alley, I wondered, *does he think I'm a hippie?*

"Where you headed?" he asked, with a gravelly voice that seemed to emanate from a cave.

"Mexico," I said.

"Me too...get in."

I fought every instinct in my body to get into the car, but I reasoned, this could be my only chance for a ride.

"Relax, it's a long trip," he said, seeming to sense my tension.

He pulled back onto the highway, and stuck a tape in the eight-track. Led Zeppelin boomed from all directions. Reaching into the ashtray, he produced a cigar sized joint.

"Light it up," he said, passing me the reefer.

The marijuana was followed by a cold Lone Star beer fished from a cooler in the back seat. I began to feel better about my chauffeur.

"Name's Bob," he offered, without asking for mine. "Looks better if I'm not travelin' alone."

"Works for me," I said.

I took a swig of beer.

"I don't mean to pry, but I've never seen a cowboy who smoked pot, and.....

"I ain't no damn cowboy!" he interrupted.

"Well, why do you shave your head and dress like a cowboy?"

"Camouflage." He looked over and smiled. "I'm a courier. I run pot between the border and Austin. The cops like to put labels on people. To them, all longhairs are filthy no account hippies, while cowboys, on the other hand, are decent upstandin' citizens. I've been runnin' drugs up and down this road for over a year now and they ain't never hassled me. They think I'm a fuckin' shit kicker." He began to laugh.

"I guess we all do that," I said.

"Do what?"

"Put labels on people."

"Yeah...well as long as we're getting' so personal, let me ask ya...why do you look so damned ragged?"

I thought for a moment. "I guess I'm tryin' to make a statement," I said.

"Whatcha tryin' to say?"

"I guess I'm tryin' to say...the world can kiss my ass."

He shot me a sidelong glance, laughed and passed me the joint.

"Fuckin' Nam vet ain't cha?"

"Shows, huh?"

"Either that or someone sure as hell took a severe disliken to ya," he said, nodding towards my eye.

"Goddamned nasty place, that Vietnam," I replied.

I took a pull off the joint before venturing. "You a vet?"

"Hell no! My momma didn't raise two fools. My brother went and came back with his head screwed on backwards. After I saw what it done to him I got myself classified 4F."

I thought about asking him how, but his ways or whys were of no interest to me now. It really didn't matter anymore. I passed him the joint and we drifted into an unenforced silence. Time dissolved into a marijuana haze.

We dropped off the Oakville Escarpment, with its scrub oak covered, limestone ledges, at Three Rivers, crossing onto the coastal plains at Alice. Except for an occasional relic island, the land was flat again. The retreating gulf waters had long since deserted the palm studded islands, leaving them awash in an ocean of cactus and mesquite. The only evidence of man's handiwork was the scattered orange groves that stood in long rows like armies of bushy-headed aliens. I watched the scenery glide past...engrossed in his concert quality stereo.

Turning east on Interstate 186, we caught U.S. 77 South at Raymondville and arrived in Brownsville with several hours of daylight remaining...enough time for me to get settled for the night. The camouflaged drug-runner pulled up near the border crossing.

"End of the line," he announced.

"And a great ride it was," I said.

I stepped into the sun and nearly fell on my ass. After finding my legs, I walked across the bridge and got into a taxi.

"Boys Town," I said.

The cab sped through the narrow streets, turning onto a bumpy dirt road on the outskirts of town. We stopped in a cloud of dust in front of a walled enclosure guarded by a rusty iron gate. It looked more like a prison than a palace of pleasure. I paid the driver and walked through the gate. Painted women dawdled in front of open, adobe cubicles, hailing me as I passed.

"Watch us make mad love to each other," offered a plump woman in broken English, as she fondled the breast of her young friend.

"Come here...I'll makes you forgets your troubles!" a middle-aged harlot called from the recesses of her darkened crypt.

I ignored the invitations, going straight for the Chicago Club, with the promise of Ice Cold Beer and Live Entertainment. It was still early...the bar was deserted except for two drunk, middle-aged Americans at a small table pulled up to the lip of the stage. They pounded their beers on the table demanding, "We want a show! We want a show!"

A shapely nymph with eyes like pools of liquid chocolate sashayed up to the table. A red mini skirt barely covered her rounded ass. She leaned over the table revealing all but the button sized nipples that hardened against her low cut, white blouse.

"What can I get you?" she asked with a crooked smile.

I figured she had everything I needed but I ordered a Tecate' and lime instead. One beer followed another...the bar filled up...the waitresses changed...the shows came and went, but I was bored. The more I drank, the more somber I became.

The men near the stage were lost in drunken reverie. I envied their state. I wanted to shut off my brain and just go with the flow, but it all seemed so plastic...the false adoration of hookers; the faked orgasms on stage; the phony smiles from corrupt cops.

I left the bar to stroll the plaza. I hoped, maybe something would grab my fancy, or another part of my anatomy. An obliging young girl stepped from the shadows wearing nothing but perfume. Snuggling up to me she cooed, "Needs some lovin' tonight?"

I sorely did, but I wasn't sure the perfume girl could give me what I needed. She pulled me into her stall, and began to massage my back with her breasts. I tried to relax while she reached around to unbutton my shirt and fly. Pulling me down on the bed, she started slapping her breasts against my bare chest.

I wasn't sexually aroused. "Stop," I said, "I have to go."

She jumped up, grabbing her housecoat from under the bed.

"You haves to pay anyway," she said, louder than necessary.

"No sweat, I'll pay."

"What's a matter you, you likes the boys?" she taunted.

"You're beautiful sweetheart...I'm just not in the mood."

Handing her a ten, twice her regular fare, I offered, "You keep the change."

"You bets I will, queer boy."

I walked to the iron gate. A smiling policeman waved as I reached the line of waiting taxis. "Take me to the border," I said, stepping into a cab.

I had spent $25 of my $120 in one night, and for what? Maybe Mexico was not such a good idea, I decided.

It was three in the morning when I passed back across the border into the territory of U.S. customs. It was past four by the time the customs officer had searched my pack and examined every recess of my body. I walked away from the noise of the border with a sense of newfound freedom, but I wasn't sure from what I had escaped.

The early morning air was dry and warm this far inland. I decided to walk back to Corpus Christi. I figured it would take ten days to cover the distance...time enough to think about my new life and much easier on my wallet.

By the middle of the morning, I had covered about ten miles. I was exhausted...my legs and feet were screaming for a rest. I found a mesquite that hid me from traffic and rolled up in the wool blanket. The wind whistled a lullaby through the mesquite, and I was wafted away into another dimension.

I'm on point in Vietnam. All around me men are dying... stepping on mines and being blown to bits! I'm frozen in my tracks...afraid to move. There are so many mines. Finally, I step forward, and sure enough, a mine explodes in my face.

Now, I'm on a troop ship, sitting on a wooden bench in front of a row of green metal lockers. It looks like my high school dressing room, except the faces are all wrong.

Some of them I know...there's Sergeant James, Mac, Z and Jake. Others I don't recognize. Many are missing limbs, or parts of their faces. Z sits down beside me. There's a gaping hole in the back of his head, but he doesn't seem to notice.

"It's good to see you again," he says.

"Where the hell am I?" I ask.

"This is the ship of the dead," he answers.

Vietnamese start filing in through an open door beside the lockers. They are NVA regulars dressed in full uniform, VC in black pajamas and sandals, and civilians of every age and sex. Some have bloody stumps instead of arms and legs. A few look like melted plastic. I begin to recognize some of the faces, leathery skin and terror stricken eyes.

I see a small girl looking back towards the door like she's waiting for someone to enter. Her jet black hair flows

*like liquid silk down her back. When she turns towards me
a shock runs down my spine, lodging in my groin.*

*She has no face, just a gaping corpuscular wound
where her face should be.*

"What's going on here?" I ask Z.

"We're all here together," he says.

"How could we have been so stupid?"

I begin to cry.

I woke up with tears streaming down my cheeks. The
wind had picked up while I slept, leaving me half buried in
the drifting sand. I sat up and brushed the sand from my
hair, then shook out the blanket, rolled it up and stuffed it
in my backpack. Removing my Marine fatigue hat from
one of the quick access pockets, I pulled it down to hide
my wind-tossed hair and began walking towards the
highway. The sun was dying in the west. At best, I had a
couple of hours of light left. My legs ached...my stomach
growled. It was time to catch a ride to somewhere.

Traffic was heavy. I stood with my thumb in the air for
a few minutes and then started walking down the side of
the road. A greasy Mac truck streaked by, pulling an
empty flatbed trailer. I looked up at the sound of
screeching tires. The brakes of the truck had locked up,
hurling the truck towards the ditch in an 18 wheel skid. It
came to a stop in a cloud of dust 150 feet up the road.
Smoke was rolling off the bald retreads. The passenger
side door sprung open and a face peered back down the
road.

"Come on," the driver yelled...waving his arm for me to
hurry.

The truck was a battle-scarred road warrior, probably on its last mission. It had been rolled at least once, and from the looks of it, someone had used a sledge hammer to beat it back into shape. Long strips of green enamel were curled up around the cracked rear window, revealing ancient coats of red over white paint. The split rim wheels were rust welded to the retreads.

When I reached the cab, I noticed a faded, hand painted sign on the door: Deatherage Express, Joe Deatherage, Driver/Owner. My mind registered the name as Death Express, and I wondered, *Is this the physical reality of my death ship dream?*

I climbed in and slammed the door. The hollow thunk was filled with broken glass and I knew the window was down for good.

A youngish looking driver with long brown hair pulled back into a ponytail sat nervously tapping on the steering wheel...looking straight ahead. He was wearing a Marine fatigue hat.

"Thanks," I said.

He pulled onto the road without checking traffic. "Saw your hat," he said. "You an ex-Marine?"

"Yep."

"Been to Nam?" he questioned.

"Just got back this year."

"Me too," he said. "I spent my last month there on convoy duty, drivin' supplies up and down Highway 1 from Da Nang to Khe Sahn. We got caught there for 30 days durin' the siege."

"I heard it was bad up there," I said.

"It was real bad, buddy...heavy artillery day after fuckin' day! My last trip out, my cargo was dead Marines and I was full up."

He began to nervously gnaw at his knuckle.

"I've never been so glad to get out of any place in my life." His voice trailed off and his mind and eyes went blank.

"Bought this truck after I got home," he said, after several seconds of uncomfortable silence. "Fixed her up myself. She ain't pretty...but she runs good."

He looked at me for the first time. "How far ya goin'?"

"Corpus Christi. Where you headed?"

"Tulsa," he said, "I'll be passin' through Corpus in about two hours."

"Sounds good," I said, shifting my weight to fit between the exposed springs of the worn seat.

We picked up speed as he ran through the gears...*too much speed maybe*, I thought; but hell, he'd driven worse roads.

North of Raymondville, Highway 77 narrowed from four to three lanes...one for each direction, and a center passing lane. We were highballing down the passing lane.

Reaching into his shirt pocket, the driver produced a joint. He let go of the wheel, steering with his knees to light it. After taking a couple of deep drags, he passed it to me. I took a hit and passed it back.

Black pavement flowed like a ribbon of asphalt beneath the truck. I lost perspective. Were we traveling over the road or was the road being pulled beneath the truck? Cars appeared and slid past my window like ponies on a carousel...and they were going in the same direction! A tap on the shoulder snatched me back to reality. I looked over to see the driver trying to pass me the joint.

Jesus, this is good stuff! I thought. One hit and I'm in La La Land. I glanced at the speedometer as I took the reefer. Ninety-six miles per hour! Maybe it's just the angle, I hoped, surely we're not going that fast.

I looked up just as the driver pulled his air horn. We were bearing down on another semi traveling towards us in the center lane. The other driver hit his horn. We both had a car on the outside lane and neither trucker seemed willing to give in. I could see the other driver's toothy grin through his bug-splattered windshield. My driver was laughing maniacally.

Seconds before impact...as if by some prearranged plan, both trucks swerved to the right, forcing a car into the ditch in each direction. Only inches separated the trucks when they flashed by one another, the drivers laying on their horns as they passed. I looked off to the side of the road. A sign announced: "Kingsville 23 miles".

"You better let me off in Kingsville. I have some last minute business I need to get done before I hit Corpus," I said.

"Okay, if that's what you want," he agreed, taking a hit off the joint.

I held on to the dash until the driver locked up his brakes on the outskirts of Kingsville. I stepped out of the truck, watching in awe as he pulled into traffic, forcing an oncoming car into the ditch. He ran through the gears, disappearing quickly over a hill. I listened expectantly for the sound of a crash until he was out of earshot.

I needed a beer real bad.

Brownsville provided the physical border between the U.S. and Mexico, but Kingsville was the cultural boundary. Everything south of Kingsville was dominantly Mexican in origin...to the north the Anglo culture flourished. A Naval Air Station and Texas A&I University provided most of the Anglo influence.

I had lived in Kingsville my first couple of months after leaving the Marines. Cindy was the reason. She was a student at the university. I met her at a Charlie Pride concert while I was still at the Naval Hospital. They gave away free passes at the hospital, and hauled us to the concert on a bus. I met her in the lobby while we were waiting for our seats. She was wearing tight jeans and a frilly blouse. I was in pajamas and a blue cotton robe. She made a joke about me being a snappy dresser and we hit it off.

Over the next few months we got pretty serious. After my discharge, I rented a small apartment near the university and we got engaged, but as my hair got longer and my patience shorter, our relationship began to sour.

Things started coming apart while I was still in the hospital. I began to get letters from buddies back in Nam. They told me who had been killed or wounded, who had come down with malaria, and how much they needed me back there. At first I was glad to be home, but I felt increasingly out of place. All my friends were in Vietnam. I knew what it took to survive in Vietnam...I wasn't sure I could survive civilian life.

Sometimes I'd hear a chopper or be inexplicably engulfed by the stench of death and "boom", I'd be right back in Nam. At night, I could hear gunfire off in the distance. Even though I knew it wasn't real...I couldn't make it go away. I spent a little time with a Navy shrink, but he assured me it was just a matter of time before everything would be back to normal. Unfortunately, I couldn't remember ever being normal.

I finally requested a transfer back to my unit in Nam...sending the request through the ranks all the way to the commandant of the Marine Corp. A sergeant in the Commandant's office wrote the reply: "We appreciate your patriotic desire to further serve your country but, as you know, only the very best can become Marines. Your most recent medical evaluation indicates you are no longer fit for active duty. Your discharge papers are presently being processed. As a former combat Marine, I'm sure you will understand."

He was wrong on both counts, I didn't understand, and I had long since disclaimed my patriotism. My only allegiance was to my friends still in Nam.

After being denied a transfer, I quit writing to the guys. In my own mind, I had failed them. I didn't want to hear about their problems if I couldn't be there to help. I started to grow my hair and beard even before my discharge was final...the Marines didn't care. I was just human waste waiting to be dumped back into the civilian mainstream.

There were a lot of us guys without legs or arms or balls...some who had blown their minds. We lingered there in a casual company...cleaning the barracks during the day and hitting the EM club at 16:30...drinking cheap pitchers until they closed.

My only respite from the growing darkness was the time I spent with Cindy. I thought it might be enough, but I felt out of place with her college friends. They had never seen a man torn apart before their eyes or held a man in their arms while he died crying for his mother. They hadn't humped through jungles and rice paddies with leeches hanging off their butts. What did they know about life if they hadn't experienced death?

I tried to hide my feelings in a bottle. I would take Cindy to a college function and pretend to enjoy myself. After taking her back to the dorm, I'd hit a bar and pour down the beers, sometimes hauling the barmaid back to my apartment after they closed. I felt inadequate...sure that Cindy would eventually dump me for a college boy.

As the darkness encroached, I threw the furniture out of my apartment, leaving only a mattress on the floor. I gave away the fancy clothes Cindy and her mother had picked out and bought jeans and denim shirts...all the same color, all the same fit. Worst of all was my anger. I expressed it through jealously...going into a rage whenever Cindy spoke to another guy. I was a grenade with the pin pulled, just waiting to explode.

It all unraveled one sunny Saturday afternoon at a football game when I beat the hell out of a fraternity brother for spilling beer down my back.

Cindy's best friend was dating one of the brothers and it was important to Cindy that we "fit in." I was sure she was looking to ditch me for the guy with the perfect smile and the crew neck sweater sitting behind us. When the team scored a touchdown, and the errant brother jumped up to cheer, his beer sloshed down my back. It gave me the chance I was looking for to vent my anger.

"You son-of-a-bitch! You did that on purpose!" I accused.

"It was an accident," he said, shrugging his shoulders and raising his hands in protest. "It was only beer."

He looked at the boyfriend of Cindy's best friend for support and added carelessly, "What's wrong with this guy anyway?"

That was all it took. I snagged him by his golden locks and head-butted him right between the eyes. It broke his nose. His look was one of total amazement. He grabbed his nose and went into a fetal curl. I kicked him once and just got lost in the release of emotion. The next thing I knew, I was being pulled off of the guy and Cindy was being dragged away by her friend.

"You're crazy!" She screamed, "I never want to see you again!"

That night, I gathered the few belongings I could carry from my apartment and returned to the familiar ground of Oklahoma.   At least I had a few old high school buddies there.

Now I was back. It hadn't been my intention to return. The death express had delivered me.

I cut across a field from the bypass to Business 77. I knew the Brass Monkey would be open by now. It was the most popular watering hole in town...a place where sailors and college students hung out with local hippies.   The music was rock, and the beer was cold.

I found an empty stool at the bar and ordered a beer. The bartender brought me the beer and stood nervously looking from eye to eye as he waited for me to pay. I had forgotten the eye patch. I hadn't worn it since San Antonio. It created a problem for people out there wondering which eye I was looking through.

"I'm over here," I said, raising my left hand.

"Sorry, but it's kind of confusin'," he said.

It felt good not wearing the patch. Its rubber strap caused my naturally kinky hair to stick straight out to the sides, like Larry of the Three Stooges. It was also tremendously hot. I had to continuously dab away the sweat with a hanky. Dabbing irritated the wound, causing the eye to swell shut. I didn't owe it to anyone to hide the wound. I knew it would be hell on my sex life, but I wanted someone to accept me for who I was - a totally confused, one-eyed guy.

The beer went down extremely fast. I ordered a second.

"I know, you're over here," the bartender joked as he delivered the beer to my left hand.

People began to fill the bar. The band set up and began playing. I relaxed...it was good being back in the Brass Monkey. This time I didn't feel like an outsider. It was okay just being me.

"Four beers please."

The voice stirred me like the sound of a mountain stream stirs a thirsty man.

I peeked to the left...she was beautiful. Dressed in the blue gather top blouse I had given her for her birthday and a short pleated skirt I didn't recognize. She looked as juicy as a July peach. Her short brown hair framed her blue eyes, long nose, and soft, full lips. I suddenly remembered how much I missed her touch.

I turned my body toward hers.

"Hi Cindy," I said, flashing a smile.

Her own smile disappeared. She flushed, stumbled backwards, almost dropping one of her four beers, then abruptly left as the bartender tried to hand her the change. The silver crashed to the floor, bringing stares from nearby patrons.   I watched her return to a table where two guys and another girl waited.   She sat down, putting her hand into the lap of one of the guys, her eyes averted from the bar.

"What happened to her?" the bartender asked.

"She must have seen a ghost," I said.

It was like one of those dreams where I'm in a crowded place in my underwear. I wanted to leave but I didn't want to be seen. Surely everyone had seen the snub...they must be laughing. I decided to finish my beer then slip away. I drank slowly, trying to regain my composure. When the last drop was gone, I retrieved my pack from the floor and ducked quietly out the door.

As I shut the door behind me, noise from the bar dissipated into the fragrant gulf air. A half block up, on the other side of the road, I saw a faded neon sign. "The Anchor Bar," it blinked. There was only one rusty car sitting in the parking lot. That's my kind of bar, I decided.

Chapter Eleven
Charlie's Place

"Kill them all, let God sort them out."
Message on a lighter in a Da Nang PX, March 1968

Except for a forty-something looking barmaid with caked on makeup and a hair-do that would hold up in a Gulf hurricane, the Anchor was empty. She sat like a fixture behind the bar, idly filing her nails.

A burn scarred pool table with worn green felt dominated the middle of the room. Besides the ten or so unoccupied barstools, several unused tables line the pine paneled wall. A dusty Wurlitzer sat quietly against the back wall. The air, as thick as blood, smelled of spilled beer and cigarette smoke. I wondered, *what is it that draws me to these places?* I shut the door to my past, and strode up to the bar.

From the shadows at the end of the bar, a gray bearded man stuck his head into the light, craning his neck to see who had dared violate his sanctuary of silence. The old man's appearance startled me. I hadn't noticed him when I walked in.

I sat a few stools down from the man, and waited for the painted lady to ask my pleasure. She remained oblivious to my presence. I waited patiently for the better part of a minute before demanding loudly, can I please get a Bud?

She walked to the cooler and retrieved the beer. She held it against her body like she didn't believe I intended to pay. I pulled a five from my jeans and slapped it on the bar.

"Give me an extra dollar's worth of change for the jukebox," I said.

When she returned with the change, I felt my way through the darkness to the jukebox. The music was all Western...mostly names I'd never seen. I dropped two quarters in the slot, and pushed buttons at random until the "you have another selection light" went out. I walked over to the pool table and squatted to put a quarter in the slot.

"Play you for the championship of the world?"

The old man's booming voice interrupted my concentrated unawareness. I hid my surprise, answering, "And a beer on the side."

"And a beer on the side," he agreed.

He flipped a quarter, let it land on a table...then quickly covered it with his palm.

"Call it for the break," he said.

I looked into his eyes...their clarity was astounding. They were as green as the South China Sea, with the same translucent quality. He was a small man, but his muscles showed through his flowered shirt...not big muscle, but well-defined, like a runner's. His gray hair was chopped short. He had several day's worth of even grayer stubble that looked as prickly as a Texas cactus.

I won the toss, collected the quarter, and broke. The one ball careened into a side pocket. I lined up on the five, using back English to get shape on the three. The five fell into the corner pocket, but there was too much backspin. I was snookered behind the fifteen ball. I tried to save the shot by banking the three, but my angle was off and I missed.

As soon as the old man began to shoot, I could see that he was no stranger to a pool table. He made his first shot and each shot thereafter became a short straight in. He quickly ran the balls and finished with a bank shot on the eight.

"Okay, you're the champ of the world," I said, watching the eight ball fall into the corner pocket.

"Let me buy you a beer anyway," he offered as he pulled the chair out from a nearby table. I sat down across the table, looking straight into those green eyes.

Pointing towards my pack, he asked, "Where you headed?"

"Corpus Christi...eventually...the government is sendin' me to college there."

"You're a veteran then?"

"Yeah...that's how I got to be one eyed."

"You saw some combat in Vietnam?"

That opened the floodgates. Nobody had asked me about Vietnam. It was a taboo subject even amongst most veterans. I began to tell him about Vietnam...about the lies the government was feeding the people back home...about the depravation and hopelessness. As I talked, I got cold inside...a chill that couldn't be stilled by backing up against a hot woodstove. He listened intently, never interrupting.

When I finished he looked at me with those soul piercing eyes and said, "Yes, these are dark days for white knights, but even so," he paused, looking me in the eye, "Vietnam could be the best thing that ever happened to you."

I was instantly angry. Did he know about my VA pension or the college? Did he think it was a fair trade, giving up your beliefs and your body parts for an education and a little cash?

"How do you figure?" I retorted boldly.

"You went to Vietnam full of ideas and beliefs that were not your own." He paused, drummed his fingers on the table then continued, "The government, your teachers, your parents and others you respected...they all told you what to believe, and you took their word for gospel. You thought you'd go off to war and be a big hero. Now you found that they either lied or they didn't know the truth themselves. Its left you disillusioned...you're empty. Your time in Vietnam has given you the opportunity for a fresh start."

"I don't understand what you're sayin'. So you think it's good to be empty?"

"I'm saying...it's time for you to take responsibility for your own life."

He sat back waiting for me to digest his statement, then he continued, "Sufis in ancient Persia believed that no man can gain understanding except through direct experience. There were no preachers or gurus...each man had to seek out his own truth. This can be your formula for building a new life. Don't believe anything except through your own experience.

"You've been fortunate enough to see that the government, corporations, and most people have a personal agenda and are constantly seeking followers by telling others that their way is the only way. They create the barriers that cause the wars.

"Your time in Vietnam has shown you that each man perceives reality based on his own unique set of beliefs and values, and that those values are based on personal experience. Don't misunderstand...there are some universal truths, but as of now, you have no experience of them.

"You have experienced the duality of man...you have released the primal instinct within yourself...your inner beast. Once the beast is free there will always be a struggle for control between the man who seeks beauty and understanding and the beast for whom survival is its only concern. Once released, this beast is near impossible to re-cage. It will always lurk at the edge of darkness, like a stalking tiger just beneath the edge of consciousness, waiting to lurch out and seize control. Many are doomed to a life of darkness...unable or unwilling to tame the beast. The beast slowly consumes the man until he loses all sense of wonder...craving only to fill his primal needs. In you, I see a man who seeks to control the beast, a man who seeks the truth and beauty he has lost."

I didn't know a Sufi from a soufflé, but the old man had my attention. Maybe I wasn't ready to accept that Vietnam could possibly be the best thing that had ever happened in my life, but up to then, the time I had spent there had no value. I thought, if I could derive something from the experience, maybe my life wouldn't seem so wasted.

"How do I experience these truths?" I asked.

"By paying attention," he said.

He paused...his eyes seemed to look inside me. "But frankly, between your drinking, drugs, and your constant self-pity, you have very little time left for paying attention."

He was starting to piss me off again. Where did this old man get off tellin' me how to act? "I do pretty well for myself," I said.

I chugged my beer, and stood up to go to the bathroom, tripping over my backpack on the way.

The old man snickered.

"Awareness is the key to understanding," he said.

I walked hurriedly to the bathroom, hoping the old man wouldn't see my reddening face. When I returned he was gone.

I walked up to the bar.

"Where did the old man go?" I asked.

The painted lady looked up from her nails. Shaking her head, she questioned, "What old man?"

I left the bar wondering about what the old man had said. *Could it be possible that I had missed the lessons of my experience?*

The Anchor Bar was near the outskirts of town. Behind the bar lay the railroad right of way...behind that, an open pasture of cactus and mesquite. I crossed the tracks and rolled out my blanket between two thickets of mesquite. I lay there looking at the stars, thinking about what the old man had said.

He was right, I hadn't been sober an entire day since returning from Nam, and now I was starting to smoke pot almost every day. I couldn't remember the last time my head was really clear. Maybe I should lay off the drinking and drugs for awhile. I fell asleep pondering his message.

The rockets came without warning. I run from my hooch, diving head first into a bunker. I huddle against the sand-bagged wall, trying desperately to melt into the earthen floor. The roar of rockets leaving their launchers sends tremors through my body. The three seconds of silence, while I wonder where the projectile will slam into the earth, is even worse. They're coming by the hundreds, exploding all around the bunker. The ground quakes...I burrow deeper, but the earth gives no comfort. They're zeroing in on my position. This time there will be no escape.

I woke up just as the train roared past. I was shaking almost as hard as the ground. I vowed never to sleep near a train track again. My stomach was in knots. I hadn't eaten a good meal since Junction City. It was becoming a bad habit. Lately, most of my caloric intake had consisted of beer...and the crackers and jerky I bought in San Antonio.

I counted my money....eighty six dollars and some change. I could afford a restaurant meal. I hid my pack in the mesquite and walked back past the Anchor, it was closed, towards downtown Kingsville. I remembered a great little family restaurant nearby and hoped it was still in business.

There was a big breakfast crowd at the restaurant, and the food was even better than I remembered. I devoured a stack of pancakes, several sausage links and a side of hash browns, topping it off with orange juice and two tall glasses of milk.

I paid my ticket and walked outside. It was a beautiful day. The winter seldom made it that far south, and already spring was in bloom. I decided to stay in Kingsville for a few days before heading up to Corpus. Maybe I would talk to the old man again.

I retrieved my pack from behind the Anchor and walked back towards town. Two blocks north of the restaurant, a two story clapboard house had a sign in the window. "Room for Rent."

I knocked on the door. A short, stoutly-built Mexican woman answered. She didn't look happy to see me.

"Yes?" she said.

"How much is the room?"

"Are you a student? I don't allow no parties here."

"No, I'm just passin' through."

"You'll have to pay in advance and leave a damage deposit."

"How much?" I asked again.

"Twenty dollars a week and a one week's deposit."

"Do I get the deposit back when I leave?"

"If nothing's damaged."

I dug out forty dollars and handed it over.

"Show me to my room," I said.

The house was clean but sparsely decorated. The rooms, four of them, were all upstairs. A single upstairs bathroom was shared by all tenants. The owner lived downstairs. My room was small...there was no closet, just an ancient looking dresser with four drawers and a small armoire for hanging clothes.

The only other furnishings were a night table, lamp, and an iron-posted bed. I closed the door, pulled the shade, and crashed for 18 hours.

"You okay in there!?" The landlady was beating on my door.

"Yeah, I'm okay...what's up?"

"What are you doing in there? You haven't come out once."

"I'm sleepin'!" I said.

"You don't have no drugs in there do you? We don't allow no drugs."

"No, I don't have any drugs." She was beginning to get on my nerves. "What time is it anyway?" I asked.

"It's four o'clock."

I sat up.

"Okay, thanks for wakin' me up."

"We don't allow no drugs," she repeated, as she walked down the hall.

I wondered if my camouflaged, drug running chauffeur had those kinds of problems. I pulled out some clean socks and underwear and headed for the bathroom. There was no shower but the big claw footed tub looked inviting. I filled it with hot water and slid in up to my chin, trying to remember the last time I had bathed.

"You be sure and clean out that tub! I don't want no tub full of hair!" She was standing outside the bathroom door.

I felt violated.

"I'm takin' a bath in here!" I yelled.

"Well, you be sure and clean up after yourself. I'm not your mother, you know. And wash your towel. Everybody has to wash their own towels."

"Yeah, yeah, I'll handle it," I yelled . "Pleeease let me finish my bath in peace!" I was exasperated. This was going to be an interesting week.

I finished my bath and went back to my room. There was a handwritten note taped to the door. Across the top in big letters it read, "Rules for Tenants" and below in smaller print was a list of numbered rules. I read down the list, "No drinking; No drugs; No visitors after 7 PM; No music after 8 PM; Front door locked at 10 PM; Clean your own messes; Wash your own towels; No cooking in the rooms."

I hadn't lived with that many rules since I left home after the eighth grade. I wadded up the note and threw it on the bed, then headed down the stairs. My new warden was crocheting in a rocker near the front door.

As I walked out the door, she yelled after me, "We lock the door promptly at ten, no exceptions."

I didn't bother answering.

I walked past the restaurant. The food smelled wonderful, but my money was running low. Instead, I found an A&P grocery around the corner. Taking a cart from the front of the store, I wheeled it to the fruit and vegetable stand. I tossed a bunch of bananas into the cart, eating several while I shopped. I put the peelings behind a row of potted meat in the canned goods section and stuffed a can of tuna down my jeans. Wheeling over to the bakery section, I traded the remaining bananas for a loaf of bread, and stuck a Twinkie into the inside pocket of my jean jacket. I left the cart and the bread at the cooler, trading them for a coke. I took the coke to the checkout, and dropped a quarter on the counter.

"Will that be all?" a pimple faced girl asked as she tugged at her pigtail.

"Yeah...and keep the change," I said.

I ate my meal on a park bench near city hall. I decided not to return to my room until ten. I hoped the landlady from hell would be asleep by then.

I had several hours to kill so I headed towards the Anchor...thinking maybe the old man would be back. The bar looked the same. The rusty heap was in the same space, the painted lady was still filing her nails. She didn't look up. At the table, where I left him, the old man sat reading a paper.

"Whatcha up to?" I asked.

"Waiting for you."

I sat down, and looked into his piercing eyes.

"What's your name anyway?" I asked.

"Charlie."

"I'm glad to meet you Charlie."

"Pleased to make your acquaintance Dennis."

That threw me. I couldn't remember telling him my name. But then, there were a lot of things I couldn't remember lately. Anyway, it didn't matter...I had some questions I wanted answered. "Charlie, you said that awareness is the key to understandin'...what do you mean by awareness?"

"Do you remember what it was like to be in combat?" he asked.

"Yes."

"What were you thinking about?"

"Thinkin' about? I really didn't have time to think about anything, I was just doin' whatever it took to survive," I said.

"Your mind was completely on the task at hand."

"I guess you could say that, but what does that have to do with awareness?" I asked.

"That is awareness, Dennis, being totally on the task at hand. Most people, most of the time, exist in a dream state. They drive to work, go to the office, and handle their daily tasks without being aware of a single moment of their day. Their lives have become so routine that they don't have to think...so they don't."

He paused, while I took a drink, and continued when he saw he had my full attention. "Awareness is living meditation," he said.

"I've heard of meditation. The Buddhist monks in Vietnam were into meditation but I guess I really don't know what it is," I said.

Have you ever listened to a bird on a busy street?" he asked.

"I guess so, I don't really remember."

"To hear the bird, you must cut out the sound of the traffic. Meditation is the same. It's freeing the mind from its constant chatter by focusing on a single thought...whether that thought be washing a dish or becoming one with God."

"I may not know much about meditation but I sure as hell know there's a lot of difference between washin' dishes and becomin' one with God," I said.

"Not to the enlightened man," he said.

He was beginning to get way over my head. I no longer believed in God anyway.

"There isn't a God," I said. "How could a God let somethin' like Vietnam happen? I've seen children buried alive. I've seen good men vaporized by a 500 pound bomb. I've seen..."

At that instant, Charlie reached across the table and poured my beer in my lap.

"Jesus, what are you doin' Charlie?"

"Changing your state."

"What the hell does that mean?"

"A few seconds ago, you were angry, now you're shocked. How important could your anger be if a little spoiled water on your pants made you forget the reason for your anger?"

"But the beer's on my pants right now," I protested.

"Exactly," he said, "Right here and now...that's awareness."

I took a bar napkin and began wiping the beer from my pants.

"How did you get here Dennis?" Charlie asked.

"I walked."

Charlie laughed. "No, I mean how did you get here?" he said, drawing a circle in the air with his finger.

"What do you mean?"

"How did you get to this table, at this time, in this state of mind?" he said.

I was confused...not knowing where to begin.

"Dennis, it's no coincidence that you happen to be here today. Everything in your life has a purpose, but if you're not paying attention you'll miss its meaning. You're at a critical juncture in your life...you can wake up and live or continue to grovel in a dream state."

I sensed a subtle difference between awareness and paying attention. I wanted to ask Charlie but I glanced at the bar clock, it was already nine fifty. I would have to hurry to beat curfew. Charlie was already up and headed towards the door. My lesson was over for the day.

I followed Charlie out of the bar to say goodnight, but he was already gone. I sprinted the several blocks back to my room... arriving just as my new warden was about to lock me out. She opened the door and stood back.

"You've been drinkin'!" she said, wrinkling her nose. She looked repulsive in her quilted pink bathrobe and wrinkled nose.

"Yes, I have," I said, "but I'm through for the night."

"We don't allow no drinkin' on the premises!" she said.

I pushed through the door and climbed the stairs to my room. There...taped to the door, was the crinkled list of rules I had thrown on my bed before leaving the house. She had been in my room and she was brazen enough to flaunt it. Ripping the note from the door, I looked down over the railing. "Lady, I'll abide by your rules but as long as my rent's paid up, you better never come into my room again!" I yelled.

"This is my house,! I'll go where I please!" she protested.

"Lady... I just got back from Nam. I've plucked the eyeballs out of livin' men and tied grenades between the legs of pleadin' women," I lied. "Don't come into my room again!"

She turned and stormed towards the back of the house. I went into my room and laughed myself to sleep.

Chapter Twelve
Friendly Fire

"If you're so interested in political objectives, let the politicians fight the war. I'm not a fuckin' politician...I'm a Marine."

Z to an Inspector General after Nixon halted the bombing. November 1968.

I never saw the landlady after our argument. I heard her voice from downstairs on occasion, but she would vanish whenever I left the room. It was an arrangement much to my liking. I began a pleasant routine of sleeping late, taking a long bath, sitting in my room reading for an hour or so, then heading down to the Anchor to see Charlie. I was intrigued by his thinking and his apparent interest in my welfare.

One afternoon as I started into the Anchor, I heard laughter from up the street. Sitting on the hood of their car in the parking lot of the Brass Monkey, a group of college students were sharing a joint. Was Cindy with them? I hesitated ...wanting more than anything at that moment to walk away from the Anchor and join the crowd at the Monkey.

Charlie chose that instant to peek out the door.

"It's hard to change a lifetime of poor decisions, but it's worth it," he said.

"Charlie, those kids are the same age as me, but I'm as removed from their world as if we came from different planets."

"In every setback there's the seed for change, and a map to give direction."

"What do you mean?"

"Dennis, have you ever had a really bad hangover?"

"Oh yeah...I've had some dillies."

"And what did you promise to never do again?"

"I used to pray to God, "If you'll make the pain go away, I'll never drink again."

"The seed for change was the pain and the map was the knowing that if you quit drinking the pain would not return."

"Yeah, but as soon as the pain stops, so does the resolve."

"Unfortunately, man is a slow learner, but each time you drink too much the pain returns and if you continue to ignore the signs, the drink could kill you."

Charlie started towards the back of the Anchor.

"Let's take a walk today," he said.

We crossed the tracks into the field where I spent my first night, then turned down a small arroyo lined with prickly pear cactus. As we followed the arroyo out of town, it deepened and pools of water appeared along its course. The pools eventually coalesced into a small stream. A narrow footpath traced the course of the stream, winding through a thicket of wiry willows that almost magically transformed into a forest of giant cottonwood trees.

"Where're we goin'?" I asked, after an hour of walking in silence.

"We're here," he answered without stopping. "We've always been here...there is no place other than here."

"What are you talkin' about?" I persisted, stopping to await his answer. Charlie turned to face me, shaking his head in disbelief.

"People are so concerned with destination that they miss the essence of life."

"What do you mean?"

"Dennis...we've been walking through some of the prettiest country in south Texas and you've spent the whole time wondering where you were going. Life is not a destination...it's a journey. If you don't learn to enjoy the journey, you've missed the point of living."

"How do you learn to enjoy the journey if it takes you to shitty places?"

"By paying attention to the lessons. The best way to learn to pay attention is to practice, and this is as good a place as any for you to begin your practice, Dennis."

Charlie pointed towards a sandy area overlooking the stream and said, "Sit down and pay attention."

As he started back up the path, he yelled without looking back, "And don't leave until you've been able to count twenty breaths without your mind interrupting."

I sat down, then turned to ask Charlie why, but he was already gone.

I took a deep breath, held it for a second, then exhaled slowly...counting silently, "One". I took a second deep breath and began to wonder what my mom was cooking for supper.

Okay, I can do this, I thought, taking a deep breath and expelling it as I counted "one" again. I got all the way to four the second time before my attention strayed. By the end of what I figured must have been at least an hour, I had gotten to seven once and six twice. This was going to be harder than I thought.

"Hell, all I have to do is count twenty breaths and I can go back to my room!" I said aloud.

What time was it anyway? I wondered. Maybe it's already past ten.

I took another deep breath and expelled counting, "One." I took a second and expelled, "Two." An owl hooted from the branch of a silvery cottonwood; a shiver sped through my body and my mind went to work.

Hell, it's only an owl! I thought...*I've spent nights lyin' on the jungle floor with poisonous snakes. God I hate snakes. What kind of snakes are there in south Texas anyway? Rattlers...diamondback rattlers...those big mean suckers. Don't they feed at night?* SHUT UP MIND!

Another deep breath, expel, "One," deep breath, expel, "Two," deep breath, expel, "Three," *Why am I doin' this? Who is this Charlie that left me in the middle of nowhere in the middle of the night? How did my mind get away from me again?*

Deep breath, expel, "One." Deep breath, expel, "Two."

Finally, I gave up...I decided to rest against a tree, just enjoying the sounds of the night. It was too late to go back to face the landlady anyway.

The night smelled delicious...thick with musty wood and rotted vegetation. I wasn't breathing. I was consuming the air. The frog's deep groans filled my ears with pleasure...reminding me of the bedtime stories my grandmother used to tell. Then I was gone again.

The sky is thick with rain...cold, pelting rain that runs in rivulets down my back. I'm crouched at the edge of a clearing...my knees folded to my chest. My insides feel like they've been ripped from my throat, tied in knots then stuffed wrong side first back up my ass. In front of me, in the clearing, two still figures lay shrouded under ponchos.

A pasty fist protrudes from beneath the poncho nearest me, still clenched in a death grip. How many times have I shaken that hand? The day we arrived in-country and he introduced himself with that big shit-eatin' grin...the day at Hill 55 when he told me about Susan...last month when he told me about his baby. Brown wasn't supposed to die. He was a survivor like me.

Salt laden tears wash over my lips, but no one sees that I'm crying. The tears are hidden by the rain. Across the field, sitting off by himself, Bruce is the only one that hurts more than me. We've all been together since we joined the company, but Bruce and Brown bonded like two layers of a birthday cake.

How could Bruce have known that Brown and Matt would come in early off their LP? That they would compromise their position and be forced to move through the driving rain and the darkness...eaten by the jungle until they set off a trip flare. Bruce saw the figures caught like deer in bright headlights. His own vision was blurred by the rain and lack of sleep. He fired just three rounds, not knowing they were Marines until Brown yelled out for a Corpsman.

Matt was gone instantly...a single round just above the right eye. Brown, hit once in the stomach and once in the chest, lived long enough to die in Bruce's arms. His final pleading words, spoken as we all stood watching.

"What happened?"

Bruce couldn't answer. He just pulled Brown closer and rocked him in silence until it was over. A helicopter slides over the tree line to hover above the field, blowing the ponchos off the bodies.

Men rush forward, throwing the two bodies in a pile on the deck of the still hovering chopper. The chopper disappears back over the jungle. I listen until the drone of the chopper is swallowed by the driving rain. Jesus, I hate this fuckin' war!

I woke up in the rain, angry. When had it started? Had it ever really ended? The rain was like the war...I couldn't shake it...I couldn't find my way out. I shook my fist at the sky.

"Fuck you God! Fuck you and your Goddamned rain! Fuck you and your Goddamned little war!" Then I began to cry.

I sat there through the night, watching the creek rise, hoping it would take me with it. Just rise up and wash me out to sea. Finally, I stood up, stiff and cold, and sloshed my way back to my room. I fell on the bed, and lay there listening to the rain through the day and into the night.

What had happened to me, I wondered? I had been so anxious to come home and now that I was home, I was more alone than I had ever been in my life. There was a darkness that shrouded me from the rest of the world.

I just couldn't find a reason to get out of bed. The more I thought about my life, the more lonely I became...a loneliness that went beyond mental anguish. I was in extreme physical pain. As it grew darker outside, the inner darkness began to overwhelm me. I finally dragged myself out of bed in self defense and went down to talk to Charlie. I hoped he had an answer.

Charlie was reading his paper at the same table. I pulled out a chair and plopped down. "What's wrong Dennis...couldn't you make it to twenty?"

I didn't answer. Charlie had said I spent too much time feeling sorry for myself and now I was here to dump my problems on him. But I had to share my pain with someone.

"Charlie, I'm so lonely it hurts. I mean real physical pain. Even when I'm in a crowd, I feel alone."

"What're you doing about it?"

"I talked to a shrink once, before I left the Marines, but he wasn't much help."

"What did he say?"

"He said it was all in my head. That I should go home and forget the war and everything would be just fine. Everyone else seems to agree...they all say I should get a job and put the war behind me like veterans of other wars."

I looked up at Charlie, he was smiling. "That's not true," he said.

"What's not true?"

"That veterans of other wars have been able to quietly put their war experience behind them. World War I veterans were so angry they marched on Washington. The government used the cavalry to drive them out of the city. Disillusioned World War II veterans formed motorcycle gangs. It's been the same down through the ages, but the problems of veterans have been mostly ignored. Governments are always in need of new cannon fodder. They don't want young men to hear stories about disillusioned vets."

Charlie paused, waiting as I ordered a beer, then started again, "Dennis, I had a friend named Tom. He was walking across a beach one day when his foot began to throb. His doctors told him it was all in his head, so he went to see a shrink.

"The shrink asked Tom a lot of questions about his childhood and diagnosed him as having Repressed Pediophobic Syndrome. He said it was probably related to his mother's overbearing behavior. The shrink prescribed drugs that made Tom forget the pain...but he also forgot his kid's names. Tom decided the cure was worse than the pain and he quit taking the drugs.

"When the pain returned, Tom's preacher said it was probably a spiritual problem. Tom went to see a faith healer. The faith healer slapped him hard between the eyes, declaring him cured. For a few minutes, Tom thought the cure had worked, but when his head stopped smarting and the foot began to throb, he realized it was only pain transferral.

"In desperation, Tom went to India and limped to the top of a mountain to visit a Guru. The Guru told Tom to try a certain Yoga posture. Tom was anxious for a cure, so he found a clearing in the woods and went to work. He sat cross-legged and began to pull his feet into his lap. As he pulled the throbbing foot into place, he noticed a sharp thorn embedded in swollen flesh. He pulled out the thorn, and his pain instantly disappeared."

"Well that's a real neat story Charlie, but what does it have to do with me?"

"Your pain is real Dennis. It has a real cause and it's creating negative effects in your life. You must experience the pain to find its cause and then you can begin the healing process. Some will try to tell you that your pain isn't real. Others will try to mask the symptom with drugs or religious hocus pocus. Don't pay attention to these people. The symptoms have a cause and the cause has a cure. Find the cause and the cure becomes obvious."

"I guess part of the problem is, I just don't care anymore," I said.

"That's one of the effects. You've lost your vision for the future."

"Yeah, I guess so. I used to think I knew what I wanted. Even in Vietnam, I knew what I wanted to do when I got home. I wanted a fast car with a great stereo and to marry Alexis. That seemed like enough. But now ... Hell, I just seem to exist in a dark void. Sometimes it feels like I'm trapped in an invisible box that separates me from the rest of the world."

"Our ancestors used Vision Quests to maintain direction in their lives," Charlie said.

"What's a vision quest?" I asked.

"It's different for different cultures. American Indians went off into the woods for days at a time to contemplate and fast while they waited for a vision of how they should live their lives. As they grew older and experienced more, the vision changed...but they always sought direction. Jesus went into the wilderness for forty days seeking strength and direction to complete his life's mission. Vision Quests are as old as mankind, but modern societies have suppressed the quest."

"Why?"

"Conformity...they would rather we all share a common vision than for each man to seek his own direction. It gives them greater control of the masses of people."

"So they can keep sendin' young men away to fight their wars," I said.

"And lying to them about the reasons," Charlie agreed.

"I know a place on Padre Island that would be perfect for a vision quest. What would I need to do?"

"Stop drinking so you have a clear mind, fast while you're there to purify your body, and go with an open heart."

"What do you mean by an open heart?" I asked.

"Dennis, sometimes we learn more through adversity and hardship. Remember when I told you that Vietnam could be the best thing that ever happened to you?"

"Yeah, I remember. It pissed me off."

"I know...that's because living a vision often includes experiences we'd rather not face...but they're offered to teach us important lessons. You must enter the quest with an open heart to understand. Anyone can seek a vision... but you need courage, faith and perseverance to live a vision. Remember...the tree that grows tallest collects the most light, but it also faces the greatest chance of being struck down by lightning."

I was trying to decode Charlie's latest parable when he got up and started towards the door. "Dennis...spend some time each day in meditation and your personal truth will be revealed." he said, as he walked out the door.

He left me with a full beer and a lot to think about. I pushed the beer away. I decided to stop drinking and work at seeking a new direction for my life.

For the next few days, I spent my mornings trying to meditate, but I couldn't keep my mind focused for more than a few seconds at a time.

One night, I went to the Anchor frustrated and ready for a beer.

"You don't look so good tonight Dennis."

"Charlie, this just isn't workin' for me! I've tried meditatin' for over an hour at a time, and nothin' happens."

He laughed, but I didn't think it was funny.

"What do you expect to happen?" he asked. "Haven't I told you? Truth is not a destination...it's a journey."

"Yeah, but what does that mean?"

"Sometimes pious men spend years in a cave searching for truth only to commit suicide in utter despair. Others have found truth in a flash of insight. If we become attached to the results, we'll certainly become disillusioned with the process," he said.

"You mean I should try but not care whether or not it works."

"Exactly."

"Okay, maybe it's the process I don't understand."

"Do you ever call home?" he asked.

"Sure I call home sometimes, but what does that have to do with findin' the truth?"

"Do you know how a telephone works?"

"No."

"So you call expecting an answer even though you don't have the slightest idea how a phone works?"

"Yeah, but..."

"That's faith Dennis...faith in technology. You should have the same kind of faith in the process. Continue to meditate and live with awareness, and with the expectation that your truth will be revealed...but don't become attached to results. In fact, be open to whatever you find."

"But what am I lookin' for?"

"You're seeking insight into the meaning of life, Dennis."

"You're way over my head Charlie. What is this meanin' of life?"

"Life is like the ocean," Charlie started. "Each drop of water contains the essence of ocean...but it's not the ocean. The ocean is the oneness that contains all the drops. When a drop is drawn into a cloud it temporarily forgets the ocean, but after it falls to the ground, it begins a long journey back to its source. Along the way, it collects sediments that recount its experiences along its journey as a rain drop, a trickling stream and a raging river. Eventually it dumps the sediments onto the ocean floor and returns to the oneness from which it came."

"I don't follow," I said. "What the hell are you talkin' about?"

"Dennis...I was wrong when I said you were empty."

The sudden change in our conversation annoyed me.

"You've replaced the rubbish given to you by others with your own anger and fear," he said.

"I'm not afraid of anything!" I protested.

"On the contrary Dennis, you're afraid of many things, and you're living in a confused state because of your fears."

I buried my head in my hands and sighed. "The only confusion in my life is you," I said.

Charlie laughed. "Dennis, you're afraid to let go of your perception of reality even though you know it's faulty. And you're afraid to change even though you know you'll die if you don't."

"What do you mean? I gave up a good job to come down here and try college. Isn't that a change?"

"This is where your confusion lies Dennis. You believe you can change yourself by changing your social status. You're running from yourself, changing friends, changing addresses, and changing jobs trying to create happiness from the outside in. In reality, you must affect an inner change to make a difference."

"How do I do that?" I asked.

"You can start with forgiveness." he said.

"Forgiveness?"

"Dennis...you have to forgive everyone for everything. Try to understand that the experiences they provided were part of the process of growth that makes your life meaningful. Without these experiences you would wilt and die. And Dennis...the people and things that bring you the greatest hardship are actually your best allies. You should thank them."

"Like my stepfather?"

"Forgive your stepfather, forgive the government, forgive yourself...you must not withhold forgiveness from anyone or anything."

"And this will help me find the meanin' of life?"

"It will help you find peace."

"It all sounds good in theory, but how do you forgive someone when they've hurt you?"

"Try to perceive the world through their eyes," he said.

"What do you mean?"

"Take your stepfather. Did you ever try to understand his motivation?"

"I guess not...I just got mad when he hit me."

"That's the normal reaction Dennis, but the wrong one. Maybe if you understood why he hit you...actually looked at it through his eyes, you'd be able to forgive him."

"Maybe I could start with someone else."

"Maybe...but just get started. Forgiving is like learning to kiss a girl, it gets easier every time, and after a while, you really start to enjoy it."

Charlie rolled up his newspaper and stood up, sticking the paper under his arm.

"And Dennis...don't forget to meditate every day, and live with awareness," he said, turning to walk out the door.

I decided to try a little forgiveness. I would start with my landlady. Not a particularly tough target, but I figured, I had to walk before I could run. On the way home, I tried to imagine what it would be like to be her and to share my home with strangers...not because I wanted to, but because I had to make payments. How would it feel to have students move in and throw parties... to have people break things and not pay the rent...to have big hairy guys make vague threats...to be a short, heavy woman, past my prime, with no life beyond my own front door? I decided to buy her a bouquet of flowers first thing in the morning.

I climbed into bed, feeling better than I had in months.

I'm in a car with my stepfather. We're driving fast, down a dry desert creek bed. There are no other cars in sight, no roads...no nothin'. It begins to rain. Huge drops tumble through the air splashing against the windshield... throwing up puffs of dust when they hit the desert floor. I look over at Ray. He looks scared.

"I think I might have taken the wrong road," he says, but he doesn't ask for help.

For the first time, I realized just how alone he is. Always taking the back roads to avoid being discovered for what he is... uneducated, an alcoholic, the product of years of abuse and neglect himself. He's lost and afraid and worst of all, because of the fences he's built, he has no one with whom to share his fears. I admire his tenacity, his will to survive... and I feel compassion for his state of constant fear and loneliness. Most of all, I wish to God he'd ask for help.

"Get up in there, your rent is up!"

Her voice sent a chill through my body, then I remembered forgiveness. "I'll pay you in just a minute."

"Your rent is up, you'll have to go!" she insisted.

"Ma'am, I'm sorry we got off on the wrong foot. Please let's try again."

"If you're not out of here in ten minutes, I'm callin' the police!"

I wanted to explode, but I vowed to forgive her.

"Okay, I'm getting' out."

I stuffed my gear in the pack and started out the door. I saw an envelope on the floor. My name was printed on the envelope. Inside, I found my twenty dollar deposit. I hoped the landlady would be waiting downstairs so I could make one more attempt at an apology...but the parlor was empty.

I yelled towards the back of the house, "I'm sorry for the trouble I caused!" and I left.

I broke the twenty at the restaurant, filling up on pancakes and sausage. Then I spent the day in the park, watching the flow of people in and out of city hall.

I arrived at the Anchor at the regular time. The painted lady was talking to a balding businessman at the bar. It was the first time I had ever seen her look up from her nails for more than a few seconds at a time. Charlie was not at the table.

I ordered a coke, and sat down to wait. I was hoping Charlie would put me up until I could find another place.

The bartender and her businessman were whispering private, indecent proposals in one another's ears when I walked up, interrupting, "Where's Charlie tonight?"

"Charlie who?" she frowned at the interruption.

"You know...the old man." I said.

"What old man?" she asked.

"Just give me a Bud please!" I said.

I closed down the Anchor at two. The plotting couple spent the last half hour staring a hole through my back, loathing me for keeping them from the entanglement they had planned. When I left the bar, I started back towards the tracks, but, remembering the train, I walked out to the 77 bypass. I decided to get an early start for Corpus come morning.

Chapter Thirteen
Fly Boys

"Shoot over their heads. If they run, they're VC."
Sgt. James, explaining the intricacies of determining the good guys from the bad guys, before Operation Junction City, July 1968.

I woke up wet and cold. It was drizzling with heavy rain in the offing. I needed a ride before the heavens opened up. Walking along the highway, I turned to face passing cars, but the flow was sparse.

I remembered, it was the beginning of a long holiday weekend, most people would be home with their families. I began to think of Alexis...remembering the plans I had made in Vietnam for a home of my own.

Whenever darkness threatened to envelop my soul, I would build a cozy space in my mind. It was our home, just big enough for the two of us, with a big overstuffed chair where we snuggled in front of the fireplace. My fantasies never included sex...there was plenty of that in Vietnam...just the warmth of her affection. Alexis never answered my letters. We had a big fight before I left for Vietnam, and she was engaged to a boy back home. But, she unknowingly helped me survive the darkest times.

My first day back home after Vietnam, I was sitting in the living room of my grandmother's house when someone knocked on the door. My grandmother answered, turning to me with a big smile. "Someone's here to see you," she said.

I wasn't in the mood to see anyone, but I begrudgingly went to the door. Alexis stood waiting on the porch. She smiled nervously, her big brown eyes glistening with the hint of a tear. She wore a cotton print dress. Her sandy-brown hair was swept back in a ponytail. She had the fresh, clean look of a cover girl with just a hint of rose colored lipstick to set off the natural blush of her cheeks. This was the girl I had dreamed of for the past eighteen months. Now she was standing on my porch...and I felt like there was a wall between us.

I hugged her tentatively and we drove out to the river. So many memories were hidden there, but they didn't seem real in the wake of Vietnam. I didn't know what to say, so I kissed her. It was an empty gesture. I was too far gone...there were no dreams left. I took her back to her car with the promise I would swing by later that night. I got drunk instead.

Her wedding announcement was in the next week's paper. I thought about going to the wedding and yelling out "that's my girl!" But, I had caused her enough pain. She deserved more than I could give. I did park across the street to watch as she left the church with her new husband. She was a beautiful bride...more beautiful than even I had imagined.

Rainy days made me morose and thinking about what might have been only made it worse. I forced Alexis out of my mind for the thousandth time.

A yellow Corolla pulled off to the side of the road. I ran up to the car. Inside, a young woman with short brown hair and blue eyes smiled warmly. I climbed in, throwing my pack in the back seat.

"Thanks, it's gettin' awful wet out there. How far you goin'?" I asked.

"I'm going to Corpus to visit my parents for a few days," she offered.

"You a student here in Kingsville?"

"No, I'm a teacher. I teach first grade in Brownsville."

She was a pleasant woman, not beautiful, but certainly attractive. She needed to talk...and she did...all the way to Corpus. She said it was her first time to live away from home and that it had been very lonely for her in Brownsville. She loved teaching, she said, but she had a hard time making new friends. When she began to tell me about her class of seven year olds, her voice rang with excitement...but the rain had triggered a switch in my mind.

I'm lost in a monsoonal downpour, an annoying trickle dripping from the end of my nose. Blood is gushing from Jake's stump, swirling into the tainted paddy water. Cold, white toes protrude from his shredded boot laying several feet away in the mud, "Mama, mama, it hurts so bad!" he cries, but she can't help. There's not enough morphine to ease the pain and helicopters won't fly in the deluge. Jake will die whimpering in the paddy, and I'll have one less friend.

Forty miles evaporated into a misty nightmare, and we pulled into the parking lot of the Pussy Cat Club at the intersection of Aires and Padre Island Drive. I looked at the driver...she was beaming.

"I really enjoyed talking with you," she said. "Let me give you my phone number in case you have some extra time this week."

She was really a lovely woman. I remembered what Charlie had said about people becoming so preoccupied that they sleepwalk through their lives. Certainly, I had missed an opportunity. I took the phone number, thanked her for the ride and stepped out into the rain. Watching her pull back into traffic, I crumpled the slip of paper, dropping it into a puddle.

An amateurish sign painted on the blackened, picture window of the Pussy Cat Club promised "Live Entertainment Daily". I decided to keep that in mind. The club's parking lot was separated from a shopping center by a battered, wooden fence. The center was built around a Post Office. Next to the Post Office, a Mexican restaurant featured a $1.49 all you can eat special. I couldn't afford to pass it up.

Taken individually, the food wasn't anything special, but piled all together, it was scrumptious. I inhaled the first round, then ran up a little Mexican flag at my table. When the waitress appeared, I ordered two more of everything. I stuffed several sopapillas in my jacket pocket for later.

After finishing the meal, I walked back to the alley behind the shopping center. The rain was coming down in torrents. I desperately needed some shelter. An oversized metal dumpster, overflowing with cardboard boxes, appeared to be my best choice. I pulled half of the boxes out of the dumpster and climbed in, closing the double doors to keep out the rain.

Boxes at the bottom of the dumpster were relatively dry, and they provided a nice cushion. The only drawback was the shiny black roaches that had scurried deeper into the dumpster with each box I removed.

Rain pelting the metal doors sounded like a jet engine revving for takeoff. I decided to wait out the storm while I dried, hit the Pussy Cat Club until closing, then sleep in the dumpster. That was my plan, but the next thing I knew, it was morning.

Waking up in the darkened box, I freaked. *Had they dumped me into the silver casket?* I screamed and pushed my arms up to throw open the heavy doors. They flew back, banging loudly against the walls of my metal coffin.

The day had dawned clear and bright. I stretched and sat up, looking out into the alley. A stock boy, wearing a dirty white apron, stood staring at the dumpster...his eyes as wide as saucers.

"Good mornin'," I said, in a booming voice, breaking into laughter. He turned and fled towards the shopping center.

I smelled like wet cardboard, but I was dry. I climbed out of the dumpster and walked to the post office. After renting a box, I mailed a pre-addressed authorization form back to the VA. Dan had given me the form so my checks could be sent to Corpus.

I walked back out to the road and stuck out my thumb. Hitchhiking down Aires Boulevard towards Del Mar College, I passed crumbling subsidized apartments and peeling clapboard houses. In contrast, the red brick buildings on campus stood in neat rows...like Marines waiting for inspection, their polished glass gleaming in the sunlight. The grass was still wet but already men and their machines were manicuring the lawns.

I approached two students engaged in a heated debate about the symbolism of Melville's whale. Both students were as impeccable as the campus, dressed in pressed slacks and identical white, short-sleeved shirts...their well shorn hair neatly groomed. I wondered if they were wearing standard issue student uniforms.

"Excuse me, could you tell me how to find the administration buildin'?" I asked, after listening to a few seconds of their gibberish.

They looked insulted. "First building on the right", one of the students finally offered, jerking his thumb in the direction of a wide cement walkway.

The inside of the building was as orderly as one would expect from seeing the campus. Several students were busy cleaning windows in the double entryway, where I found a building directory.

"Admissions Room 101," was the first listing. I walked down the freshly waxed corridor to sign up for college.

A petite lady in granny glasses sat behind the receptionist desk, her lips in a permanent purse like she had sucked a lemon dry. Her black skirt fell well below her knees and her dazzling white blouse was buttoned to the collar. She was typing so fast, I figured she must be faking it just to impress me. Finishing the letter, she pulled it from the typewriter, and without missing a beat, asked, "May I help you?"

"I'm here to see Mr. Bitterman."

"Is Mr. Bitterman expecting you?" Her voice had a machine quality...formal and precise.

"The VA office in San Antonio called last week to make an appointment."

"And you are?"

"Jackson...Dennis Jackson."

"If you'll be seated, I'll let him know you're here."

She disappeared down the hall... reappearing several minutes later.

"If you will follow me, Mr. Bitterman will see you now," she said, looking down over the top of her glasses.

She floated down the hall like an apparition...not a hint of movement from her neck to her knees.

Bitterman's office walls were covered with military memorabilia...pictures of him standing next to a Phantom jet on the deck of a carrier, commendations for flying combat missions over South Vietnam and a diploma from the Naval Academy. Bitterman sat hunched over his desk, thumbing through a stack of papers.

"Sit down" he said, without looking up.

I sat in a chair against the wall and waited. Bitterman spent several minutes poring over the papers, letting out an annoying grunt every few seconds.

"I see you're not a high school graduate," he said, looking up for the first time. "What makes you think you can succeed in college?"

He looked like a newspaper man who had just asked the president about an affair with the chamber maid.

"I survived Vietnam and the man at the VA said the government owes me an education for losin' my eye," I said.

"The government doesn't owe you anything, young man." He was beginning to sound like an officer. "I flew over 50 missions in Vietnam. We all had a duty to serve our country...to give our lives if necessary. Already, too many veterans like you are taking advantage of the government...signing up for a few courses just to draw easy money, rather than getting back to the business of building a stronger America."

He pushed back in his chair, apparently finished with his speech.

"Where were you stationed in Nam?" I asked.

"I was stationed aboard the USS Champion," he said, pulling back his shoulders.

"So you were never really in Nam then."

"I told you, I flew over 50 bombing missions over Vietnam."

"How many people did you kill?"

He raised his eyebrows. "I have no way of knowing that," he said.

"Did you ever see the results of one of your bombing missions? Did you ever see the bodies of burnt children? Or smell burnt flesh?"

"What's your point?" he asked, suddenly fidgeting with his tie.

I leaned over Bitterman's desk, looking directly into his steely blue eyes. "I watched you flyboys streak over a village to drop your load, then streak back home for a cold beer and some hot pussy while we cleaned up your mess. Your hands never got dirty. The government screwed every one of us poor boy grunts they sent to Nam. We were there just to keep a corrupt government in power so big corporations back here in America could get richer. Now I'm damn sure going to take advantage of every opportunity I'm entitled to," I said.

I felt a rush of adrenaline. Bitterman's face was red. He looked back down at the papers.

Without looking up, he said, "You will have to make at least an 18 on your ACT...even then you'll only be granted provisional admission for the first year."

"No sweat," I said. The adrenaline was talking now.

"And," he looked up with a smirk on his face, "Del Mar has a strict dress code. No hair below the shoulders, no facial hair, no blue jeans or cutoffs, and all shirts must have a collar."

Bitterman had changed my state of mind as effectively as Charlie had with the beer down my pants. Was this a college or a preppy military school, I wondered? Did Dan, the VA man, know about the dress code when he recommended Del Mar?

"No sweat," I answered, trying to hide my dismay.

Bitterman scheduled me for the ACT in August, two weeks before the beginning of the fall semester. I signed paper work authorizing the VA to pay my tuition and books, and stood up to leave Bitterman's office.

"You'll have to be a serious student and work hard or you won't last the semester," he warned.

"No sweat," I answered for the third time, but the confidence was gone from my voice.

The sun was at its zenith when I got back on Aires Road. I started towards Padre Island Drive, holding out my thumb as I walked. Traffic was heavy, but no one stopped. The humidity was oppressive. Sweat gushed from every pore of my body. I was as soaked in the afternoon sun as I had been in the previous day's downpour.

I stepped into a bar across the street from a row of barracks-style, government subsidized apartments to wrap my sweaty palm around a cold brew. The contrast between the darkened bar and the bright sunshine sent my pupil into shock. The door slammed shut, leaving me feeling vulnerable in the few seconds of total blackness. It was like trying to see through my thumb.

When my vision returned, my vulnerability was replaced by fear. Activity in the bar was frozen in time to the instant I had stepped through the door. Pool players were leaning motionless across the table. Men at the bar were caught in mid-swig...mugs perched at their lips. All eyes were glued on me, the only white man in the bar.

I wanted to make a quick exit, but I suddenly remembered the dogs on the way to Brady's house.

Brady had been my best high school buddy back in Oklahoma. He lived on the south side of the tracks in the older part of town. To get to Brady's I had to pass the Rodriguez's house and their pack of blood-thirsty hounds. The dogs could smell fear. If I ran, they'd give chase, biting my ankles and calves all the way to Brady's house. But if I stayed cool, swaggering past like I wasn't afraid of the devil himself, they'd bark, then go back to chewing their bones (sometimes I wondered whose bones they were chewing). Even then, I made sure I had a big stick and a pocketful of rocks. Here, I had nothing but false bravado to carry me through.

I looked for the biggest man at the bar and slid onto the stool next to his. He was shaped like a coke bottle with arms as big around as telephone poles.

If this was a biker's bar, his name would be Tiny, I thought, feeling kind of giddy.

I ordered a beer and turned to face the pool table. The players looked up, then strutted over to stand on either side of me.

"Whatcha want whitey?" the man to my right asked while slapping the thick end of his pool stick into his palm.

He was tubby...with a thick neck and a roll of fat protruding from the bottom of his sweat-stained tee shirt. I figured one good whack in the gut would take him to his knees. But his friend was thinner, with well defined muscles and a pinkish-colored facial scar that ran the length of his left cheek. He looked like a man who had seen his share of street fights.

"Can't you see this is a brother's bar?" the chubby man asked.

I was trying to think of a cool comeback, when the coke-bottle shaped man wheeled around on his stool. "Let the man be so's he can enjoy his beer," he said.

"What's he to you, jive ass?" the thinner man interjected.

Tiny stood up, towering above the two antagonists.

"He's just a man tryin' to enjoy himself a cold brew," he said.

The two younger men backed away towards the pool table, and went back to their game without a word. I turned towards Tiny.

"Thanks man," I said.

"You should drink up and move on...them boys is plenty bad," he warned.

I slugged down the beer and walked slowly to the door, not daring to look towards the two pool players. Stepping back into the glaring sun, I closed the door and ran the first two blocks to put some distance between myself and the bar.

It took me another hour and a half to reach the intersection of Padre Island Drive. I crossed to the southbound lane of Padre, and stuck out my thumb. A canary-yellow Lincoln, with three scraggly longhairs and Oklahoma plates, pulled off to the side of the road. I climbed in back with a glassy eyed hippie who appeared to be about my age. I hoped the driver wasn't as stoned as my back seat companion.

The front seat passenger turned, handing me a cold bottle of Coors. "We're goin' to the beach," he announced, grinning broadly.

The driver chimed in, "To the beach!" They clanged their bottles together, spilling beer down the front seat as we pulled into traffic.

"This your first trip to Padre?" I asked.

"First time any of us ever seen the ocean," the driver answered.

"You'll love it," I said.

"You from Corpus?" the hippie in the back seat wanted to know. From the look of his eyes, I was surprised he could still communicate.

"No, but I lived here for awhile. I can show you the way," I said.

The driver cranked up the stereo and everyone started singing along with Steppenwolf's "Born to be Wild". I joined in. After all...we were all Okies.

We drove past the Naval Air Station and out onto a thin, sandy peninsula. We crossed the steel drawbridge, and took the turnoff to Bobhaw Pier. The smell of the ocean and the warmth of the sun brought back good memories of weekends with Cindy on the beach. The ocean had always lightened my spirits.

The Okies were bouncing in their seats, babbling excitedly about the ocean and the girls. We passed the pier and the public bathhouses and then, to my surprise, drove straight into the surf. The stereo was blaring "Innagoddadavida" as the waves broke over the hood, spilling into the car. I climbed out the window, and waded to shore, leaving my three stoned companions just as the beach patrol pulled up.

Walking south on the beach, I came to a hamburger stand that offered five hamburgers for a dollar. I ate five and salted five away in my pack for later. I bought a gallon of fresh water, then continued south, past the last of the parked cars. When I was out of sight of the last bather, I undressed and went swimming in the nude. After lying in the sun to dry on the cool, wet sand, I continued trekking south.

Five miles south of Bobhaw peer, a driftwood shack sat deserted in the dunes. At least it had been there when I last visited Padre. A group of hippies, led by a self proclaimed messiah, had lived there. Actually, there had only been four of them: Johnny, the leader, a thirty something year old power freak, Pea Pod, a balding long hair with a love for acid, and the two Debbies. Young Debbie always wore a tiny bikini, Johnny said he liked to keep her as close to naked as possible...she was 16. Dancing Debbie, a pert woman in her late twenties, provided the means for everyone else to live the communal life style. She was a topless dancer at a bar in Corpus. I'd met them on the beach one weekend, and spent a few days at the shack.

Johnny had built his flock by finding people with a poor self image, then making them feel totally worthless without his affection. He dished out praise, sex and drugs to the faithful, and withheld affection whenever he didn't get his way. He reminded me of preachers who rant and rave about hell and damnation, then set themselves up as the only hope for salvation. Fear and reward... the carrot and the stick...and why not, it works on jackasses.

Johnny was an astute observer of human nature. He saw the makings of a convert in me. His plan was to make me feel special by providing shelter, food, booze and women. He failed to recognize my distrust of power.

The commune broke up when dancing Debbie, tired of playing second fiddle to a 16 year old, ran off with another man. The free ride was over... everyone had to go to work. I was delighted to hear later that young Debbie had also deserted her messiah, leaving him with just one devoted acid freak.

The dunes shift with the winds and tides. The shack could be lost with the many Spanish galleons buried beneath the sands of Padre Island. I cut back behind the dunes, crisscrossing an area as wide as a football field as I continued south. When I found the rusty skeleton of the MG, I knew I was at the site of the commune. Sand had built a wall against the seaward side of the shack, but the structure remained intact. Inside, two canvas army cots stood against the back wall separated by a metal footlocker once used as a night stand. It looked like it was waiting for someone to come home...and now I was back.

Chapter Fourteen
Life's a Beach

"Don't tell my momma what we've done here!"
Jake, after stepping on a mine in Arizona Territory SW of Da Nang,
October 1968.

Sometimes the solitude of nature was the only thing that stood between me and raving lunacy, and I desperately needed some time to reflect. At night, there was nothing but the symphony of howling wind and pounding surf. Day brought the piercing cry of the gulls, as they circled high above the billowy clouds. I swam every morning, walking the four miles back to the hamburger stand for food and fresh water each afternoon. At first, I talked to the man at the stand, but later, talk seemed an unnecessary triviality...except for those few times I caught myself discussing life with the ocean, sand, or gulls, the only sounds were those of nature.

One day I found a spiraled conch shell on the beach. I picked it up and turned it over and over in my hands. I looked at that shell like I had never looked at anything in my life. My conscious self was swept away...there was nothing but the shell. When I sat it down, over an hour later, I knew what Charlie had meant by focusing the mind on a single thought. I had used the conch as a mantra. Now that I had experienced meditation, I understood.

I tried to meditate every morning before swimming, but I couldn't duplicate the same focus I had with the shell. After several days of morning meditation, then walking to the hamburger stand in the afternoon, I realized the beach was becoming my routine, as sure as if I were a businessman performing the same boring task day after day. I was existing in that dream state Charlie had warned me about, often walking the four miles to the hamburger stand without any awareness of my surroundings. I wanted to wake up and pay attention but the harder I tried, the more deeply I lapsed into mental apathy.

I changed my routine, going for hamburgers in the morning and swimming in the afternoon, but that soon became a new routine. I was growing increasingly disoriented and angry with myself over my inability to control my own mind. Finally, I settled on doing absolutely nothing...completely eliminating my trips to the hamburger stand.

The first day of not eating, I spent staring at the ocean. It seemed desolate, even though I knew an abundance of life thrived beneath the ceaseless currents. Its somber appearance cast a gloomy pall over my temperament. I felt irredeemable. As darkness enveloped the world, I fell asleep on the beach.

I've been on this red clay road before. It connects our base camp at Hill 55 with an abandoned Arvin outpost. We're on our way in from operation Starlight. It's been an uneventful operation. We lost Lieutenant Sumpter to a mine, but for the most part, we've spent the past ten days humping 80 pounds of gear through rice paddies, jungles, and bombed out banana plantations.

Captain Matterson holds up the column. It's late afternoon. Across a rice paddy, a small village sits nestled into the edge of the forest. I can see people watching us from the windows of their thatched huts. They're eating dinner and relaxing after a day in the paddies.

The captain calls the platoon leaders together. *"I don't want to carry all this ordinance back to camp,"* he says. *"Deploy your men, and we'll use it here."*

We line up along the road...M-60 machine guns, 60 millimeter mortars, a 3.5 bazooka plus the M-79 grenade launchers and M-16s. People in the village watch...they're curious but not concerned. We're only a mile from base camp and we walked through their village on our way out to Starlight. Aren't we here to protect them from the VC?

"Fire on my command!" Captain Matterson yells. *"Fire!"*

We open up on the village. They look surprised...diving for cover in their bunkers. Cheers go up when a mortar round drops into the middle of a hut. Everyone is testing their marksmanship. I shoot holes in the bucket hanging from a rope on the village well. The well was paid for and dug by Americans as a good will gesture.

"Save your last clip," the Captain yells above the plop of mortars, rattling machine guns, and the pop of small arms fire. The shooting stops. The village is in ruins, several huts are burning. There are no villagers in sight.

"Saddle up!" the captain says.

We take the road on in to base camp, thankful for the lightened load.

Now, I'm in the belly of the beast, hovering a few feet above a rice paddy. The tall green rice grass gyrates in the prop wash. We jump into the paddy, running hard to put distance between ourselves and the Chinook. We lay in at the edge of the paddy, watching Phantom jets strafe the village. Silver high explosive bombs fall from the wings tearing huge chunks out of the village. The white canisters *of Napalm tumble along the ground, dragging a ball of fire behind.*

The jets bank away and we sweep into the burning village. Charred bodies lie scattered in the carnage. Are they human or livestock? After months of C rations, the smell of burnt flesh makes my stomach twitch. Whether it's hunger or disgust, I can't really tell.

An unexploded bomb protrudes from the ground in front of the tangled remains of a hut. I enter where the door used to be. An old man sits on the ground in a puddle of blood with his ancient eyes staring blankly at the shattered remains of his leg. Sergeant James is talking to a Corpsman near the back of the hut. The Corpsman shakes his head and leaves through the fallen back wall. James walks up behind the old man, waving me to the side. He pulls his 45 from his holster, points the piece at the back of the old man's head, and pulls the trigger. The man's head explodes. He lurches forward and tumbles sideways onto the packed earth floor. His jelled brain oozes onto the red clay. "He was suffering," James says, holstering his 45.

I'm running towards the paddy dike. Bodies of Marines are strewn along the dike. Dawson, our rocket man, lies face up in the mud, his eyes staring into the merciless heavens. I grab one leg and Newsome grabs the other. We begin dragging him back towards the river. Bullets kick up geysers of mud as they smack into the paddy at our feet. We run as fast as our adrenaline can take us, jumping into the river when we reach the bank. I float the stiffened body across the river, and drag it face down up the opposite bank. I flip him over when I reach the top of the embankment. His eyes are still wide open, his nostrils filled with mud. I'm wishing I had his mustache.

James walks up. "You and Barnes take care of the villagers," he says.

We pass a big bunker on the way to the edge of the village, where the Vietnamese are gathered under guard "Move out!" we command, but they pretend not to understand. I grab people, jerking them to their feet and shoving them forward. We herd them to the big bunker, but they waiver at the door. Barnes and I stand on opposite sides of the entrance, funneling people into the bunker. We use the barrel of our M-16's like cattle prods, urging the frightened children forward. Some are crying, others move forward as if in a trance. I push a hesitant young girl into the darkness. From the rear she looks like Mai Ling, with long silky black hair. I pray she doesn't look back.

The last villager disappears into the bunker. We pull the pins on our grenades and toss them into the entrance. The villagers scramble to escape, but the explosions push them back. Afterwards, we listen intently to the eerie silence, then turn away to rejoin the company.

I woke up crying.

When had the boy, dreaming of glory, become a cold-blooded killer? I went back to the beach hut and wrapped up in my blanket on one of the cots, but I couldn't still the chill. These dreams were making me crazy. I mulled over my experiences in Nam, trying to discover the exact moment I lost my humanity...like searching for a pinhole in a slow leaking tire. I figured if I could find the exact instant, I could repair the damage.

Was it the time I dragged the woman and her children from their home so we could dig up the floor and kill the father? I remembered the way the small children fought and kicked and the woman cried for mercy.

"Get them out of there!" James had ordered, but every time I dragged one out of the hut, another would run back in. We finally had to physically pin them to the ground. I subdued the little boy while Mac and Z dug out the bunker entrance and killed the man. When the shot was fired, the boy jerked and went limp...as if the bullet had torn through his skull. I left him there whimpering, wondering if all we were accomplishing was creating enemies for our children.

Maybe it was the time we dug corpses from their graves to search for weapons beneath the bodies...bloated bodies that burst like over-ripe melons when we accidentally hit them with our entrenching tools...rotted flesh that fell from the bones like greasy spaghetti off the back of a spoon.

Maybe it was the first bodies I helped to mutilate, the gold teeth we pulled to augment our combat pay or the first village I torched, dragging screaming women and children from their homes, killing their livestock, pouring kerosene on their food stores, breaking every dish and piece of furniture and then piling everything together and burning it, while the distraught inhabitants cried for mercy.

At first I was appalled by the perversion of our mission. I watched in horror while James tortured a villager to get information on the VC. Intervening, I angrily asked, "Aren't we supposed to be helping these people?"

James took me inside the villager's hut and pulled a straw mat up from the floor. Under the mat, a series of tunnels concealed several fifty pound bags of rice.

"This man is supplying food to the VC," James said. "What he knows could save your life. I don't like this any more than you do, but these people don't want us here. It's them or us."

After a few weeks in the field, I became a part of the treachery. A human being could not endure the mental anguish...an animal fighting for survival could. Survival was the only thing that counted.

I spent the next two days on the beach struggling to pinpoint the exact instant I had lost my humanity. As the second day faded into night, I was overcome by fatigue. I fell asleep on the dune against the back wall of the hut.

The darkened sewer is filled with rats and roaches...millions of them scrambling over one another. A brightly colored butterfly flies into the sewer, its beauty a stark contrast to the murky catacomb. The butterfly begins a metamorphosis. Its wings turn black. It becomes too heavy for flight and falls into the seething mass of rats and roaches. At first I'm afraid I'll be devoured, but instead, I become a cockroach. Frightened by the change, I run from the sewer, but no matter how far or fast I run away, I remain a cockroach.

I woke up trembling in the warm night air. The moon had not yet risen and the ocean looked as black as death. The roar of surf was muted by a receding tide. Sitting in the stillness, I decided to go out with the tide. There was no reason to live if I couldn't retrieve my humanity.

Stepping into the ocean, I felt its chill against my naked flesh. I waded out until the water was chest deep and then began to swim toward the first sand bar. The retreating ocean was only ankle deep over the bar. I walked seaward again, until the water deepened enough for me to swim to the second bar. The ocean sloshed knee deep over the bar. I dove from the bar swimming out to the last sand bar between the beach and the dark fathomless ocean. I stood in waist deep water on the last bar, almost a mile from the beach, my heart pumping wildly and a buzzing in my ears. At that moment, I was more excited about facing the unknown than I was afraid of death.

I looked back towards the beach. Except for the boundary between cold water and warm night air, everything was uniformly enveloped in blackness. Overhead, the stars radiated with intense clarity, like brilliant gems scattered across black velvet.

I started swimming seaward. My progress was slow, but there was no schedule for reaching my final destination. I laughed out loud, thinking no one would ever know what happened...I would just be gone. "Disappeared without a trace", they would say around the campfires back home. My life hadn't amounted to much, but my death would be a mystery people would talk about for years.

Then I felt its presence. It was huge, and I knew it was aware of my presence. Somewhere, lurking in the darkness of the ocean, it stalked me. Until then, I had been surprisingly calm and serene in my decision to sink slowly to the bottom of the ocean, but the thought of being ripped into bite-sized chunks sent chills down my spine. I began to hyperventilate, more frightened than I could ever remember being.

To survive, I had to remain calm, and my will to survive had returned with a vengeance. I seized control of my breathing, forcing myself to take slow, even breaths. I stayed virtually motionless, exerting the minimum effort to stay afloat. I had to get back behind the third bar, but in my fright, I had lost all sense of direction. If I made a mad dash for the bar, swimming in the wrong direction, I would die in a violent struggle. My head was spinning...surrounded by utter darkness, I couldn't decide which direction to swim.

Suddenly remembering the stars, I filled my lungs with air and pushed onto my back. Floating there beneath the stars, I saw Orion's Belt low on the horizon. If Orion was setting, the big dipper had to be off to my left. I found the Dipper. Following a line through the two stars forming the edge of the dipper, I located the North Star. If I kept the North Star to my right and Orion to the left, I would eventually reach shore. Time was growing short...I sensed that my nemesis was hungry.

I had no conception of the distance between myself and the third bar. Trying to remain calm, I started with short breast strokes, dragging myself slowly in the direction of the beach. I concentrated...taking deep breaths and then exhaling slowly through my nostrils.

A loud splash sent me flailing through the water, stroking towards the safety of the bar before razor-sharp teeth ripped the flesh from my bones. Something hit my knee. I screamed, rolled over on my back and began kicking violently toward the attacker. When it touched the back of my thigh, I pushed down and away with both hands. Wet sand slipped through my fingers.

I had swum onto the bar. Scrambling over the bar, I quickly rechecked my directions and then continued stroking towards the beach. I wasn't a strong swimmer, but I wanted out of that ocean more than I had ever wanted anything in my life. I swam onto and over every bar, continuing until the water was too shallow to buoy my weight. I ran to the beach from there and collapsed on the wet sand. It felt good to be alive, and in my heightened state of awareness, everything was clear. I could hear the ocean, smell the salt air, feel the individual sand grains against my back. I could see every star in the heavens.

It was the same feeling I had experienced in Nam after a fire fight...what Charlie had called total awareness.

A bright light came from the east. At first, I thought it was the moon rising. As it grew and moved over me, I was enveloped by the most intense light I could ever imagine. I became the light...every atom of my body became its own point source for the light. I saw, or rather experienced the atoms of sand as particles of light. I melded with the sand...the particles of sand light and body light became interwoven. I was the earth...the earth was me. I became the universe. I am an intelligent, amorphous energy field...all things are one within the field. · A stirring within pulls particles of stuff together and substance materializes from the homogeneous mass. This substance is being, in all, or any of its manifestations. This substance forgets that it is one with the mass. When the substance has finished with its being, the stuff of its being dissolves back into the mass. Experiences gathered as being become part of the Oneness that is all things. The protoplasmic mass grows through the gathering of experience. Everything that the one is...I am. All of its accumulated experience is available to me...If I remember what I am.

Then it was gone. I was sitting on the beach dumbfounded. I had experienced the moment of insight Charlie talked about. I knew the meaning of life and death. I wanted to talk to Charlie about my experience, but I was alone on the beach.

"I am the essence of God!" I said aloud. "Creative energy and light flow through me like a current of electricity. I am greater than the sum of all my experience, the experience of all creation flows through me."

I couldn't find the exact moment when I lost my humanity, but I had discovered my source...a source much greater than my individual humanity.

I watched the sun rise over the ocean. The water changed from its blackness of the night to a translucent green...the color of Charlie's eyes. Now I understood Charlie's ocean analogy.

The gulls circled above, searching for breakfast. I was hungry, too. It was time to leave Padre Island.

Chapter Fifteen
Cops and Robbers

"When I get home, I'm gonna put this shithole behind me."

D. Jackson, after an ambush during Operation Mead River, Arizona Territory SW of Da Nang, November 1968.

I gathered my things from the driftwood shack. Looking back as I left, I knew it would soon disappear beneath the sand. It had been there for a purpose, I knew that now. Walking to the pier, I stopped several times to recuperate. I hadn't eaten or slept in several days and events of the previous night had drained me of any energy reserve. When I finally reached the hamburger stand, I ordered ten burgers, but I could only eat two. I fed the rest to the gulls, letting them snatch pieces of bread from my fingers.

At the pier, the night's catch was hung from a vanity rail. An eight foot gray reef shark, its black eyes looking into eternity, swung there with blood dripping from its snout. A broken two-by-four was stuck between its jaws displaying a jagged row of diamond shaped teeth. I had survived. Had my nemesis died in the night? Before leaving the beach, I stopped at the public bath house and took a shower. The water was cold, but it felt good removing two weeks' worth of sea salt and sand. I dressed in the cleanest clothes in my pack and started hitchhiking toward town.

It was still several weeks before my VA check was due, and I only had $43. I would have to find some sort of part time work in Corpus.

A faded blue Valiant pulled off to the side of the road. The driver rolled down the window with a big smile.

"Hop in...it's too damned hot to walk."

I stepped in and we pulled back into the sparse traffic. The drone of the air conditioner masked the noise of six cylinders hitting on four. It looked like the car was held together with bailing wire and masking tape, but it was cool inside and the AM radio even worked.

"My name's Hank," the driver offered, sticking out a large, callused hand.

He had a gap between his front teeth which was constantly exposed by his big grin. His long, wavy hair was slicked back and tied in a pony tail. A scraggly red beard was doing its best to cover his square chin.

"Been to the beach?" he asked.

I wanted to come back with some wisecrack like, No, an alien craft just dropped me on this road...is there a beach around here?

Wake up Hank, this is the beach, I thought. "Yeah, I been there," I said.

"Bitchin' ain't it. I never seen so many young things."

"I've been back in the dunes, away from the crowds," I said.

"Why? Man that beach is paved in babes," he laughed.

"I was lookin' for somethin'," I answered.

"Did you find it?"

"Not really."

"Maybe you were lookin' for the wrong thing in the right place." He laughed again.

"How do you mean?" I asked.

"I came here lookin' to get laid, and I found all I wanted."

His hair trigger laugh went off again.

"Where you headed now?" he asked.

"You can let me out anywhere along Padre Island Drive," I said.

"I'm in no hurry...I'll take you wherever you need to go."

"Well, if you see a construction site along the way...that would be great."

"Are you lookin' for work?" he asked. "If you are, you should come to Houston. I have a carpenter buddy there who's lookin' for help."

"I'm expectin' some money in the mail...I really should stick around Corpus," I said.

"You can have the Post Office forward your mail to Houston."

"I don't have a place to stay...or a car," I said.

"My buddy would drive you to work and you can stay at my place until you get your first check," he offered.

I was out of excuses. The truth was, I wasn't interested in a full time job. I hoped to slide by until the VA check arrived, then live it up until school started. But $43 wouldn't be enough. "Can you stop by the Post Office so I can give them a forwarding address?" I asked.

"Sure thing," Hank said, "Houston's a happenin' place, you'll like it there."

We pulled into the shopping center. Hank wanted to hit the Pussy Cat Club, but it wouldn't open until after one.

"Maybe we can find a titty bar on the way," I suggested.

"I like the way you think," he said, laughing.

I went into the Post Office, checking my box on the way to the window. There was a yellow envelope inside.

I took the instructions out of my wallet to open the box. The envelope was from the VA. *Probably something about school*, I thought, trying not to get too excited. I opened the envelope.

It was a check for 1,417 dollars.

"Hallelujah! Praise the Lord!" I yelled, startling the other postal patrons.

This was a sign, I decided. No way would I take a job, but I would ride to Houston with Hank. It might be fun having some cash in a "happening" town.

We found a place on Ayres Drive to cash the check, then continued on out of town across the High Bridge.

From the top of the bridge, I could see the white sandy beaches of Padre Island stretching to the horizon. Beneath us, a ship blew its horn as it headed for open sea.

What is it about man that makes us long for the ocean? I wondered. I once heard that man is 90% sea water and that our blood has essentially the same chemical composition as the ocean. Are we like that rain sucked up from the ocean that Charlie had talked about, carried inland, where we live with the constant longing to return to our essential nature, our oneness with the ocean?

We crossed the inter-coastal canal, stopping in Rockport at a crossroads tavern overlooking the beach. The tavern was little more than an open driftwood shack. There was no glass in the windows, just wooden shutters that were pushed back to let in the sea breeze. The plank wood floor was covered with sawdust and peanut shells. The bar itself was constructed of planks laid over wooden kegs.

Hank ordered two beers and a plate of raw oysters. I declined the oysters but paid the tab.

"How can you eat those slimy things?" I asked, frowning.

"Like this," he replied, sucking one of the wrinkled, brown blobs of muscles and internal organs down his throat. "Hell, haven't you heard, they're good for your sex life."

Hank's thin frame and rugged good looks did seem to draw female attention. It wasn't long before one of the female patrons had asked him to play pool. Hank introduced me, but she avoided eye contact. I still wasn't wearing the patch. It was rolled away in my jacket pocket, in the bottom of the pack, out in the trunk of the Valiant. It didn't matter anymore, she wasn't worth the trip.

I drank my beer, staring out at an empty section of beach. At first, I was feeling a little sorry for myself. *It wasn't that long ago that she would have asked me to play pool*, I thought. But the beach, with its warm breezes and fragrant air, was like a balm soothing my emotions. Over the past weeks, the beach had embedded itself in my psyche. It was like an old and dear friend.

Hank disappeared into the back seat of the Valiant with his new friend while I drank a second beer. He returned, his smile wider than ever, and ordered a six pack to go. I paid the tab.

"My plates are expired and this old car's on its last leg," he said, after we were in the car. "I'm just gonna drive it until the cops catch me or the car dies... whichever comes first. We'll have a better chance of avoiding cops if we take the coastal route to Houston," he explained.

"What's the down side?" I asked.

"It's slower...the roads are bad and if we break down, we'll have a hell of a time getting any help."

"But what's the down side?" I repeated.

Hank laughed. "I do like the way you think," he said.

We took the coastal route from Rockport through Port Lavaca. We crossed narrow causeways and wound past sandy beaches, but Hank was good company and he had some good weed. I was in no hurry. We stopped for seafood in Freeport then cut inland to Houston, parting company in front of a seedy looking bar in the Westheimer District. Once the home of wealthy Houstonians, the district now sported a plethora of bars and restaurants.

"This is where it's happenin'," Hank said, as I stepped from the Valiant.

"Thanks for the ride, Hank, it's been great."

"If you change your mind about work, give me a call," he said, handing me a rolled up piece of paper.

I unrolled the paper. Hank's name, address, and phone number were scribbled on the paper, a joint was rolled inside.

"Thanks a lot," I said.

As the Valiant pulled away from the curve, I stuck the joint in my shirt pocket and dropped the paper in the gutter. Taking my money from the pack, I stuck all but 10 dollars in my sock and walked up the sidewalk towards the bar. "The Hut" was painted on a sign nailed above its double wooden doors.

The bar was raucous...a throng of people of every shape, color and sexual persuasion brought together by drugs and rock and roll music. It was a true egalitarian society. The life style of everyone in the bar was equally feared by the main stream.

I found an empty chair at a long wooden table fronting the bar. It gave me a good view of a pool table that sat between the bar and the front door. There was a double row of quarters from the corner to the side pocket. Too many to keep track of, I decided.

Across the table, a girl with curly blond tresses and deep crimson lipstick was trying to get my attention. Her flowered print dress clung to her breasts revealing hardened nipples. She was in full bloom and I instantly wanted to taste her nectar. I couldn't hear over the music, so I leaned across the table, straining to focus on the sound of her voice.

"What happened to your eye?" she asked.

The question flattened me quicker than a needle stabbed into an over-inflated balloon.

"Vietnam," I answered, falling back to my chair.

She frowned then turned to say something to the pig-tailed hippie on her left. He looked my way, but averted eye contact. I was trying to figure out what they were saying when the waitress tapped me on the shoulder. I looked down the table. There were four pitchers of beer in various stages of fullness. "Give us four more pitchers and a Bud," I said.

The crowd at the table grew friendly when the pitchers arrived. They all lifted their mugs and toasted their new benefactor. Even the blond loosened up and smiled a thank you.

I leaned towards her and asked, "Why did you look at me that way when I told you I lost my eye in Vietnam?"

"I hate the war and what it's doing to the people of Vietnam," she said.

"Well... what's your name?"

"Brenda."

"Well Brenda, I don't think you could possibly hate the war any worse than I do... unless you've lost someone you care about over there."

"My brother went to Canada and I quit writing my boyfriend when he went to Vietnam," she said.

"Why? Do you blame your boyfriend for the war?" I asked.

Sparks shot from her eyes...I had touched a sore spot.

"I know what you guys do over there," she said, with emphasis on the "know".

I was interested in wrestling with the girl but with the direction the conversation was headed, a fistfight was more likely.

"Look Brenda, I'm not here to justify the war. I hate what's goin' on over there just like you. We're on the same side." I paused, lifting my beer. "Cheers," I said, tapping my bottle against her mug.

"Cheers," she said.

Out of the corner of my eye, I saw two black guys ditty bop through the door. They both wore their hair in Afros. The taller one had a pink, big-toothed comb stuck in his hair. A tattooed, coiled snake lay ready to strike from the bicep of the shorter man.

The tattooed man began working his way down the other side of the table, stooping to speak into as many ears as would listen. Each conversation ended with the person at the table shaking their head and the man moving down to solicit someone else's attention. The tall man followed, nervously checking the room as his buddy talked. When the pair moved around the far end of the table, I turned my attention back to Brenda, until I heard someone yell in my ear.

"Want some good pot man?"

I looked back. The tattooed man was standing over me. His taller friend was behind him with his back turned.

"Want some pot?" he repeated.

"How much?" I asked.

"Ten dollars for a good four finger ounce."

"What is it?"

"We got dynamite Mexican and some Thai stick if you want."

I only had the one joint. Maybe I could talk "'anti-war Brenda" into something intimate if I had some dynamite pot, I decided.

"Sure, give me a bag," I said.

"We ain't got it in here... you'll have to come out front."

"I'll be right behind you."

I waited until the men left the bar before taking a twenty out of my sock. It was the smallest bill I had. If they didn't have change, I would buy two ounces and throw a party for the whole table. I left my change from the $10 on the table and stood up to leave. "Save my place Brenda, I'll be right back," I said.

The men were standing at the edge of the road talking to two more black men in a white Chevy Impala. When I started towards them, the Impala pulled away.

"Let's go...our car's parked around back," the tattooed man said. I walked to the edge of the road.

"The pot's in the car," he said, starting toward the corner.

I followed...the tall man fell in behind me. We turned down a side street. Parked cars lined the street, but there was no traffic.

"Where's the car?" I asked, becoming somewhat suspicious.

The short man whirled around, sticking a steel blue .22 caliber pistol in my face. "Give me your money, honky!"

He was agitated, squeezing the handle of the pistol and waving it erratically back and forth under my nose. I reached in my shirt pocket and slowly removed the twenty. He snatched it from my fingers, more greedily than even the gulls on the beach.

"Is this all you got? You better not be holdin' out on me or I'll blow your head off!" he threatened.

"That's it. Do I look like a guy with a lot of money?"

He stuck the pistol under my nose, pushing my head back with the barrel.

"You better not be lyin' to me, honky, or I'll shoot your nose off!"

I knew he couldn't miss at that range.

The tall man with the pink comb began to rifle my pockets. I turned to look back.

"Look at my face and you're dead," he said.

It was the first words he had spoken, and he sounded serious.

When he started frisking my legs, I protested, "You have all the money I came with, let me get back to the bar before they start to miss me."

"Shut up or I'll blow your head off!" the gunman said again.

Lifting my pant leg, the tall man exclaimed, "What's this?"

"Man, don't take that," I pleaded.

"Shut up, honky...I should kill you for that!" the short man said.

The tall man took the money. "Let's blow", he said, his voice retreating toward the street.

The short man walked around me, slowly sliding the barrel of the pistol across my forehead, around the side of my head, past my ear.

"Don't look back or I'll kill you," he said.

At point blank range he couldn't miss, but once he stepped away, the short barreled pistol would be useless. I waited until I heard him running. Turning around, I saw a metal "House for Sale" sign on the lawn. I pulled the sign, and took off after the men. Before I could make up any ground, the white Impala screeched to a stop at the corner. Both men dove into the back-seat as the car sped away. I ran to the corner and watched the Impala and my money melt into traffic.

Returning to the bar, I counted four dollars and seventy five cents laying next to my lukewarm half bottle of Bud. It was all the money I had left in the world. I sank into my chair, cradling my head in my hands.

"What's the problem?" the guy to my left wanted to know. I hadn't noticed him before...Brenda had sucked up my attention like a Texas twister. He had dark, almost black eyes, like his pupils were fully dilated. Long black curls spilled across his shoulders from beneath a leather cowboy hat cocked over his bushy eyebrows. His mouth was lost behind a full beard and mustache.

"I got robbed."

"Robbed?"

"Yeah, those two niggers had a gun. They took almost fourteen hundred dollars."

"Fourteen hundred dollars!"

He sat back, pulling at his beard.

"Well, save what you have left. We'll take care of you for the rest of the night."

He introduced himself as Robert. He was with Brenda and the pig-tailed hippie sitting next to her. His name was Danny.

As news of the robbery spread down the table, my beers multiplied. Everyone had appreciated my generosity. They were happy to return the favor.

I pounded down the beers...my mind in a turbulent flux. One moment it was a crucible, melding the experiences of the past few days to reconcile everything in light of my new reality. The next it was a boiling cauldron of rage and apprehension. How could I have let two niggers dupe me, and what would I do now? Suddenly, I remembered Hank's phone number, I stood up to go out and look for the slip of paper.

"Where're you goin'?" Robert asked. "We're headin' down to Rowdy's here pretty quick...you wanna go?"

"What's Rowdy's?" I asked.

"It's an all night jam...lots of women, drugs, and rock and roll."

"I dropped somethin' outside...I'll be right back," I said.

With the music and crowd noise behind me, I began searching the gutters for the lost phone number. I felt like kicking myself for throwing it away. Hadn't Charlie warned me that nothing comes by accident? I searched from corner to corner on both sides of the street, but the slip of paper was gone.

I started back into the hut just as Robert, Brenda and Danny came out the door. "It's almost closin' time, let's go to Rowdy's," Robert said, handing me my pack.

I got into the front seat of a blue Torino with Robert. Brenda and Danny were in the back. I heard a sucking sound from the back as soon as we pulled away from the curve. Looking over the seat, I watched Brenda light a small brass pipe. She passed it to me. I took a hit and handed it to Robert. He held the pipe until we left the intersection, then took a hit and handed it back to Danny. By the time we parked, just off the square in downtown Houston, I was properly stoned.

I had never seen anything like the square. Rock and roll bars completely encircled the open mall. Hordes of hippies in costumes of every color, fabric, and design swarmed the streets...congregating on corners to smoke pot and practice free love. Houston City Police cars were cruising the square but they seemed oblivious to the throng of hippies.

"Cops don't bother us here...there's too many of us," Robert said, in answer to my unasked question. "Just don't let them catch you alone away from the square."

We stepped into a line that stretched around the corner from the entrance to Rowdy's. "This place is always packed," Robert noted.

The line moved slowly. Each time someone left, the doorman would let an equal number of people enter. It took us over an hour to get in.

Rowdy's was a microcosm of the square. People were squeezed belly button to asshole like Marine recruits lined up for chow. Smoke hung in hazy curtains...not all of it was from cigarettes. A live drummer kept beat with the ear splitting hard rock from a platform built over the dance floor, illuminated by flashing strobes. His wailing arms trailed a thousand specters. Red, green and blue blinking lights intensified the illusion. Beneath the drummer, dancers possessed by the beat writhed like a ball of mating water moccasins.

There were no tables or chairs. Mats scattered across the floor served as crash pads for people in various altered states of awareness. As we stepped around and over people, they seemed oblivious to our intrusion...zoned out on drugs and the pounding drive of the rock and roll.

After we squeezed onto a mat near the dance floor, Robert grabbed my shoulder and pointed toward a wall near the stage. Following his finger, I saw a man working his naked thighs up and down. The legs of the woman beneath him were wrapped around his waist.

"Anything goes in Rowdy's," Robert yelled above the music, then added "Except sleepin'."

I laughed. "How could anybody sleep in here?"

"People crash from too much drugs," he said. "See that goon?" He pointed to a powerfully built man standing against the wall with his arms folded across his chest. He looked out of place...dressed in a white shirt and black tie, a scrawl across his cleanly shaven face.

"Yes," I said.

"He's a bouncer. They catch ya sleepin' and they'll put ya out on your ear...no questions asked."

I wanted to leave anyway, the music assaulted my head and the volume of smoke was nauseating. They only served soft drinks and they wanted a dollar for a small glass. But, if I could just hang on until morning, I could put Houston behind me. It was a happening place, like Hank had promised...but not my kind of place.

I tore the corners off a paper napkin, stuffing them deep into my ears. The music was bone jarring...the thump of the bass could not be stilled by a wad of shredded pulp.

Danny led Brenda onto the dance floor, and Robert stumbled off toward the bar to hit on a redhead. Their departure left me with space to spread out and extra pillows. I laid back against a   pillow, trying to recall the last time I had slept. Two nights ago the dreams had kept me awake, last night the ocean, now the ... Music? I closed my eye, remembering the peacefulness of the beach hut and the ocean breezes whistling through the driftwood planks.

I felt something in my ribs. He wasn't kicking me so much as just digging in with the point of his boot and jostling.

"Get your ass out of here," he said. It was the bouncer I had seen against the wall.

"I wasn't asleep," I lied.

A second bouncer, his stretched shirt bulging with muscles, appeared on the scene.

"You got some trouble here?" he asked the first bouncer.

"Will be if this hippie don't get his ass out of here!" the first bouncer answered.

They both looked down at me. It was time to go.

I looked around for Robert. I needed to get my pack out of his car, but the crowd blinded me to individuals. I was reminded of the seething rats and cockroaches in my dream. *Why would anyone live like this*, I wondered?

The bouncers grabbed me, one by each arm, and started dragging me towards the door.

"Wait a minute, I'll go! Just let me get my things."

I tried to pull away. The two men took me by the collar of my jean jacket, almost lifting me off my feet.

"Don't give us any trouble, hippie," the muscle bound one said as they threw me out the door.

I landed on my knees in front of a crowd of people waiting to go in. Jumping to my feet, I turned to rush back towards the door. Both bouncers stood blocking the entrance.

"And don't come back!" the first bouncer warned, then waved for one of the crowd to come in. I walked back to where the Torino was parked. It was gone.

"Shit! I've lost everything!" I yelled, turning to kick at the red brick building.

I walked away from the noisy square feeling totally depleted.

Three blocks from the square I came to a small park where bolted-down, wooden benches surrounded a lighted fountain. Scattered oaks cast eerie shadows across the grounds. A low hedge separated the park from the sidewalk. Finding a darkened corner of the park, away from the fountain, I rolled up under the hedge as far as possible. A police car slowed as it passed, shining its spotlight into the park, but I was sure they hadn't seen me. I went to sleep there...glad the day had finally ended.

I slept fitfully, replaying the events of the past several days over and over in my mind.

"Come on out of there!"

I wasn't sure if it was a voice from without or part of a dream.

"Come on out of there, I said!"

A boot caught me in the back, forcing the air from my lungs. I rolled into the fetal position, trying to catch my breath. I looked up to see my tormentor, but a bright light blinded me. From out of the light, a hand grasped my collar.

"Get on your feet."

Another hand took me by the arm and the two hands jerked me to my feet. The light left my eyes, running down to my shoes then back to my face. Squinting, I could see the outline of two uniformed cops with flashlights in hand.

"What do we have here? Looks like one of those Goddamned hippies," one of the cops said, as he stepped behind me.

"Spread 'em, asshole!" the cop in front ordered.

"Got any ID on you, faggot?" he asked, as the cop behind began to frisk me.

Before I could tell them about my lost pack, he found the joint. I had forgotten it was in my pocket.

"He's in possession," the cop said, sounding like a school boy telling off on a classmate. "Marijuana's against the law in Texas, faggot; didn't you know that?" the cop in front asked, not expecting an answer.

I decided to oblige him.

"Whatcha doin' here, anyway?" he asked.

I didn't answer.

"Oh, we have a wise ass on our hands," the cop behind me said. "Speak up or we'll kick your ass!" he warned.

I stared blankly ahead.

The first blow caught me below the ribs, doubling me over in pain. Before I could react, the cop behind me had my arms pinned. The cop in front began to work me over, his anger and frustration becoming more apparent with every blow.

"You goddamned hippies are everywhere!" he yelled, hitting me again in the stomach.

I shifted my body, causing his uppercut to brush past my shoulder. "You're causin' us to lose the war!" he screamed.

The cop holding my arms tightened his grip. I saw it coming, but I couldn't avoid the roundhouse right.

"I'd like to line you all up and blow your asses away!" the angry cop yelled, as the blow crashed into my jaw, grinding my teeth to powder.

The taste of powdered tooth enamel and blood caused me to vomit. The cop holding my arms released his grip, and I fell to my knees, spewing vomit on my assailant's spit-shined shoes.

I looked up just as he swung his flashlight down towards my head, yelling, "You bunch of faggot communists make me sick!"

I managed to catch the barrel of the flashlight and jerked it out of his hand. The cop behind me yelled, "He's resistin' arrest!"

Then the lights went out.

Chapter Sixteen
Black Angel

"I get his poncho liner. He was my best friend."
Z, following the death of Jake, Arizona Territory, October 1968.

"Love is the light of the world."
The voice was loud enough to wake me...but it seemed to originate from within.

I opened my eyes slowly...pain surged through my head with every heartbeat. I smelled the pungent odor I equated with death before I saw the puddle of congealed blood. I reached up to touch my head...the bandages were soaked. Pushing my hand beneath the bandages, through the matted hair, I felt the open lip of a wound on the back of my head. Both my eyes were swollen and a crust of dried blood covered my face.

I slowly pulled myself up against the wall. The room was cramped, with a solid steel door and four suffocating, gray walls. The only furnishings were a stained porcelain toilet and the metal platform upon which I rested. Sitting against the cement wall in my underwear, the room felt physically and emotionally cold.

What did it mean? I wondered. *Love is the light of the world.*

From my experience on the beach, I knew that the light was the realization of my oneness with creation. Didn't this mean that love was the essence of the light? And since I was one with the light...wasn't my true essence also love? To live an enlightened life, I had to acknowledge this love by letting it be the filter for all my experience. If it increases love, it's enlightening...if it decreases love, I've colored it with my own fears or false perceptions. If I could put my petty emotions aside, and open my heart, like Charlie had said, then my soul would become an open channel for the light... love would flow through me into the world. I was excited. It seemed so direct....experience life through the essence of God that resides in me.

A sliver of light appeared through the steel door. "You awake in there?"

I could see two blue eyes through the narrow slit. "Yes...I'm awake."

The door opened. A man in a brown jailer's uniform threw in my clothes.

"Get dressed and come with me," he said.

The clothes reeked of vomit and dried blood. I dressed and walked out into a long yellow corridor. Dim fingers of light reached into the darkness from the widely-spaced, bare bulbs lining the ceiling. The jailer was leaning against the wall, smoking a cigarette. He snuffed out the butt with the toe of his shoe and started walking down the hall.

"Let's go," he said.

The clicking of his heels against the linoleum floor echoed off the faded walls. I had a hard time keeping up, my head pounding with every step. When we reached the end of the corridor, the jailer opened a lock and threw open a steel door. The light was blinding.

Stepping aside, the jailer said, "Get out of my sight."

I looked at him quizzically. *Weren't they going to press charges for the pot?* He seemed to understand my hesitation.

"You weren't worth the time or money to run a finger print check. Now get lost!"

The exit at the back of the courthouse fronted a long flight of stairs to the street below. My head was spinning... I clung to a metal railing to negotiate the stairs without falling. Passing police officers shot sidelong glances of contempt.

When I reached the street, I collapsed onto a bus stop bench. A black man in an army field jacket sat at the other end.

"You look terrible brother...what happened?" he asked.

"Cops beat me up."

"You gonna make it okay?"

"Not really...I'm havin' a hard time keepin' my head up."

"Where you goin' man, you live around here?"

"I just got in last night...I think it was, but I don't know how long I spent in jail."

"Let me get you down to the Salvation Army, they'll put you up," he offered.

A Houston Transit bus pulled to the curb. The black man helped me board. He paid both our fares and we found two seats near the back of the bus. I slid in next to the window. My own strong odor was soon absorbed into the smell of diesel fuel, cigarette smoke and cheap perfume. *This is the real Houston*, I thought, *not the glitter of downtown or the bars and restaurants of the Westheimer District, but the minimum wage workers who keep the city alive...the garbage collectors, clerks, and secretaries that ride a smelly bus to an over-priced apartment to share chicken pot pies with a spouse and four hungry children.*

Like a pyramid needs a broad base, so it is with a city. The valued few build their fortunes on the sweat and toil of the forgotten many.

I looked at my companion. He rode the bus like a seasoned cowboy sits a horse...his body flowing with the bumps without conscious thought. His arms were folded across his chest and his dark eyes lost in deep thought.

"Thanks man, I really appreciate the help," I said.

He shook his head as if to snap himself back into the present. "Sorry man, what did you say?" he asked.

"Thanks for the help."

"It's nothin', I've been down myself," he said.

Noticing the First Cavalry insignia on his jacket sleeve, I asked, "Have you been to Nam?"

He looked at me. His nose was crooked...like it had been broken and not set properly.

"Yeah...I just got home last month," he said. "You too, I'd guess," he added, looking towards my missing eye.

"Yeah, I've been home almost a year now." I paused, and then said, "Don't take this wrong, but you look a lot older than most vets."

"It was my second tour. I spent twelve years in the Army...I was gonna make it a career, but they said I had flat feet and forced me to take a medical discharge."

"You were a lifer?" I asked.

"There ain't much else for a black man to do in Houston. I ain't been able to find a steady job since I got home. Last week, I had to separate from my wife and kids just so they'd qualify for public assistance."

"Sounds like you've hit a string of bad luck," I said.

He looked at me and laughed, "From the looks of things, I'd say your luck ain't been none too good."

I extended my hand.

"What's your name anyway?" I asked.

"My name's Grady; what's yours?"

"Dennis," I answered, shaking his hand.

Grady helped me off the bus in front of a decaying, four-storied, red brick building a block off the square. A red Salvation Army emblem was painted on the side.

"They open at five," he said, sticking three dollars in my shirt pocket. "You can pick up day wages at the Man Power office two blocks up on Main.

"I'll probably see you there tomorrow," he said, as he stepped back onto the bus.

"Thanks, Grady, I'll pay you back."

"No sweat...we're all brothers," he said.

I sat down on a crumbling cement stoop that fronted a boarded up entrance to the building. Several other men shared the stoop, waiting for the center to open. Except for a few blacks, about my age, they were mostly older men.

"Care for a toot?" a leathery faced man with a thick growth of stubble asked, shaking a bottle of Tokay wine in my direction.

"Sure...thanks," I said, taking a pull off the bottle.

It burned all the way down...but it was a good burn.

We hung there for most of an hour, waiting for the doors to open, then paid seventy-five cents for our meal and bedding. Inside, a large lobby soon filled with the dregs of society. As I listened to them talk, I discovered that many of them were veterans...some were college educated. All had given up on the American dream.

I found a bathroom where I washed the crusty blood off my face and discarded the bloodied turban. One of the older men gave me a sock hat to cover the open wound on my head. When a whistle announced supper, a long line formed near the entrance to the chapel. After we were all seated in the chapel, the manager of the mission delivered a mandatory ten minute sermon on temperance. We sang a few hymns then filed downstairs to the dining area for a bowl of beans, a slice of cornbread and a lukewarm glass of powdered milk. I couldn't remember food ever tasting better.

"Tomorrow we get potatoes," one of my new friends announced excitedly.

After supper, we had an hour to lounge around the lobby and watch TV. We were not allowed to leave the building unless we were willing to stay on the street for the night. I vowed never to spend another night on the streets of Houston.

At seven, we were each given two sheets, an army blanket and a towel. We were sent upstairs to the dorms...huge open rooms with evenly spaced rows of cots. There was a large communal bathroom in the middle of each floor with several Johns and a shower. I showered and washed my clothes in a sink, hanging them to dry outside a window at the head of my cot. Listening to the men talk as I drifted off to sleep, I knew these men were truly kings of the road. They knew, "every handout in every town and every lock that ain't locked when no one's around."

Reveille was at five-thirty. We had to be out of the building by seven. I dressed, my clothes were still damp, and went downstairs, watching TV until they made us leave the building. I walked a block over to Main Street, and then turned south toward the Man Power Office. There was already a line forming. Grady was the first man in the line.

"How you feelin' this mornin'?" he asked.

"I feel great, thanks to you, Grady."

The attention embarrassed him.

"I didn't do nothin' anyone else wouldn't of," he said.

Grady left his place in the front of the line and joined me...sharing a cinnamon roll from the pocket of his army jacket. Sugar accumulated in his thick mustache. When I pointed it out, he laughed, saying, "I save it there to sweeten my coffee at lunch."

As he wiped it away, I noticed a sprinkling of gray already salting his mustache and sideburns.

For the next two weeks, Grady and I worked together...drawing up our pay each evening and parting company. He visited his family every night, taking home the money he had earned that day. He had to do it on the sly, he said, or the government would cut off his ex-wife's assistance. I returned to the Salvation Army each afternoon.

I liked the work. It was different every day. One day we loaded boxcars with fifty pound bags of concrete, the next we loaded drill collars for the off shore drilling rigs. We cleaned up construction sites and set steel forms in high rise office buildings.

Grady started bringing enough lunch for us both. His wife would add an extra piece of chicken and pie or an extra meat loaf sandwich. One day, while we sat under an oak tree enjoying his wife's cooking, I asked, "Grady, are you a religious man?"

"I go to service every week, if that's what you mean."

"But do you ever think about God, or the meanin' of life? Like...why does God let some rich drug dealer live in a mansion and you can't even live with your own family?"

"I used to wonder about things like that until my last week in Vietnam," Grady said.

"What happened?" I asked.

"My commanding officer relieved me of duty and sent me to graves registration. One day we got word that somethin' had gone down in the A Shau. I got there just as the dead started rollin' in...helicopter after helicopter full of bodies. My job was to wash them off in a shower with a high pressure hose."

"Jesus, Grady...that sounds awful!"

"My first week at graves, they gave me a bucket and a scoop shovel. I cleaned out the showers, takin' all the spare body parts to the incinerator. Believe me Dennis...hosin' down the bodies was the best job there." He paused to collect his thoughts. "Anyway...the bodies from the A Shau were chewed up somethin' awful. I washed down twenty or more before I recognized the first face. It was Jenks, the medic from my platoon. The platoon sergeant that replaced me had called in an air strike on his own position. It pretty much took them all...includin' the company commander that sent me to graves."

"So you figured God saved your life by havin' you transferred?" I asked.

"No, in fact, at first I felt responsible. It wouldn't of happened if I'd still been there. It was the darkest time of my life. I couldn't talk to anyone for several days...then I remembered something Jenks had said. As our company medic, he saw a lot of guys die. He said some of them died crying for their momma and others died with their jaws set... determined to fight to the end. The only thing they had in common was death. Putting it into a bigger perspective, Jenks saw that all any of us really have in common is the inevitability of our death. Jenks said that death wasn't a phenomena restricted to Vietnam. Thousands of people die every day around the world, but in Vietnam, we tended to focus our attention on death. Jenks said he had decided to quit worrying about death, to focus his attention on living. He said, it's not when you die, but how you live that really matters. Even with all the death he witnessed, I'd say he was the happiest man in our platoon. Thinking about what Jenks had said, I realized that men have been dying since the beginning of time and obviously it's part of God's plan. I figured, God gives a man the experiences he needs to fulfill his destiny and I don't question His wisdom."

"You think everything is predestined then?" I asked.

"My preacher says we all have free will to choose whether or not to listen to God...but God continually sends us messages to help us find our way. He says if we miss the easy messages, the voice of God gets louder and louder until we're forced to take note."

"How do you mean?" I asked.

"Well, the preacher uses an example about a man who buys a new car and parks it under a tree. The next morning he comes out to find the car covered with bird manure. The man cusses the birds, washes the car and parks it right back under the tree the second night. The next morning he finds it covered with manure again, but this time the paint job is ruined. The man is pissed about the paint, but he washes the car again and parks it under the tree the third night. The next morning, the man comes out to look at the car and the tree falls down and kills the man. God didn't want him to park under that tree."

I laughed at the parable. "Sounds like a pretty cool preacher ...all mine ever did was scream and yell, tellin' us to repent or we'd all go to hell."

"Yeah...I've had preachers like that too. Seems they're always passin' the plate and talkin' about sacrifice...then leavin' in a Cadillac. Our preacher works as a butcher all week and still takes time to visit people in jail and the hospital. All the money in the collection plate goes to buy food and provide shelter for poor folks that can't afford to pay for their own."

"Does he think God's an old man livin' off in the sky somewhere that sends down a bunch of temptation, then passes judgment on those of us who can't resist?" I asked.

"Naw, preacher says it's not like that at all. He says God's more like an intelligent force that pervades all things."

"I had a mystical experience not long ago...somethin' like that, but it's kind of hard to put into words," I said.

"What happened?" Grady asked.

"It was really strange... like I was the universe. I guess what happened was, I had a realization that we're all one with Creation."

"That's about what our preacher says and Jesus himself said, '"I and the father are one". Preacher says the Hindus bow to one another to acknowledge the essence of God in one another."

"Your preacher studies the Hindus?"

"Hindus, Buddhists, Taoists, Essences, American Indians...you name it, he studies it."

"What kind of religion does he belong to?"

"It ain't so much a religion as it is a spiritual practice. He says he's searchin' for the truth that ties all the religions together."

"Has he found it?"

"He thinks he's close. The oneness with God that you experienced is one principal that most religions have in common and they all talk about the importance of love, forgiveness and tolerance. Where they mostly differ is in their creation myths."

"Creation myths...what does that mean?"I asked.

"You know...how the world was created. Preacher says it really doesn't matter if the world was created in seven days or an Indian woman pulled some mud out of a lake. The important thing is that we're here...let's try to get along and understand why. He says most of the world's conflicts occur because of religious dogma."

"What's a dogma?"

"It's a religious rule, used to control the people." He looked at me to see if I understood.

"Have you ever heard of the Gnostics?" he asked.

"No, who were they?"

"They were the original Christians. They believed that each man was responsible for his own salvation."

"What happened to them?"

"They lost out when the church set up a hierarchy of priests to control the people. These priests set themselves up as the only link to God. They decided what would go into the Bible to establish their religious dogma. They dished out salvation like a mess sergeant dishin' out chow...and you couldn't get fed unless you came to their kitchen. Suddenly man was no longer responsible for his own salvation. Preacher says most of man's problems began when he broke his personal link with God. That's why he don't put much faith in the Bible as a whole. He says the Old Testament and New Testament conflicts so much as to make it all confusin'...and that most people interpret the scriptures in ways that best fit their own wants and needs, anyway."

"What about Jesus?"

"Well, the preacher says that Jesus was dead set against established religions. He was always warnin' people to beware of pious actin' men, warnin' they would steal you blind. He told us to pray in private, to never call another man master and to be humble...to never cast your pearls before swine."

"I've heard that before, but never really understood what it means," I said.

"Well, the preacher says it's like a man with a wallet full of money who goes into a bar. It's better if he don't go flashin' his full wallet around. Others will either want to take his money or think he's a pompous ass. He says it's the same with people who have received God's blessings. It's better if they don't flaunt them in front of people who's spiritually impoverished. Least, that's what the preacher says."

I thought about my experience with the light.

"You know...if you really understand the oneness, you don't have to be convinced to act a certain way. You know you can't hurt someone else without harming yourself," I said.

"Yeah, preacher says the real test of a man's faith is how he chooses to live his life. He says love is the light of the world and once you understand that, and live your life accordingly, the love of God will flow through you into the world."

A chill ran up my spine hearing the very words I had heard in the drunk tank just before meeting Grady.

"I'd sure like to talk to your preacher some day," I said.

"Our church is open to anyone," he invited.

I was amazed at the inner peace Grady seemed to enjoy in the face of his hardships, especially considering he had pulled two tours in Vietnam as a rifleman. He had seen the horrors I witnessed and more. Why hadn't they affected him the way they affected me? I asked him one afternoon while we went cleaning out an apartment complex. "Grady, did you ever do somethin' in Vietnam you were ashamed of?"

He thought for a moment. "I guess in retrospect I'm kind of ashamed of the whole episode," he said.

"No, I mean somethin' personal."

"Like what?" he asked.

Oh...I don't know, I hesitated, then blurted out, "like killin' civilians?"

"I saw a lot of it, but I refused to take part. I turned my company commander in for orderin' the company to kill a bunch of village people outside Bien Hoa."

"How did you manage to stay clean? I mean, everyone was doin' it."

"My momma told me when I was a kid that I was responsible for each and every one of my actions. She said that if I was arrested for stealing a car, it wouldn't matter if everyone else was doin' it...or if we was hungry and I needed the money to feed my family. I'd go to hell all the same."

He paused, leaning against his broom.

"She was a Southern Baptist...fire and brimstone Southern Baptist. I didn't believe everything she said but I did learn about personal accountability."

"So...you did your time in Nam and stuck by your principles?"

"Yeah...I guess I did...but it cost me a career in the Army."

I wanted to ask him about how he left the army, but the boss stepped in the door and we went back to work.

I spent the rest of the afternoon thinking about the concept of personal accountability. In retrospect, I had been taught to go along with the crowd...that there were certain important beliefs we held in common to insure our survival. Most of these I had found lacking, or outright lies, but I was taught not to question authority...not the preacher, the history teacher or government policy.

To blame my actions in Vietnam on the way I was raised would be a denial of my personal responsibility. It would be like taking the insanity plea for murder. Sure I did it, but it wasn't my fault. In reality, I knew I had made a personal decision to participate in every atrocity. If I had said no, I may have gone to jail...or worse yet, my buddies may have turned their backs on me...but the price I was paying for participation was much higher.

That weekend, Grady and I got hired by a construction company to work on a high rise. Wet weather had gotten them behind and they needed to pour cement on one of the upper floors to be ready for the union carpenters on Monday. The job was not paid through Man Power. We would draw our salary directly from the company...over twice what Man Power paid us through the week for the same work. We jumped at the chance to make a little extra cash.

I had just started pig tailing steel rebar, the supporting network for the concrete, while Grady unhooked bundles of steel, lofted to the roof by a crane. The crane operator, six stories below, was being directed by a cocky young company man. Grady was bent over with his back to the company man unhooking a load. The company man, bragging about a fight he had the night before, began gesturing wildly with his hands. Mistaking the arm movement for a signal, the crane operator pulled away. The cable securing the rebar tightened around Grady's arm, jerking him into the air with the bundle of rebar. The load spun out of control, dragging Grady off the building. He dangled from the bundle six stories above the street.

My eyes locked on Grady's eyes as he hung there. There was no fear...just silent resignation. I immediately thought of the eyes of the old villagers as they walked into the bunker. Before I could close the distance between myself and Grady, the crane operator attempted to lower the bundle, banging the edge of the rebar against the building. The load tilted precariously...steel began sliding from the cable. Grady grimaced as the torque between steel and cable twisted his arm. Suddenly, the load released, sending Grady and a thousand pounds of steel rebar plummeting toward the street below. We all ran to look over the side. Grady's legs protruded from a tangled mass of steel. He looked like a toy soldier buried under a pile of "pick-up sticks".

Everybody rushed toward the elevator to get down for a closer look. I stayed up. I had seen enough dead men to know there was no such thing as human remains.

Whatever it is that makes us human leaves the body at the time of death. The police cordoned off the building and we shut down for the day. I went back to the Salvation Army.

I sat alone in the lobby while the others went to supper. Afterwards, I went up to the dorm and laid on the bunk, staring at the ceiling. I had not seen a single dead body in my first 17 years of life. In Vietnam, I had seen more violent deaths than I cared to recount, but Grady was the first friend I had seen die in the U.S. What was it his friend Jenks had said? "The only thing we have in common is the inevitability of our death." Certainly, Grady had been right in his assessment...death is part of the divine plan. Perhaps death and rebirth are God's way of experiencing creation. The cycles of destruction and renewal of each substance are interwoven with all others to create the universe as we experience it. Like the cogs of a watch...each wheel driving the other to create the flow of time.

Charlie had said each man has a personal destiny and if we are guided by spirit, we can know our life's purpose. Grady seemed to be at peace with his own death. Maybe he had fulfilled his life's purpose. Still, I could find no personal solace in his passing and I knew his family would be devastated by his death. I had never met his wife, Jane, or the kids, but I knew I had to do something to help them through their sorrow.

Early the next morning, I went to the construction site to see about drawing up Grady's pay. I knew Jane would be too devastated to come downtown for twenty-five dollars...but I also knew she needed the money.

The building was deserted, but I heard the air conditioner running in the company office. I knocked on the door of the white, aluminum-sided trailer. "It's open." I recognized the company man's voice.

Inside, he and the foreman were drinking coffee. The building's blueprints were rolled out on a drafting table where the foreman sat. The company man was standing on the other side of the table.

"I came to see about gettin' Grady's check...his wife'll be needin' the money."

"He didn't work the full day," the company man said.

I was wondering how fast I could get over the table and get my hands around his throat. "He would've if you hadn't killed him!" I said.

"Hell, that stupid nigger should have had the load unhooked," he said. "What's he to you, anyway?"

Taking a deep breath, I remembered that I had been that company man just a few weeks ago.

Grady had taught me to value a person for who he is...not because of his color. The company man had not had the good fortune of knowing Grady.

"He was my brother," I answered.

Turning my attention to the foreman, I asked, "What are the chances of me drawin' up Grady's pay?"

"Sorry...it's against company policy for me to give you another man's check."

"Well then, just let me have my check."

He looked at me, shaking his head.

"You didn't work long enough to draw any pay," he said.

I wanted to scream. The memory of a young Marine who died his first day in Vietnam crossed my mind. He hadn't had time to burn a village or be in a fire fight, but he had given all he had to give in that single day. Surely Grady had earned a full day's pay in that short half hour of terror.

I left the trailer without saying a word. Walking away, I felt the same sense of freedom I experienced when I left Mexico. Anger would not guide my actions. I had been putting away money in the Salvation Army safe...I would give it to Grady's family.

I waited until Monday morning, hoping Jane would be up to a visit by then. I caught a bus on main, beneath towering pinnacles where business executives made million dollar decisions every day. On a frontage road tracing the route of the Gulf Freeway, the bus passed body shops and auto supply stores where small businessmen made a decent living. Turning under the freeway onto Brailsfort Drive, I was appalled by the sudden poverty. With the skyline of Houston as their backdrop, half naked children played in the streets in front of one and two room, unpainted shanties. Many of the buildings were burned out or boarded up. Gangs of working age men sat loitering on the porches or prowling the streets. Block after block for miles, we passed poverty as bad as any I had seen in Vietnam. I began to understand why some of the black Marines had said the Vietnamese were their brothers and the American government their enemy.

I reluctantly left the bus in front of a moldering government project. The buildings were built barracks style...long rows of clapboard buildings with peeling green paint and big numbers stenciled on the sides. I found Building 5, apartment 3 and knocked on the door. A heavy set woman with graying hair and-red swollen eyes answered. She looked surprised to see me.

"Whatcha need?" she asked, with a get off my porch look.

"I'm Dennis Jackson...Grady's friend."

Her features softened. "I'm sorry...I thought you was the building manager come for the rent. Please come in."

The apartment was clean but cockroaches scurried down the faded walls and across the threadbare rug. The furniture was past worn. Holes where stuffing had long since disappeared were covered by hand stitched doilies. "Sit down, Grady talked about you all the time," Jane said. Noticing a picture of Grady posing with a group of black soldiers, I asked, "Is that a picture of Grady in Vietnam?"

She looked at the picture.

"Grady was gonna make a career of the army till that General throwed him out."

"I didn't know he was thrown out of the army."

"Yeah...he turned his commandin' officer in for killin' civilians, and the army suddenly finds out he's got flat feet. He done been in the army 12 years...two tours in Vietnam and suddenly...his feet's too flat!"

"I guess he did tell me about that." I watched her lovingly stare at his picture.

"He was a great guy...the best friend I had," I said.

"He said the same about you. Funny thing is...he never had a white friend before. Came back from Nam pretty much disgusted by the whole race, but he said you showed him there was good and bad white people...just like there's good and bad black people."

I was struck by the fact that I had been a teacher for Grady, just as he had been for me.

"I'm really gonna miss him, and I wanted to thank you for all the love you put into those lunches. I know it was a hardship," I said.

"It wasn't nothin' at all," she said, looking down at the floor.

She sat in silence for several moments. I felt awkward, not knowing what else to say to comfort her. Looking around the room, I saw a worn Bible on a shelf near the door.

"I guess I'll be goin' now...is there anything I can do?"

"No, there's nothin' nobody can do," she said, without looking up.

I stood up and walked to the door. Looking back, I saw she was lost in sorrow. I took an envelope from my pocket. It contained $200...all I had saved in the past two weeks working with Grady. I slipped the envelope into the Bible and left the apartment.

Chapter Seventeen
Final Lessons

"How could we have been so stupid!"
Jackson to Z, aboard the ship of the dead, 1969.

By the time I departed the bus in front of the Salvation Army building, I had decided to leave Houston. I paid my 75 cents and got in the chow line for the last time, just as they filed into the chapel. The pews were filled at the back but I found an empty seat on the front row. After the ten minute temperance sermon, we sang "The Old Rugged Cross"...the one church song I knew by heart. The chapel fell silent and we started to rise to go downstairs for supper, when a man behind me yelled, "Let's sing "Rock of Ages", number 115."

The chaplain was happy to oblige...tickled to have someone looking for salvation, but no sooner had we finished the song, when the man yelled out again, "Let's sing "Shall We Gather At the River", number 211, it's one of my favorites."

"We have a man in the spirit tonight," the chaplain's voice rang with approval.

I figured the man was certainly under the influence of strong spirits. By now, the throng was getting restless, but we sang the hymn, finished the song and then hurriedly stuffed our hymnals into their racks.

The high-spirited man was living dangerously.

"Let's sing just one more." He paused, thumbing through the hymnal, "How about "Onward Christian Soldiers", number 177," he yelled.

This was the only meal of the day for many of the singers and they were hungry. A rumble passed through the room. Men on both sides of the "would be" choir boy threatened to stick a sock down his throat if he didn't shut up. Looking back to watch the row, I saw those translucent green eyes. Charlie smiled and winked.

The chaplain asked for quiet.

"We'll sing this one last song and go to supper," he promised.

We sang the last hymn and then rose to leave the chapel. I waited and got in line next to Charlie. "I think they were ready to kill you Charlie," I said, smiling.

"Singing is good for your soul," he said.

"Yeah, Charlie, but a broken neck is real bad for the body."

We ate our beans and cornbread in silence and retired to the dorm. We picked adjoining cots near a fourth floor window and crawled out onto the fire landing. The night air felt good. Music from the square dissipated into the sounds of heavy traffic passing below. "What are you doing here, Charlie?"

"I'm here to see you," he said.

I laughed..."How could you have possibly known that I was here?"

"Synchronicity."

"What does that mean Charlie?"

"Do you remember when I told you that nothing occurs randomly? Everything happens for a reason, at a specific time and place?" he asked.

"Yeah, I remember."

"That's synchronicity. Sometimes we're not in a position to see the significance of an event. Like watching just the goalie at a hockey game, if we don't take a wider view and see from a broader prospective, we never understand what he's doing out there on the ice. You may not see the significance of us being here together right now, but know that it is significant...and work to understand its meaning."

"Well, I do know your timin' couldn't have been better. I really needed to see a friendly face today."

"There you go Dennis, maybe that's it. I'm here so you won't feel so lonely." He leaned toward me. "So tell me Dennis...why do you need a friend today?"

I told him about the past month, the light on the beach, the dreams and Grady. He listened intently, piercing me with those wonderful eyes.

When I finished, he sat in silence for a moment, digesting my words before he spoke.

"You've learned a lot in a short period of time," he started. "'When I tried to explain the oneness of creation using the ocean analogy, I knew you had to experience it yourself. Without experience, our intellect can never truly understand. Remember this when you try to help others."

"So teachers aren't of much value?" I ventured.

"That's not what I'm saying...Grady was your teacher; wasn't he?"

"Yeah...I learned a lot from Grady."

"And what did you learn from the shifting sands of Padre Island?"

"What do you mean, Charlie?"

"The sand was there to teach you something. Didn't you understand its lesson?" he asked.

I thought for a moment.

"Nothin' ever stays the same?" I guessed.

"I don't know Dennis...it was your lesson. The point is...teachers come in many forms. If you pay attention, every experience and person in your life will become a teacher. Don't make the mistake of searching for a Guru. Don't let anyone tell you what to believe or how to live your life. Each of us has our own lessons to learn. Let life flow through you...like flowing with the current of a river. Trust only in your own intuition, it's the Voice of God speaking directly to you. But Dennis...always remember, it's a personal message for you...not all mankind."

"Charlie, I'm not sure I want to flow anywhere. Livin' in ignorance sometimes seems like my lost bliss."

"You have no choice, Dennis. Now that you've awakened, you must continue searching for truth. To stop is certain death."

His seriousness scared me.

"What do you mean by death? Do you mean physical or spiritual death?"

"Physical death is imminent for us all. But let me explain what I mean with a story about an inquisitive ant."

He leaned back against the rusty railing and began. "There was an ant that lived in the hold of a wooden cargo ship. It was very dark down there. The light never penetrated into the hold. The ants there toiled ceaselessly to bring bits of food to the queen. One day this certain ant was searching for food when it happened upon a fly caught in a spider web. It was an old fly, past its fear of death...but it was lonely. The fly asked the ant to stay for awhile and talk.

"But I have to feed the queen,'" the ant protested.

"If you'll stay, I'll tell you about the world outside this darkness," the fly promised.

"This was a wonder to the ant, it had no idea anything existed outside the darkness of the hold. The ant agreed to listen. The fly told the ant about the sun that shined upon the deck of the ship.

"'It's the source of all life," the fly said. "To bask in its warmth for but a moment brings ecstasy beyond imagination."

"The ant couldn't tarry any longer, it had work to do, but no matter how hard it worked, it couldn't forget what the fly had said. Eventually, the ant started asking other ants about the sun.

"What is this foolishness?" they would say. "Get back to work. The queen is hungry!"

"One day the ant had to know the truth. The fly had told it how to reach the deck through a small crevice in the planking. It was a dangerous journey...with many spiders along the way. The ant toiled as he had never toiled before to reach the small crevice the fly had described. Finally, after days of hardships, fear and loneliness, it found the crack in the planking. A small beam of light streamed through the crack...the first light the ant had ever experienced. It was excited as it first stuck one feeler then the other through the hole. Wiggling its antennae in the open air of the ship's deck, the ant became aware of tantalizing new delights. It pulled itself through the crack, onto the deck. The warmth of the sun was ecstasy...its light radiant. The ant began to dance with joy at having found the truth, then a wave crested over the bow of the ship, washing the ant overboard.

"Suddenly, the darkness of the hold seemed like a lost paradise. The ant sensed that creatures in the sea would eat it, and the ant wasn't a good swimmer. Certainly all was lost. But just when the ant was ready to give up hope, a piece of flotsam appeared. The ant scrambled onto the raft, thankful for its rescue from the sea. The ant found bits of food and small droplets of water on the raft. It felt good again. It had broken its bondage of feeding the queen, found the sun, and had enough food and water to survive.

"The ant drifted at sea for days, until an island appeared on the horizon. As the raft drifted nearer to the island, the ant could see it was paradise. Everything an ant could want...the island would provide. Sadly, the ant realized that the currents were taking the raft past the island. The ant had to make a decision. If it stayed on the raft, there would be temporary safety, but the food and water would soon be gone, and death was imminent. If the ant took a chance and swam for the island, it would face the perils of being eaten by fish or drowning...but if it reached the island, paradise would be at hand.

Charlie fell silent, looking into my eyes.

"Well what did the ant do?" I wanted to hear the end of the story.

"Each ant must decide for itself, just as each man must decide for himself."

"What do you mean?"

"Right now you're at a crossroads. You've toiled most of your life under various false perceptions. You became restless and began seeking out the truth. Hardships have come your way, not to detour your path, but to teach you lessons. Whenever darkness seemed ready to prevail, something has appeared to pull you back into the light. Now the question is...do you have enough faith in this truth to continue the search or will you hold on to the small portion of truth you've collected and return to the darkness? Faith will see you through, fear will bring darkness."

I understood his analogy. Like the ant, I had grown up with the false perceptions handed to me by society, perpetrated for the purpose of upholding the established power structure...to feed the queen. Vietnam had destroyed my myths but it took this emptiness to make me search for the truth of my own existence. Every obstacle had provided new insight and when the road seemed too rough to continue, something always came along to renew my faith in the journey: In Kingsville it had been Charlie, on the beach it had been the realization of my oneness with all creation, in Houston...Grady.

But the death of Grady seemed to nullify everything I had seen, learned and experienced in the past weeks. It was unfair by any terms.

"Charlie...I still don't understand why good men like Grady have to die...at least like he died...and what about his wife and kids? What will happen to them now that they're left to fend for themselves?"

"Tomorrow we'll learn about life and death," he said, rising to his feet. "Tonight let's get some rest."

Charlie left me on the landing to ponder his words. I smiled at his preposterous idea. After all those nights as a child, laying there in the dark...alone and afraid because I didn't know what life meant...and all the meaningless death I witnessed in Vietnam, tomorrow Charlie would clue me in. But, Charlie had insights into things I could only imagine. *Maybe tomorrow would be enlightening*, I thought, with a tinge of excitement, as I returned to the bay.

Charlie was shaking my cot in the quiet of the dark.

"Hurry, let's go before the sun rises," he said.

I hated to get up before the sun. It reminded me too much of the Marines, but today, I would learn about life and death. *I dare not tarry*, I thought, smiling a private smile.

Charlie led me out the door and turned away from the square, where zonked out hippies tried to stay awake while police cars circled like vultures, waiting for them to crash. We walked down to the edge of Buffalo Bayou then along the course of the stream, away from the muffled music, until the only songs were those of the frogs and crickets.

"Sit...watch and listen to the earth being reborn," Charlie said, pointing to a grassy knoll near the bank.

"I thought we were gonna talk," I tried to protest.

Charlie pointed to the knoll and repeated, "Sit, watch and listen."

The grass was wet with dew. It soaked through my jeans and all I could think about was my cold, wet butt. Then I remembered Charlie's instructions to sit, watch and listen. I took a deep breath and slowly exhaled...then another. It brought me back to the bayou and my purpose for being there.

I became aware of all the sounds...the night creatures and the gurgling bayou. My eye adjusted to the dark, and I watched a raccoon wash its face in the river. Then the color of the sky began to change and so did the sounds. One by one the frogs and crickets gave way to the morning songs of the awakening birds. Then the sky was pinkish orange and I began to anticipate with some excitement, the rising of the sun. *How long had it been since I was excited about the risin' of the sun?* I wondered.

When the first rays of the new born day cracked the city skyline, to my amazement, small white flowers began to pop open all around me and turned to face the sun. As the city awoke, the sound of traffic began to drown out nature. Charlie picked that instant to rouse me from my reverie.

"All of the earth's living things...except man, take note of the new day. They know that each day is a miracle of rebirth. Sadly, man has forgotten his place in the flow of life. He's forgotten the meaning of life."

"Okay Charlie...I'll bite. What is the meanin' of life?"

Charlie shook his head like a teacher who keeps getting the wrong answers.

"All right...one more time," he said.

Charlie picked up a muddy piece of plastic pipe that had washed up on the bank and walked down to the water.

"This is man in his perfect state," he announced, holding the pipe up for me to see. "And this bayou is the essence of God."

Charlie pushed the plastic beneath the water so that it flowed evenly through the pipe.

"This then is the ideal relationship of man to God...a constant flow of energy," he said.

Charlie sat the conduit aside and plucked an empty beer bottle from the muddy bank.

"Unfortunately, most of us exist in a bottled up state," he said, as he filled the bottle with water.

He held the bottle up to the sun and swirled the water for me to see.

"We have this God energy, or what some call a soul, within us...but we're separated from the flow.

"How do we open ourselves up, Charlie?"

"Actually, it's our natural state. We've had to cut ourselves off from the flow. Anger and fear, and our desire to control others or to physically separate ourselves from what we might consider a lower class of people...these are the sorts of things that can bottle us up. We have to embrace all of life and be willing to flow with the current and learn from its lessons."

"And death...what is death Charlie?"

Charlie leaned over the river, draining the water from the beer bottle back into the bayou. Then he smashed the bottle against a rock.

"The essence is returned to its state of oneness...only the vessel is destroyed. Unfortunately, we have become more attached to the vessel than to the essence of God that gives it purpose."

Charlie turned toward the bayou and spread his arms.

"Look at this polluted river. It's like man living in a separated state. Each piece of trash represents someone's fear or anger...greed or prejudice. If man lived in his natural state of oneness, God's energy would flow clear as a mountain stream. Fortunately, every time someone realizes what they really are...the energy becomes purer."

"I guess that's what happened to me on the beach...I had the realization of my oneness."

"Then you know all there is to know."

"Well maybe so...but I still don't understand."

"Don't you...really? I think you understand perfectly, you just refuse to acknowledge the understanding because it would force you to take action. You're like a kid who knows cookies cause cavities, but he still eats cookies because he likes the taste.

"You see Dennis...the key ingredient to wisdom is action. Wisdom without action is like a car without a motor...it can't take you anywhere.

"Wisdom is the sum of knowing, plus action. If you know cookies rot your teeth, so you quit eating them, you're living with wisdom and your reward is good teeth. Likewise, if you know that you're one with all that is, then you know that to harm anything is to harm yourself. If you're wise, you'll learn to live in harmony with all that is. And Dennis... harmony begins within. It can't be broadcast like the message of a larcenous radio preacher. It must be a reflection of the harmony that exists within. And, just as you can't express harmony that doesn't exist within, neither can you love another until you learn to love yourself. To love yourself you must realize what is lovable...the essence of God that dwells in all men...the seed from which all things are made whole."

"Sometimes the things we do in the name of God are not very lovable," I said, thinking of my time in Vietnam.

"We will continue to evolve," he said, "but the more love we bring into our lives, the faster we evolve. This is your quest Dennis...to fill your heart with love. But remember...you cannot truly love others until you love yourself and you cannot love yourself until you forgive yourself. You must never withhold forgiveness from anyone or anything. We are all one in the perfection of God."

"I understand what you're sayin' Charlie, but how do I continue my quest? Where do I go from here? What do I do?"

"No one can tell you that. You must listen to your intuition and remain attentive to all lessons. Remember what I told you in Kingsville...awareness is the key to enlightenment. Have faith, and never abandon the path of truth. We are all working toward the perfection of the spirit. When enough people are willing to live in the light, the Oneness will evolve to a higher state."

We left the bayou, getting back to Main Street just as the city came to life. Charlie sat down on a bus stop bench and I sat beside him, silently observing the throng of people beginning their work day.

I was in a kind of ecstasy... a detached state of loving understanding I had never before experienced. For the first time in a long time, I was more concerned with the plight of people I didn't know...that I would never know, than I was with my own problems. I could see they all shared my loneliness. Each encapsulated in a shell created by their own fears. I knew love was the only solution strong enough to dissolve these shells. I began to project love and to smile at each person that walked by. Most remained impassive...some were outwardly hostile. I was either invisible or their shells were truly impenetrable.

I began to get discouraged, and mumbled, "What's the use... I can't make a difference."

"Dennis...are you becoming attached to results? Ten minutes of trying and you're already going to give up on the human race?"

"Well, I've always heard a smile was infectious...most of these folks must be immune."

"In this work, you can't be influenced by the sourpuss attitudes of others or by things you can't control. You can't change others...change comes from within...only when that person is ready for change. But you can and you will influence others by the way you live your life. It's just a matter of what kind of influence you'll be...and Dennis...it's not what you say, but what you do that counts."

We returned to the Salvation Army shelter in time to sing for our beans and then spent the evening sitting together on the third floor fire landing. We sat mostly in silence...occasionally pointing out an aroma or sound to one another. I had never felt so close to someone without feeling like I had to say or do something to keep their attention.

We climbed back into the room long after everyone else had gone to sleep.

"How long are you gonna be here?" I asked Charlie, as I climbed between the sheets of my cot.

"I'll be on the 9:05 to Memphis in the morning...there's someone there I need to see."

He smiled, and his eyes twinkled in the moonlight.

"Maybe I'll tag along, if you don't mind."

"Maybe," he answered, as I fell asleep.

I'm back on the ship of the dead, sitting next to Z. The Vietnamese begin to file into the room.

Their gaping wounds and bloody stumps are grotesque. The young girl with the silken black hair turns to face me. I want to look away so I won't have to see the hole where her face should be.

Suddenly, I know what to do. I walk over to the Vietnamese and begin to hug each one. As I do, their wounds are healed. The last one in the line is the faceless girl. When I hug her, I begin to cry...my tears falling like a hard rain down into her hair. Then she begins to cry. I step back to look at her. The tears have left a sparkle in her eyes and a smile spreads across her beautiful face.

I woke up eager to share the dream with Charlie.

The first rays of a new day were breaking across the room. I looked over at Charlie's cot, but he was gone, his bedding stripped from the mattress and the mattress rolled up against the head rail. There was no indication anyone had slept there.

I dressed quickly and left without breakfast, hoping to catch up to Charlie before he caught the train. I walked down to the tracks, following them to where they passed under the highway. I felt lost. I didn't know where to go from there.

My mind began to wander: Maybe I could still catch Charlie before the train pulled out, or I could hitch a ride to Oklahoma and go back to work at the dam. Or maybe, I should go back to Corpus and get ready for college.

I wanted to do the right thing, like Charlie had said, but nothing seemed to make sense in light of all that had happened in the past few weeks.

It was early Sunday morning. There wasn't much traffic on the freeway so I decided to rest awhile and think through my options. I found a peaceful nook near an abandoned roadbed close to the freeway onramp.

Sitting there in silence, I tried to listen to my intuition but I didn't know what an intuition sounded like. Out of the corner of my eye, I saw movement along an old barbed wire construction fence. I focused in on the movement. There were thousands of ants racing back and forth on the bottom strand of wire. Ants going to the right had forage clamped between their jaws...food for the queen. Ants going to the left were hurrying off to gather more food. On one of the upper strands, a solitary ant carried a giant white larva back and forth along the wire.

There were cross wires leading to the bottom roadway on each end of the short strand where the ant was lost. It would race to one end, wiggling its feelers around trying to decide whether or not to take the cross wire, then back track to the other end and repeat the process. I watched for several minutes as the ant scurried from one end to the other...confused by its options. From my vantage point it was obvious...the ant could reach its destination going in either direction, it just needed to make a decision and stick it out.

I realized that I was that ant. The larva was my burden of decision. But now, I knew that it really didn't matter which route I took. I would reach my destination as long as I persevered.

I walked up to the freeway and stuck out my thumb. Almost immediately, a Volkswagen bus pulled off to the side of the road. A bearded passenger with long braids hanging from beneath a red bandanna opened the back door.

"Climb on in here," he said, reaching out to give me a hand.

A red headed girl with laughing green eyes and a sprinkle of freckles across the bridge of her nose looked up from the back seat.

"Where're you going?" she asked.

"I'm goin' all the way," I said.

About the Author

Dick Jackson was born in the Oklahoma panhandle in 1949. He grew up on the Great Plains of Kansas, Oklahoma and west Texas. Dick spent his seventeenth birthday on a Greyhound bus traveling to Oklahoma City for his Marine Corps physical. He left the Marines in 1969, after being wounded in Vietnam. Dick attended college on the GI Bill, graduating from Texas A&I University with a B.S. degree in 1977, and from Idaho State University with an M.S. degree in 1979. He met his wife, Julie, while attending Idaho State, and together they have lived in Idaho, Nevada, Texas, Wyoming, Colorado, Arizona, Kansas and Missouri. Their abodes have varied from a five bedroom, tri-level in the suburbs of Denver to a 63 Chevy school bus parked in the forest of Arizona. During their adventures, Dick has worked at different times as a petroleum geologist, a mud logger, a carpenter, a newspaper editor, a college teacher, a freelance writer, a real estate agent and a sailing instructor. Dick earned his USCG Captain's License while teaching sailing. Dick and Julie have three children and five grandchildren. They presently live on a small farm in the Missouri Ozarks, where Dick works as a senior petroleum geologist.

For more great stories, visit our website at

www.BadgleyPublishingCompany.com